Under the Dead Man's Hat

KILLING TIME Book One

Under the Dead Man's Hat

A Dr. Jude Avery Thriller

ROBERT W. WALKER

PROSPECTIVE PRESS

Winston-Salem

P R O S P E C T I V E P R E S S LLC

1959 Peace Haven Rd, #246, Winston-Salem, NC 27106 U.S.A.

www.prospectivepress.com

Published in the United States of America by P R O S P E C T I V E P R E S S LLC

TRADEMARK

UNDER THE DEAD MAN'S HAT

Library of Congress Control Number: 2017947519

ISBN 978-1-943419-52-4

Second P R O S P E C T I V E P R E S S trade paperback edition

Printed in the United States of America

The text of this book is typeset in Minion Pro
Accent text is typeset in DCC Ash

Samuel Evan Dewalt could hardly remember a time when he had been called Sammy. So, after a tour of duty in Iraq and his third tour in Afghanistan, he'd decided he'd go by that name. Sammy, his childhood name. Just being called Sammy reminded him of happier times; times when he didn't hear the voices inside his head.

They weren't evil or angry voices, but instead they were just damn sad voices. They never once gave him a recipe for just how to join them, and they never once suggested that he hurt others. They were the voices of fallen comrades inviting him into their world, the place of peace, the other side of life, the other side of the River Styx. It'd be painless. They said suicide is painless. They assured him every day now how easy it'd be to simply give into their well-meaning pleas for a better life for him on the other side—among his brothers.

Sometimes, the voices did make him feel ashamed to have clung to life that day when their Humvee was hit by a roadside bomb. He'd been the only one who'd *not* passed over, and the guilt had continued to eat him up, as the saying goes. "Eating me up," he said for the hundredth time that day.

Now he was a homeless vagrant, an adult runaway who'd left no word of his whereabouts with family. Why should he? After all, no one in the family understood or ever would. Not really, not truly. Not even his Vietnam vet father understood, as his father had not lost buddies in Vietnam. The old man had been stationed in a safe zone, doing clerk's work, supplying the real soldiers who went on combat missions. His dad had never actually gone on a single raid or mission, had never been under fire.

The only people Sammy knew who halfway understood him were other homeless vets. One or two he'd met *got it*, but even they were gone over now. One had *offed* himself several months ago, another had been murdered, killed by some kids wielding baseball bats, a marauding band of young animals the news guys said. The cops had caught some gang members, and word on the street said it'd been a sick gang-initiation rite of some sort, but none of it had as yet been proven.

Sammy thought the punks ought to be sent to Afghanistan and used as walkers to do their time, scouting in front of a Humvee, using *their* bodies to test the ground for bombs and to attract sniper fire. Of course, nothing of the sort could or would be done. They'd go to a prison for life and be out in fifteen, no doubt, their crime forgotten. What was the life of a homeless vet worth, anyhow?

Sammy had become known in the area where he spent most of his time, but tonight he'd ventured out farther than ever, seeking out Dumpsters at the rear of restaurants for castaway food. All in all, he thought, it wasn't a bad life thanks to the kindness of others. Still, thinking brought on his persistent friend, guilt—emotional quicksand that snatched him deep into the dark place where the voices were loudest. Even so, his core self fought on, a warrior still struggling with a twisted inner enemy. From moment to moment, from day to day, the struggle to *not* think, to not recall, to just survive, on the pain itself perhaps. The blank look on his face, that others took for brain damage, wasn't physical. His wounds had been to his lower extremities. He'd lost half a foot, so his left shoe had had to be 'special made,' and the VA doc made a big deal of how 'special' he was. A kindly lady doc she was, but her kindness only made him feel sicker and guiltier than ever. Still, the fitted shoe helped a great deal. Did nothing for the destruction the bomb fragments had done to his private parts, but that was altogether another story.

The restaurant he spied had a quaint sign, rattling on chains and swinging in the Chicago breeze. It read:

The Red Lion Inn

The place was a bar and grill, but not an inn in the real sense of an inn with rooms to rent. The cuisine was distinctly British, but not the night cook. Dark skinned with a thick mustache and the name Miguel Jose Lamas marked the kind young fellow as Mexican. He was in fact a second generation Mexican-American. Understanding hunger from his youth, Miguel had promised to save some scraps for Sammy; scraps that would be fresher and more sanitary than what might be discovered in the Dumpster.

But Sammy's attitude was at odds with such kindness shown him. You g'damn don't deserve any kindness, one internal voice said. Not so much as a salute, came another. Much less a handout. The voices were adamant on this point; they repeatedly reminded him of how undeserving he was. After all, he'd been the one who'd gotten all his buddies killed when he insisted on taking a stray dog back to base with them. In the time it took to catch the mutt and secure it, darkness had descended. On their way back from the mission, which had accomplished nothing save capturing the dog, they missed a turn under the moonless Afghan night. While making a three-point turn to go back to the missed road, they struck that mother of an *effing* bomb. Everyone, even the dog, all killed. All but Sammy.

So when Miguel sneaked out and offered Sammy a Brit burger on a bun with all the trimmings, chancing the loss of his job, Sammy tried to brush it away as something he didn't want or need even as his eyes, his watering mouth, and his grumbling stomach ferociously debated with the voices inside. Not taking and savoring the offering from Miguel was just punishment, a deserved retribution, or so his mind dictated.

Miguel had bagged the burger along with a hefty helping of what he called chips, but looked a lot like fries, and it all smelled wonderful. Miguel kept insisting he take it. "For payment to you and all the soldiers, Sammy. Come on, man, take it. You earned it many times over, amigo."

"All my friends are dead, Miguel, because of me and that damn dog."

Miguel knew nothing of the dog or the circumstances, but he knew when a man riddled with demons needed to eat. He shrugged in response and added, "Hey, man, can't dwell on shit messin' wid your head, man. Eat up!"

"If we'd left on time," Sammy said in a guttural whisper.

"My wife, she is always late for evvvrything, ha!"

"Left me to the punishment. Don't you see?"

"I don't know, man."

"So—so I don't deserve your generosity or respect."

Sighing, Miguel opted for Spanish swear words under his breath.

Sammy knew just enough Spanish to understand; the short order cook was upset with him. The two men stared into one another's eyes, exchanging a knowing look. Sammy knew that Miguel had gone through his own war.

"Take it then, for my peace of mind, Sammy."

Sammy grasped hold of the bag, crushed it into the crook of his huge arm, and rushed off without thanking Miguel. The cook thought it was like a whipped dog grabbing a handout and too fearful of the hand that fed it to stay around. He shrugged and went back inside, exchanging the noise of the street for that of the kitchen.

A couple of blocks away, Sammy found a small, deserted park. Sitting on a child's swing, he tentatively munched at the thick, juicy burger. It's size and taste, even the Kaiser roll it was on, all reminded him of his wonderful childhood, the life he'd had before going off to war, a life that in memory was his only respite from the constant enticement to kill himself.

The burger was fully loaded—even had bacon across the top, a thick tomato, still-crisp lettuce, and it swam in mayo and mustard, a mix his dad called 'Hillbilly butter.' A thought swept over him. If a simple burger could bring back a flood of good memories as this was doing here and now, perhaps there was more to live for than to die for.

"Perhaps I should go home, try again, start over," he said to the night. "Get that job at Franklin's auto shop in Decatur." He smiled at the sudden, unbidden ambition, something he'd had no experience with for several years now. Funny, he thought, how a home-made 'Brit' burger cooked by a Mexican can bring such feelings on.

He wasn't sure the shockingly unfamiliar sense of future happiness and possibilities might last, but he even began thinking about Sharon back in Decatur, and how she tried so hard to help him, and how hard he had pushed her away. He'd felt like Hamlet back then, shouting at his girl and making her cry at every turn.

Maybe it was the warm night breeze, the rustle of the leaves in the park, both those on the ground and those still clinging to life, but he dared to think a positive thought. He dared to think that a thin sliver of hope for Sharon and himself—together again—existed.

With his mind focused on this single thought, what little light he had to see by, a park lamp with an orange glow, was suddenly gone. Someone stepped between the light and him, standing at his back.

"Sammy, that you?" came a shaky, high pitched voice.

For a millisecond, Sammy had the silly thought it was Sharon all the way from Decatur, but even as he turned to see, he knew better. It was a pair of young men, hardly more than boys, perhaps in their early twenties. They'd approached Sammy on occasion before, so he recognized their faces, although he could not recall names.

"Yeah, what'd you want?" he asked.

They'd approached him, earlier in the day, asking if he knew where they could get some weed. He'd pointed out a street vendor who did some sales on the side. The two younger men had been hanging around the neighborhood, and they'd sometimes ask Sammy questions about the other homeless characters in and around the old market area that had once been a hubbub of a street market—Hamlin at Van Buren. The young guys also wanted to know where they could get military stuff—high-quality, real-thing 'stuff' as they called it. They wanted clothes, boots, yes, but they also wanted ordinance—grenades and guns.

Sammy had advised them against doing whatever stupid thing they were planning. He'd told them stories of how war had ruined him for anything approximating a normal life. He'd told them of the depravity he'd witnessed, the body parts flying by him, and those parts that had struck him. He confessed to how the war had turned him into an alky and a junkie. He assured them that they did not want to play at war or to rob a bank, or to do anything stupid.

The taller of the two now confided in Sammy. "Thought we might rob a commuter train."

"The one that goes out to the northern burbs," said the shorter one.

"We figure those passengers'll have thicker wallets."

"And why're you telling me this, fellas?" Sammy asked.

"We want you to go with us, help rob the train. Come on, Sammy. It'll be like we're all in a Western movie."

"Yeah, 'cause we're going to film it. The whole thing on camera, see?" The dumpy, shorter fellow raised a camera and began shooting film of Sammy's stunned look. The kid then added, "Now, Keith. Do it, now!"

The second kid raised a baseball bat spiked with large nails at its end, and he brought it down on Sammy's head, blood exploding from the impact.

Sammy staggered back, threw what was left of his food in the baseball-wielding kid's face and heard the cameraman on a GoPro laughing. "I got that!"

Stunned by the initial blow, Sammy knew the pain slowed him to a crawl. Crawling he was, too, on all fours. The pain was a *god awful* pain, so awful it made him sick to his stomach. Confused, somehow getting to his feet, dirt, debris, dead leaves clinging to him, he found himself hugging a tree as if to hide behind it. Foolish, but holding onto the solidness of the tree steadied the veteran.

"Mitch, zoom in closer for this one," said the bat wielder to his sick cameraman.

"Why? Why're you doing this?" Sammy pleaded as the kid came down with the bat again, squarely at the same spot on the vet's skull.

Sammy slid down the tree, gone. The second blow sent him not only into unconsciousness but into oblivion.

The kid with the bat set his feet apart, blood pumping madly, determined to get a good third swing in, till a dog off his leash came wildly at the boys, barking and chasing them off. The dog walker who'd only seen the last part of the altercation did see two young men harassing a homeless man in the park. "Sic 'em, boy, sic 'em!" he'd ordered Pongo. And the dog needed no further telling, going straight after the punks.

While his dog was running the hoodlums clear out of the park, Thadeus Wilson hoped that Pongo would tear off some flesh while at it—evidence for the ID people. "Serve the bastards right," Wilson shouted as he rushed to the victim amid the trees. The sheer amount of blood, purple in the dim light, told the story. No one could survive that much blood loss from his head, no one. The blood had painted the tree trunk, had filled in every nook and cranny in the bark like rain saturating a valley bottom. The ground around the body was soaked in the rich purple blood as well, not to mention the dead man's face. It, too, was painted in blood. Even so, Wilson recognized the murdered man as a local homeless vet, a white guy that everyone called Sammy.

"Bastards took you by surprise, big man, didn't they?" Thadeus asked the corpse. He was a nurse practitioner at nearby Northwestern. He'd seen a lot of death, as he, too, was a vet. He had to use the tree to right himself now after leaning in over the body. He was a bit unsteady given that one of his legs was prosthetic. "Sons of bitches," he muttered even as he dialed 9-1-1 on his phone.

◆   ◆   ◆

Jude was what her loving parents called her. Her father, a former military forensics doctor, whose cases were often fodder for fascinating bedtime stories, doted on her and spoiled her only in the area of love, as did her mother. Her mother had been a military mom, but she had her own life as an agricultural scientist and botanist. Dr. Judith 'Jude' Avery had lost them both to that horrid thing called cancer, which her mother battled. Alongside her father, Jude had to helplessly watch her strong mother's awful debilitation and final days—a thing that contributed to Jude's father's own death—the result of a broken heart, Jude was sure. Natural causes, his doctors called it, but she knew better. Jude had to work hard to block out this period in her life. To do so, she often called on thoughts of her early days as a child growing up on an army base with other 'army brats.' She recalled a time when she and the other children came across dead animals in the woods near the army base, their curiosity about death had been aroused, but none so much as hers.

Now a medical examiner herself, Dr. Judith Avery had two more John Doe's left on her schedule, one she called John Doe of the Big

Toes, and the other John Doe of the Fedora Hat. For the moment, she sank her gloved hands deep into her work—into the open corpse of Big Toes. Her fingers worked busily over the body of the man with no name. Likewise, her mind was at work with familiar questions that came rushing in whenever the victim was unknown. While enumerating his condition aloud for the record, Jude quietly played twenty questions in the back of her mind.

What was it authorities in Great Britain called a John Doe? Oh yes, A. N. Other or Another! Big Toes had been the sixth John Doe in as many days, along with a Jane Doe who'd made it seven. Only The Hat was different. The other unknowns had died of heatstroke and related complications such as dehydration. Were they too weak to seek help? Found beneath bridges and in the subway tunnels, had they no recourse whatsoever? Still there was that one about a month before who'd been savagely attacked and beaten to death, as it looked like The Hat had been as well. Both of these two had died horrible deaths, bludgeoned to death with some ungodly weapon that had yet to be identified.

All the other homeless deaths that Dr. Avery had recently seen had been the result of the staggering, stifling Chicago heat wave. One that'd continued for two and a half months. The daily newscasts had begun to keep count of the numbers overcome and hospitalized from heatstroke.

Will there be more homeless and nameless people, she silently asked herself coming in for a brief visit with me? To see the Assistant Medical Examiner of Cook County, Illinois? When will this damnable heat wave end? A heat wave in early fall!

Assistant Medical Examiner for Cook County, Illinois. The title had sounded so wonderful while the reality had become, thus far, rather banal until The Hat had arrived.

She made a mental note to talk to Dr. Shanley about the details of her autopsy of the homeless vet, also beaten to death a month earlier. Perhaps a comparison of their findings was in order. Whoever Shanley's John Doe was, he'd never been identified and had been interred in a Potter's Field at taxpayers' expense. Still, the possibility of there being a connection to the more recent murder nagged at Dr. Avery. The earlier autopsy simply held too many patterns—a similar MO. It all left her with a dry throat and a fear that they had a serial killer on the loose. Or else her imagination was in overdrive.

She felt a wave of fatigue and impatience building from within as she examined Big Toes's lungs. The organs were saturated with the distinct odor of tobacco with a hint of *Cannabis sativa*—pot. For the record, she used the formal name, adding, "Unmistakably so."

She ran through the remaining organs, and then paused, tired but eager to get to the next case. "We're finished with Big Toes for the time being, Ralph. If you don't mind, put him to bed."

Ralph watched the exhausted Dr. Avery step out of the autopsy room, and then poke her head back in to add, "It's not too late. We'll start in on the complete autopsy next."

"The Hat, oh yeah. After my break, doc."

Before she made her first cut on the next cadaver, John Doe of the Hat, Dr. Avery had examined the crime scene photos, as she had with photos taken of the discovery of Big Toes. In the photos of Hat, she noticed that the dead man's prone body was twisted like a pretzel. The image telegraphed his pain in the last moments of his life at the foot of a tree, whereas Big Toes had died in a peaceful if blistering setting. Jude had also taken note of the fact that the fedora hat looked nailed to the deceased's head, bloody and embedded in a wound, again unlike the death of Big Toes.

Earlier, when the body had been wheeled into the morgue, what few belongings the dead man owned had been tucked into a cigar-sized valuables box and placed inside the body bag. All but his crumpled hat. Apparently, it'd been removed from the head or had fallen off when the body was turned or lifted, and was retrieved after the body was bagged. The hat had been treated as an afterthought—duct taped to the bag at chest level.

Before beginning the autopsy, she learned the name of the detectives on the case, and she'd gotten one of them on the phone. She asked the man, Wayne Stephens, to explain what'd happened with the hat at the crime scene. Stephens laid it out in quick brush-stroke fashion that when the body had been turned to be searched for identification, the hat came away and was grabbed up by a dog. "It was the devil to get that dog to give it up, but the owner, something of a witness to the killing, managed to get it back, but by then your ETs had already bagged and placed the body into the van. My partner, Dennis Marks, he gave the hat to the techs."

"And they duct taped it to the body bag," she said with a sigh.

"I have no idea 'bout that."

"That's where it was when I first took note of it. Swamped as we are down here, I didn't say anything at the time, but that's damn careless handling of crime scene property."

"No one can predict what a dog will do."

"The dog ate your homework. I get it."

"Hey, now, doc—"

She'd hung up on the detective. Busy as she'd been with Big Toes, Dr. Avery had not questioned the carelessness regarding the bloody hat when it'd come through the door. She'd instead removed the hat and had zipped open the body bag to lift out the valuables box. She placed the bloody hat and the valuables atop a steel counter, readying to go to work. She stopped, stared hard at the hat and realized just how important it was, as important as what the hat had once covered—the victim's head while it was being smashed.

She needed a break badly, and she forced herself from the autopsy room to find a sandwich and a drink she'd left in the small refrigerator in her office. Ralph, too, had taken a break along with Lionel. When she returned, that dead man's hat was gone. This gave her a gasp, and at first, she thought that perhaps she'd placed it elsewhere, but unable to find it, after asking Ralph about it on his return, still the hat was nowhere to be found. Ignoring the mystery for the moment, she asked Ralph to unzip the body bag anew and cut it away to prepare the body for autopsy. When he did so, they discovered the hat. It was pulled snugly over the cranium of the dead man as if he'd gotten up for it and replaced it there.

Once it dawned on her just how badly the hat had been mishandled, Jude felt increasingly frustrated with this latest example of the ongoing lax attitude toward both evidence and human remains. She took action, calling down to the ET supervisor's office, wanting an official record of her complaint. She then made a mental note to follow up with an email. She explained the careless handling of the hat, and that the two crew members who'd transported the body to her morgue needed re-training in proper procedures. At the very least, the hat should have been placed in a dry paper bag and delivered separately into her hands with an explanation. The supervisor's less than keenly interested response was brief, "Hey, we're overworked and underpaid. Whataya 'spect, doc?"

Groggy from being overworked herself, and with the damage done, Jude thought there was nothing more to be done save move on. She soon discovered that the pattern of blood on the hat, inside and out, while compromised due to the mishandling, held useful clues. Mud caked in the dead man's hair was also caked onto the under rim of the hat. The darkest, largest blood stains surrounded holes in the hat where something like nails had penetrated the fabric and had gone directly into the skull and brain. This made the loss of the hat as evidence worse than ever. "What a screw up!"

Working now more slowly and steadily, she continued the autopsy, reminding herself again to make a cast of the teeth and to look for any implants that might help identify the dead man. In the back of her mind, Jude wondered again if the other, similar corpse that Dr. Shanley had autopsied might not have similar contusions and abrasions to the skull, and if so, could there be a link between the two dead men. Was this murder for fun or something personal? Someone with a grudge against the victim with the hat, or was the killer a stranger to the victim? Whichever, John of the Hat had, from what little she'd seen of Shanley's victim, similar wounds to the back of the head. "Messy work; very messy," she muttered, speaking of both the wounds and the unprofessionalism shown by Grant's evidence techs in the field.

Dr. Dean Grant's Chicago and Cook County ME's office was a huge affair, and Grant had seen to it that he had experts of every sort on his team. Clothing went to a team supervised by Dr. Shanley. Her team minutely examined a victim's clothing from head to toe, hat to heel. Shanley's Hair and Fiber department could take a splotch of carpet, even just a few fibers, or a minute piece of a tee-shirt, differentiate human or animal samples, blood from V8 juice, as well as animal fur from human hairs, and all manner of magic down to the genetics from cells left on the cloth or carpet or seat cushion, cigarette butts, crumpled wrappers, and disposable cups. Shanley's people were in charge of seeking out dried tissue, blood, hairs, fibers, broken fingernails, matter under fingernails, and fragments of metal, as well as all types of other materials, for a detailed report. Their report would follow her autopsy, both of which, ultimately, would find their way to a detective's desk.

So the hat mattered. It mattered a lot.

In fact, it mattered to more people than Jude. Handling the hat anymore than absolutely necessary, even with gloved hands, was not only highly unprofessional, but it also contaminated any evidence that might be found, rendering it, in some cases, useless. Anyone who had handled the hat must now be ruled out as a suspect. A real time sink. This manhandling of the hat from the crime scene to the morgue needed to be recorded and addressed.

Not long after the unsatisfying discussion with the ET director, Dr. Avery had come to the unofficial conclusion that her mystery victim had not been killed by a blunt object but by some sort of large spikes penetrating his skull and brain. This superseded her earlier suspicion that a crow bar had been used. The icepick nature of the wounds had ruled out many a weapon.

Her final analysis had the killer using some kind of ancient, metal-spiked battle ax. Or one mimicking the age-old weapon—like a modified baseball bat decked out with spikes the size of sixty-penny nails. A baseball bat with spikes protruding in every direction. The image of a mace or a spiked ball on a chain flitted through her mind.

That's what the hat said, speaking loudly and clearly to her, agreeing with her current assessment. The holes in the hat proved a perfect match to the location of each wound.

The heatstroke victims still awaiting processing would have to wait. Murder came first.

After another back-breaking hour of close work over John Doe Hat, Jude called it quits. "I'll have to finish later," she confessed to her lab assistant. "I'm beginning to make mistakes."

"It's fine by me, Dr. Avery."

She asked Ralph to place John into his temporary quarters—a lab freezer drawer. "For now it's see you later, Johnny," she said to the corpse.

Ralph, a big man with meaty hands, grabbed the wheeled Stryker slab and moved it to the freezer units, opened an empty drawer, and tilted the tabletop to deposit the corpse. He righted all the limbs before shoving the drawer inward. Drowning out the humming air conditioning, the resounding noise of the coasters, the unit door slamming shut, and then the handle falling for a final thud, all announced the official check-in of the dead.

With a morbid sense of humor, Ralph patted the door, saying, "Sweet dreams, buddy." Ralph then began whistling a Bob Dylan tune as he fell into the routine of readying the slab for the next autopsy while Dr. Avery left for a dinner break.

Later that evening

With the constant airflow overhead that promised to keep the room as antiseptic as possible in terms of air quality, and with the water hose at the ready, the sounds of the autopsy room played in Dr. Judith Avery's head even as she worked late into the night. With Ralph's help, she'd cleaned the horrible gash in the man's head. "My god, I'll be doing this in my sleep soon," she said.

John Doe had a full, thick head of hair. Ralph was given the nod and he began shaving the victim's head. The noise of the clippers got Dr. Avery thinking about taking a vacation. She needed it despite having been on the job in Chicago for only a few months. This Cook County job was taxing, non-stop death, and wearing on even the strongest among them. She thought about how Ralph, beside her, and Lionel, who only came and went as needed, moved like automatons, doing the job with silent, practiced efficiency when Ralph suddenly began an actual jig as he cut the dead man's hair.

She was getting that way, too, going from overtired goofiness to being completely jaded to the point where each body she autopsied was the same as the one before. It made her think of a line in a poem an old English teacher once read in a class, a poem called *The Misery of Mechanics* by some observant poet whose name escaped her now. The misery was in the daily grind, the business of inspecting cars and changing oil and light bulbs, draining oil pans, and going across the bridge from the job to home and wife, and how saying, 'Hello, honey, I'm home' as being the same as going to the men's room. It all began to have a grim sameness about it, becoming dull, gray, and meaningless.

Judith had always combated such depressive thoughts, such horrid emotions arising from mankind's worst enemy—boredom eating away at you from within. She had always vowed that if her work should ever make her as horribly depressed as the mechanic in the poem, that she'd step off, move away, and retool and reinvent herself. Of late, given the heat wave and the relentless parade of death it had brought to her autopsy work, she felt that deep misery creeping in. She feared her true talents were being wasted on heat-stroke victims.

Now the murder case, it just might be the thing, she told herself as the wound was cleaned. Cleaned of all blood and the hair surrounding it—*gone*. Ralph had done a perfect job. Respecting the dead man here and now, not leaving him absolutely bald. He'd left his professorial-looking ponytail intact as it was nowhere near the wound, so John Doe, wherever he wound up, would go to his Maker with that ponytail to distinguish him.

Ralph next cut away the clothing, and Lionel began to bag the trousers and shoes for Material Forensics examination. Her concern was with the body, and as soon as Ralph cut away the shirt, a tattoo revealed that John Doe was former military. The ink told the story. He'd had his unit emblazoned across his left shoulder. The discovery gave even Ralph pause, and he said, "This fella's a veteran. Afghanistan."

They saw the extensive damage to his left foot, which was half gone. They saw the stitches to major shrapnel wounds in his hip and side.

"Guy survives a war zone only to be murdered in Garfield Park. Sucks." Ralph sighed and took in a deep breath at once.

"Maybe we can at least ID him, given the tattoo, through military channels?"

"Lionel's good at tracing. He'll get on it."

Lionel didn't hesitate, taking a photo of the tattoo using his phone. He added a text message as directions, and he then immediately sent the shots to someone he knew in the service.

Judith began a close examination of the ugly wound to the head. She pulled over a light on a swivel arm to illuminate the wound and give it definition. As to the exact killing weapon, in this case, there was no way to know without a thorough examination of the wound, now cleaned and revealed. "There's at least two, maybe three blows here, but they're so close on one another, it's hard to tell. Hand me a depth gauge, Ralph."

The gauge was in her gloved hand in an instant. She dove into the measurements, explaining each step to Ralph. Going from side to side, up and down, all around. Then onto depth measurements of the same wounds to the cranium. Dr. Avery soon had the number, size, and depth of each blow.

She scanned for where the instrument of death had sunk into the skull. Like John Doe's hat, there were multiple deep wounds. Wide holes, deep holes. She pictured thick ice picks, and then she pictured thick, long nails one could purchase at any hardware store. Then she pictured the spikes on an ancient battle ax, the sort a marauding Viking might have wielded in the 13th century.

Ralph, who had been taking night classes for 'forever' to become a medical examiner himself—or so the joke went around the lab—watched Dr. Avery's every move as she again measured the depth and width of each wound, comparing them to the holes and stains on the hat. "Are they the same size?" he asked her.

"Precisely so. I have a suspicion the killer used something like a baseball bat spiked with nails."

"Shit...horrible...bastard."

"Agreed."

"I think Dr. Grant's going to want to hear about this one," said Ralph.

"No doubt."

"He may want to take over on it, too. He does that a lot, Dr. Avery."

"Is that so?"

"High profile cases." Ralph shrugged.

"Hold on. Just a sec." She switched off the overhead recording device. "Now tell me more about Dr. Grant."

Ralph displayed an exaggerated, emphatic shrug. "He gets off on the publicity, I think."

"I've heard that about Grant."

"Some think he's writing a book on his most spectacular cases."

"*Hmmm*...how do Dr. Shanley and others get along with him?" she ventured to ask, and then quickly added. "He's been awfully kind and generous where I'm concerned. Seems to trust me to do the work."

"Well...he's taken cases out of Dr. Shanley's hands. That's all I know. Doesn't do it with the male docs, only Shanley. She's been pissed with him for some time now."

"Thanks for the details and warning. Appreciate it." Even as she said thanks to Ralph, she wondered about his motive in speaking so candidly about the goings-on here. She recalled a Mark Twainism: You have two enemies. The one who goes behind your back, and the one who brings you the news. While she could not recall Twain's exact words, her memory had it close enough for the given situation.

"How're your night classes going, Ralph?" she said to test him.

"Not so good. I *hadda* quit again. Money run out."

"Can you look into getting a grant? Some Obama money? I admire you for continuing your studies."

The talk had veered away from the autopsy, and part of her appreciated this fact. Ralph stared deeply into her eyes and said, "I ought to look into a grant."

"I still owe a small fortune in student aid," she confessed.

"Some folks here take me as a joke, Dr. Avery. Thanks for...for you know."

She switched the recorder back on and continued with the autopsy. Using her recordings, Lenora Whitley would be transcribing the autopsy into a viable report for Grant and the Chicago PD. It'd been for this reason that she had switched off the mic when the conversation had drifted from the deceased to Dean Grant.

She knew the cause of death, the blows to the head with that deadly object, but protocol meant she had to continue with a complete autopsy even if just to determine that John Doe was in absolute, complete good health and there were no other contributing factors to his death. This meant a full cavity search of his organs, that he had to be opened up via a Y-incision. It meant the removal and examination and weigh up of the 'rack' of organs that inhabit the thoracic area. It meant the whole nine yards. She opened him and began.

Later, she examined the heart she'd removed, weighing it, studying its color, texture, size and heft. She continued speaking for the record as she searched but found only minimal signs of damage. She said, "A tinge of gray, but nothing serious. He had a strong heart that likely would have continued to beat for another forty or fifty years had he not been murdered."

Ralph watched her every move, wishing to learn more from her.

"Heart disease has become so commonplace," she said. "It's taken over as the number one killer in America, so I'm giving The Hat's heart a thorough going over, but look closely at it and tell me what you see."

"The heart in your hand looks good."

"Obviously, this fellow didn't die of natural causes. His heart stopped, yes, but it had lots of help to get there."

In fact, the bloodied back of the skull and brown muck of matted hair, stiff with dried blood—which she'd had Ralph photograph before shaving and cleaning it—was cause enough to stop a man's heart from beating. Still, she wondered if the heat wave in some tangential way had a connection here; wondered if the perpetrator, wielding his blunt object could have been acting out of what Dr. Avery called the *boiled brain syndrome*. Heat waves of this duration brought on a great deal of stress and even more violence in people than normal. Could John Doe's attacker be someone he knew, someone who snapped under the influence of that boiling point?

Murder, after all and in the end, for whatever reason other than self-defense, involved emotions. Passions drawn taut as a high wire, and those unstable on that wire generally fell to one side or the other in cases of murder as either victim or perpetrator.

"Given the *givens*, and the givens are extremely few," she said for the recorder, "the skull fractures are certainly the cause of death. Zeroing in on the exact nature of the weapon used will be more problematic. A good deal trickier than the naked eye alone can determine. Spiked baseball bat on the surface, but that notion has to be proved along with a great deal else."

It was going to be a long night. But at least she was doing worthwhile work and not another heat wave-related stroke death. She wasn't feeling the *Misery of Mechanics* anymore.

2

Dr. Avery was the new kid on Grant's block, Grant's highly honored and respected team, and one of the ET transport guys had already hit on Avery, making unwanted advances and a lewd suggestion. Something in the nature of a not so innocent question. "Ever wish to make love to a corpse or on the floor in here, doc?" The man was referring to the morgue floor.

Another had asked for a date. She'd refused any and all advances at the workplace and had made herself clear, but one of the 'boys' in particular had kept annoying her. His name was Luther Noble, the more obscene of the 'boys,' but there was nothing noble about the man. Noble had taken her office policy as a personal affront, and he had begun playing little jokes on her as a result. She imagined the business with the dead man's hat the day before was just that.

"You bet," she muttered to herself, forgetting to turn off the mic. She'd had Ralph return the murder victim to the slab. She must be thorough. Having reminded herself of the live mic overhead, she replaced her speech with thought: When did that hat get back on the dead man's head? Neither Ralph nor Lionel would've jammed the hat onto the head. At the crime scene, the hat was grabbed by the dog, and then later retrieved and taped to the outside of the body bag and delivered to the ME's in that manner. The only one who'd have screwed with it after that, had to be that idiot, Luther Noble.

It was true that Noble had been one of the two attendants who'd wheeled the body in with the hat duct taped to the body bag. The other one was a new person, a young female evidence tech. Dr. Avery believed that even if the young woman had done it, she would have done it at Noble's urging.

The guy was bad news and a loser's loser as far as Avery was concerned. He seemed to be working with a screw loose. When she had first discovered this problem with the hat atop the body bag, it did get under her skin. Exactly what would please Noble.

"Ralph, keep things in place for me here. I've got to take care of something," she said and rushed out. By the second, she was losing her calm. She'd rushed down the corridor to the break room where she believed Noble would be loitering, and she was not disappointed.

The place fell silent as if everyone in the break room had been expecting her. It was like every saloon in every western film when the Matt Dillon character walked in for the kill. She didn't hesitate. She lashed into Luther about his unprofessional behavior regarding the hat, first taping it to the victim rather than including it in either a separate paper bag or inside the body bag. Then she lambasted him for jamming the hat onto the dead man's head. "So disrespectful! We do not handle the deceased as if he's Uncle Bob Nobody or Aunt Sally No One. We work by the book, here, Mr. Noble."

Noble grinned at her like a contented cat, eyes wide as he pointed to his female partner, Lisa Coombs. "She did it, not me!"

"Is that true?" asked Dr. Avery, eyes afire.

"*Ahhh*, yes, Doctor. I didn't know where else to put the hat, and we were out of paper bags, and—and I didn't want to linger, so I put it on the gentleman's head."

"You unzipped the body bag, exposed the head from the bag, lifting it, gloved hands, I hope, and put his hat atop his head. Jammed it tight even. You did all that all by your lonesome?"

"I'm sorry, doctor, but yes, I did," confessed Lisa. "When you were on a break. Heard you complaining 'bout it earlier, on the phone."

"Lisa, you realize I'll have to report this to Dr. Grant."

"Oh...yes, I suppose you must."

"Dr. Shanley must know as well, for her examination. I—I have no alternative."

Lisa nodded, pursed her lips, but said nothing.

"This is a major breach of protocol. Any blood on the hat's been *compromised*, a dirty word in forensics. It renders it useless as evidence." Dr. Avery thought of how perfectly the puncture holes in the hat aligned with the blows to the skull.

"I am sorry and I—I understand, doctor."

"Do you? Do you really?" Dr. Avery saw that Noble was stifling a giggle, while two other evidence techs remained silent, their faces showing displeasure. They were not stifling laughter. They appeared to find no humor in this confrontation nor in Lisa's uncomfortable situation.

"Come with me. We'll go see Dr. Grant together."

Lisa complied, and the two women left the break room. Behind them, they heard Noble talking to the other men in the room, but his words were too garbled to understand. When she had gotten Lisa to a quiet corner, Dr. Avery said, "The truth now. How much of a hand did Noble play in this?"

She shook her head, avoided eye-contact, and sighed heavily. All signs that Jude Avery knew and understood. "Working with that man has to be a nightmare," Dr. Avery added. "Out with it; I need the truth."

This caught Lisa's attention and for a fleeting moment, she was about to confess when she stopped herself. "I really, really need this job."

"He's harassed you and put you up to this, hasn't he?"

No answer. Shuffling and staring at feet.

"Has he told you I am a cold bitch? That maybe I am frigid because I haven't responded to his advances?"

"I'll take my punishment, now, Dr. Avery."

"You mean *his* punishment, don't you?"

"I did it, not Luther."

"His idea? He lifted the head while you slipped the hat on, or the other way around, he has you lift the head?"

"You're so smart, you figure it out." Lisa said through gritted teeth, eyes afire now for the first time.

"Save your anger for Luther. You're going to need it."

Lisa fell silent again, eyes and head bowed, again unable to meet Jude's eyes. "You smell of cheap latrine soap, Lisa. At least you washed the blood off your hands."

"We had gloves on!"

"We, I see." Dr. Avery glared at the young woman. "Listen, if you wish to file charges against any man here, I will back you up. Especially if it'd help to get Luther Noble out of here."

She stood mute.

"All right then, but when it becomes unbearable and you've developed an ulcer from it, and you're no longer sleeping well, and you want to do something about it, I will add my voice to yours and together, we will see the door swing on that *jagoff*. Understood?" Dr. Avery lifted Lisa's chin and forced the eye-contact. "I mean it. I will stand with you. The man has gone too far."

"I need this job."

"I get it. You have kids at home, a mother in ill health?"

"How'd you know all that?"

"Call me a mind reader. It's an educated guess. Don't let that bastard bully you another day. You're better than that."

Dr. Avery started away when Lisa asked, "What about reporting me?"

"That was for Luther's sake. I'm not reporting you."

"Isn't *that* against the rules?"

Dr. Avery returned a few steps and coolly whispered, "Are you going to report *me* for not reporting *you*?" Chuckling, she turned back down the hallway and through the double doors of the morgue and autopsy rooms. There she took a moment to jot a note to herself which in cursive read: *Training seminar for all ET's and transport personnel SOON.* She then added: *Don't assume others know shit.* She recalled how her father had always put it: *Make those you lead earn your assumptions.*

The two detectives who had been put on the case of the unknown man in Dr. Avery's care were Jonathan Marks and Wayne Stephens, both homicide veterans. They'd taken the call and after the first uniformed officers on scene at Garfield Park, the detectives were the first to see the victim and walk the scene. Evidence techs later arrived and awaited the 'all-clear signal' from the detectives before they created a grid of the scene, searching for any possible evidence, however minuscule it might be. The ETs had filled a few bags with trash that might or might not be relevant. It was apparent that the victim had been eating a meal in the park when he was attacked. That much any pair of eyes could determine.

Marks had pocketed one piece of evidence, however: a white paper bag with a Red Lion logo on it. He knew the place. They'd relocated from an area in the city where no one, much less a patron of the bar and grill, could find a parking space any longer—a circumstance that'd existed now for over a decade, ever since the city decided it could make a fortune by selling parking stickers for every residential block across Chicago. No one not living on the block could park on it.

As a result, The Red Lion Inn had relocated to the Garfield Park area, and here the Lion was thriving. "Just a half block or so from the park," Marks had whispered to Stephens, who understood, saying, "Whoever handed the victim that bag from the Lion is quite possibly the last person to see him alive, other than his killers."

Earlier, the detectives had interviewed Thadeus Wilson and his dog. Wilson had said, "There were two of them. One wielding the weapon, killing the poor man while the other disgusting bastard filmed it."

"We have to take your dog in," Stephens had then informed Mr. Wilson, who grimaced. "Pongo? Whatever for? He's had his shots, and I have his license at home."

"If he bit either of the assailants," replied Stephens, "then we might get human DNA from Pongo's fangs."

"Not fangs, Wayne!" corrected his partner, Marks. "Dog's got canines."

"You won't harm him, will you?" asked Wilson.

"Oh no! We'll treat him well," said Marks, a dog lover.

"Like any witness," added Stephens.

"I got him as a pup, to help me heal after a breakup. Love him so much. Even one night apart...well, if it is necessary." He handed the dog, on the leash now, to a uniformed officer. "Get Pongo here to the MEs."

"Now?"

"Now and no stops along the way."

The detectives, after waving in the ETs, abruptly left the murder scene for The Red Lion. It was early morning, but perhaps someone who *schlepped up* around the place might be on hand for a few questions.

◆ ◆ ◆

It wasn't long before everyone in the ME's office and by extension the ambulance drivers and secretaries, down to the janitorial staff were falling all over Pongo, and everyone was also abuzz with news of the homeless veteran's terrible death at the hands of some ghoul wielding a battle-ax. Rumors ranged from it's being the handiwork of a maniac on the loose to a time-traveling, battle-ax wielding Neanderthal or Viking. Dr. Judith Avery had slept on it, her sleep disturbed more than once by what she'd seen of the man's crushed skull and the no less than three-inch deep puncture wounds that had done the damage. She'd not been there when Pongo captivated the staff or when Dr. Shanley took swabs from the dog and was told by the detectives that their victim was a veteran known about the neighborhood as Sammy.

In her sleep, her subconscious had filled in the gaps; she came to a clear picture of the blows. There had been at least two blows, driving home nine puncture wounds, but only the three deep enough to kill. She decided the nails at the end of the club or bat had to be five to a side, at least ten in all. She surmised this from the close examination of the spacing of the killing results.

Still, to be certain, a replica of the weapon needed to be done. She knew it needed to be wielded with authority. At least two blows to a ham hock or some other soft tissue with bone beneath. To simulate how the round angle of the bat drove in five nails at once, three of which went deep, two not so deep. The second blow saw only four punctures. Either that or *vice-versa*: four then five. The curvature of the bat and how it was wielded would, she believed, tell a convincing story.

To this end, she'd had Ralph secure the necessary props, and when prepared, he'd called her and said, "Dr. Avery, Jeeves and I are ready."

"*Jeeves?*"

"We gave the pig a name. Seemed only fitting."

"Then you were able to get a pig's head?"

"Yeah, Jeeves!"

"A relatively firm, fresh pig's head, you mean?"

"In a vise, awaiting your presence, yes, doctor."

Somewhere in the bowels of the building stood an entire floor devoted to ballistics at one end and a workshop and freezer unit at the other end. A place Jude Avery now searched for. It was where Ralph had fashioned the killing instrument. A Louisville Slugger with ten nails driven into and through the tip in rows of five on either side. Each nail had been carefully placed, precisely as she had imagined. Each obliterating the black marker points she'd placed on the bat, simulating the murder weapon.

It was only when Ralph had crafted the weapon and secured the poor pig's head that he called her down to the testing area. All had been arranged by Lionel and him, the 'grips' of the ME's department.

As Avery entered, Lionel, a thin, angular man, Ralph's opposite in stature and size, handed her a pair of safety glasses and some surgical gloves. All she had to do was put her safety glasses on as Ralph administered two blows to the pig's head, a prop secured from the stash of such parts in a freezer unit. The ME's department got donations like Jeeves from the many slaughter houses in the city. Chicago remained to this day the hog butcher to the nation.

Dr. Avery had instructed Ralph to make the first blow at a position in back of the pig's skull, and the second from the front. Her exacting examination of the wounds suffered by the homeless veteran John Doe showed that the nails in the first blow had angled down from the rear, while the second blow angled in and down from the front, while both blows had struck the dead man in the same specific region. In fact, two of the nail holes nearly shared the same space as they fractured the skull. "The SOB appears to have aimed for the same spot over and over," she'd told Ralph when she asked him to aim for the same spot on the pig's cranium.

Ralph didn't disappoint her. In fact, he so accurately followed her orders, that he was fast endearing himself to her. She almost wanted to pay his school bills for him.

Judith moved in close to see the results more clearly. Lionel, curious, as he'd wanted to wield the bat when Ralph had won the coin toss, also moved in for a closer look. Ralph had hefted the bat over his shoulder and stepped off, a look of accomplishment wafting across his face before he went blank again. A single grunt escaped Lionel, his reaction to Ralph's bringing down the bat.

"This is going to be quite helpful, Ralph, Lionel." Dr. Avery gave Ralph a quicksilver smile. "Get the video Lionel's made safely tucked away, and freeze the head. Dr. Grant may well wish to see this simulation, I mean, if he questions my findings. Or let us say *our* findings. Thanks, both of you."

Apparently, Dr. Dean Grant had heard the rumors about this 'special' John Doe, now being called Sammy the Vet; the one who'd come into the morgue with a slew of additional heatstroke victims as if hiding among the other corpses.

Grant had heard a few things about how poorly the body had been handled, and something about a hat, and something about sacrificial goat and blood drinking along with the new ME claiming that the vet was her purview and that she'd be overseeing every aspect of the case to the exclusion of others.

Grant suddenly showed up to find his new ME experimenting below ground and taking up Ralph and Lionel's time. When he entered, he did so with a question.

"What exactly is going on here, Dr. Avery? I am hearing all manner of reports about you and this murdered veteran."

Before she could answer, Grant, a big man with the shoulders of a lowland gorilla and a charismatic personality just as large, stepped close to the smashed skull of the pig, a head that had been secured to a table, fitted over brackets that held it in place.

"*Ahhh*, a simulation of what happened to that poor man I'm hearing about?" Grant asked.

"John Doe, 34598, yes, sir," replied Dr. Avery.

"And he's still a number?"

"Afraid so, doctor, except for a first name, Sammy or Samuel."

"What's this telling you?" he indicated the pig's head.

"A number of things, sir."

"Things? *Things*? What things? Not my favorite word, Dr. Avery. A bit too obscure. What *things* do you mean, exactly?"

"My preliminary report will be on your desk in an hour," she said.

"I don't like my labs seeming like the set of a soap opera."

She lightly laughed at this image. "I can assure you, if that is the case, it's not my doing."

"I should hope not. We're all under glass, you know. This office is scrutinized by those who control the purse strings. Anything that smacks of unprofessional behavior, any breach of protocol, well, you can well imagine the position it puts me in."

"You certainly have no reason for worry about me, sir. I believe in safety and protocol. I believe there've been no breaches of either."

"I want to see everything you have on this vet's case. This is the kind of case that can easily bring down far more scrutiny on us than we want, understood?" He then spoke to Lionel and Ralph. "And you two, this is not a g'damn story factory. I've warned you both before about gossiping about the doctors and assistants, and about ongoing cases. If I find either of you have again shot your mouths off about this case, I will give you a choice." He took the baseball bat with the spikes shimmering below the light fixture and held it high. "Your preference: I fire you or I take this bat to you."

Hyperbolic came into Jude Avery's mind.

Grant, a stormy man, left as suddenly as he had come.

"Dr. Grant's under a lot of stress," Lionel said. "Divorce is what I heard."

Ralph shook his head at Lionel. "That's exactly what he said not to do, Lionel, gossip."

Lionel's hurt look was replaced with his comeback, "It's not gossip if it's true, is it?"

Judith Avery shook her head, removed her protective glasses from where they'd been resting in her hair, and again asked Ralph to take a series of photos of the result of their experiment. She then told Lionel he should get back upstairs in case he was needed by Dr. Shanley or any of the other MEs. Lionel nodded, started to leave, but then turned and raised his hand to her, and for a moment, she thought he was going to strike her, when he plucked a piece of pig flesh caught up in her hair. He produced it in his palm. "Saving this for lunch, doc?" he joked, tossed the flesh to the table with the vise and left.

"Lionel is a joker. Watch him. That was in his hand to begin with and not in your hair."

"Thanks, Ralph. I appreciate your confidence in me."

"I could tell the moment I met you that you're good people. Some people aren't so nice or good at all, and some are just annoying while others just scare you. Dr. Grant tries to scare people, but we all know he's got a good heart."

"Is he in the midst of a divorce?" asked Judith.

"Well...I don't listen to such talk, so I couldn't say."

"Such events in a person's life do affect their work and attitude. Knowing it, if it is true, gives me reason to forgive his, *ahhh,* abruptness and rudeness."

"Oh, I don't think he was rude. He's in charge. He has to be tough."

"Well, get the video sent to me, and see to it that Jeeves here remains fresh," she pointed at the smashed pig's head.

"Fresh as a daisy. You can count on me, Dr. Avery." Ralph gave her a slight wave as she disappeared for the corridor and the elevator. Jude felt a wave of endorphins for a job well done, and she felt confident that her experiment had useful clinical results.

At the noon hour, Jude knew she had to face Grant for a second time that day, and that she had to be prepared. Lionel had finally gotten back to her regarding a lead on their John Doe. The members of the unit depicted on the man's bicep had all been killed save Samuel Evan Dewalt. It stood to reason the survivor and homeless Sammy was one and the same. Lionel had also sent out a man into the field who flashed a photo of the deceased around the area of Garfield Park, and the few hits that he got had the man's name as Sammy, who'd been a fixture in the area, known primarily by the local merchants. It was further evidence that the man known as Sammy of Garfield Park was also Corporal Samuel Evan Dewalt.

Almost on cue, Detectives Marks and Stephens visited Dr. Avery, and after pleasantries, they announced that they had a bead on the John Doe, and that his street name was Sammy. It was all anyone knew him by. They seemed puffed up to have found out this much and spoke of how he'd gotten a handout from one of the cooks at The Red Lion. She thanked the detectives for bringing her up to speed. "Any idea who could have murdered Corporal Dewalt?" she asked, unable to help herself.

"Corporal Dewalt?" asked Marks.

"You know who he is?" Stephens added.

"We do now, thanks in large part to our great staff here. You can thank Lionel next time you run into him."

The detectives hemmed, hawed, said a see-you-later and were tripping on one another to get out of her lab.

"Before you go, detectives," she said, stopping them at the double doors, "Did anyone at this Red Lion place see anyone harassing or in any sort of disagreement with the dead man?"

"The fellow who gave him his last meal, we still have to question. He's been a bit hard to find."

"I'd urge you to do so, and to get any video from the restaurant to study for possibilities."

"That's standard, but it wouldn't help in this case," said Marks.

"Seems Sammy never actually came into the place. The cook would meet him out back. No cameras on the alleyway."

"That's too bad. Well, please let me know if you learn anything else."

This time, she did not interrupt their quick exit.

Armed with an ID for their John Doe and with all the effort she had put into the autopsy, the simulation of how Samuel Dewalt was murdered, the type of weapon used, and her exacting notes on the puncture wounds, Jude felt confident she would impress Dr. Grant and remain lead forensic investigator on the case, regardless of how 'red ball' it may have become, and regardless of how new she was to Chicago Law Enforcement. When she knocked at his office door, she silently prayed to the god of Jeeves that Dr. Grant would be bowled over by her sheer compilation of information in such a short period of time.

"Enter," he said from behind his desk, not bothering to stand.

She tentatively found a seat opposite him, a shaft of light from a side window bathing her where she sat. She worried momentarily at having rushed her makeup this morning. She'd been anxious to get back to tackle this case.

Grant took a moment to rearrange a couple of photos on his desk. He turned one toward her, a photo of a boy and a girl. "Sweet looking kids, eh? Best thing I ever did, help make those kids good citizens and to keep them out of this field we're in, Dr. Avery."

"They look a little young for this work, sir."

"They're forty and forty-two now, own their own homes, all grown up. My girl went into commercial rental property sales, and my son, Devon, he's a TV news producer, works at WBBM right here in Chi-Town."

She wondered why he was telling her all this, and if it had to do with the rumored divorce. "But you keep their photos as children on your desk?" she asked. "Why? Sentimentality?"

"Something like that. Best years of my life when the kids were in it. Back then I was where you are now, an assistant ME to Dr. Jeremiah Fenger, whose family has doctors going back to the Stone Age, I suspect. Fenger, now there was a tough task master." Grant then showed her a photo of his wife who looked half Grant's age.

"Not a current photo either?" Judith asked.

"No...this was taken perhaps fifteen or so years ago."

"Is everything all right, Dr. Grant?" she asked, half hoping he'd simply say yes, that all was ducky, so she would not have to hear about how his life was falling down around him.

"Actually, my wife and I had a rough patch after the children flew the coop, but we overcame the obstacles. What doesn't kill you, all that, you know. But recently, we're having a new...*ahhh*, well another rough patch, which I suspect we'll get over."

"I suggest flowers, sir."

"It's way beyond flower stage and jewelry stage and gift stage." He sighed heavily.

"Maybe a cruise? Travel does wonders for a—"

"I would prefer, Dr. Avery, that we were," he hesitated long enough to scowl, "that we start talking about this Samuel Dewalt killing."

"Yes, of course, I'd prefer that myself, sir."

"Good, good." Grant's features tightened. "Yes, that's what you're here for. To discuss the case. Look, it's obvious that you're a hard worker, a go-getter, and we need that around here, of course."

She wondered what he could be driving toward. She instantly recalled Ralph's warnings about Grant. She fought them off, wanting to make her own assessment. "Thank you," she replied.

"It's commendable how hard you're working, Dr. Avery, and I wanted to preface anything I say with a caveat, *family* comes first around here. Always has under my administration. That is as much as the job allows. One reason you were hired is because, frankly, you *have* no family. That was a big plus in your favor over other candidates just as qualified, you see."

Didn't see that coming, she thought. This was the second time within minutes that Grant had surprised her, and she could not conceal her shock at this revelation. "I thought I was hired purely on my qualifications."

"Well you were, you were," he said. "I'm not saying you weren't. I am saying, I saw that you were single. No one else on staff here is single, and most have children. I am confessing here, Doctor, so let me clear the air. I wanted you for all those people who do have family for times when they have to be away, off duty, you see, and with this damnable heat wave on top of us, just sitting on the city as it is, you've been called on more than any two other staff members to do more and more work, and it has not been easy or fair to you."

"I've not complained, sir, and I've not been here long enough to ask for a raise," she half joked, a smile widening her face.

"No, no you haven't complained or copped an attitude, none of that! And well, I admire that in you."

Oh my god, don't let him hit on me, she silently prayed. "Thank you again."

"Look, I just want you to understand how things work around here. I've got monkeys on my back all the time, and most often, I can wrestle the bastards down, but between the press and city hall," he shrugged, then added, "and then there's the city councilmen and well, all manner of people hounding these corridors whenever we get a high-profile case."

"Hold on...high-profile case? This homeless man was an ignored wounded warrior, likely mentally wounded as well. Last night, when he came into the autopsy room with that hat on his chest, he was a non-person. So why is there such an uproar over him now?"

"He's a vet. According to Lionel, a *decorated* vet."

Strange, she thought, Lionel withholding that gem of information from me. "Lionel didn't tell me he was decorated."

"Mostly it appears for not dying."

"They give medals for that?" she asked.

"For being wounded in action. You saw the condition of his body."

"Of course."

"I meant for not dying with his buddies, they gave him a medal. Still, there was no medal on him," continued Grant. "Only a screw top from a wine bottle. In any event, the press is all over it, and they're making him out to be some sort of Chicago street martyr."

"You're taking me off the case?" she asked point-blank, again recalling Ralph's dire prediction.

"Not entirely, no. But the mayor's office wants me to take point on it. Nothing personal. It's about optics."

"Optics, I see."

"If the press is already howling, it's only going to get louder."

"Understood...sir."

"Reflects badly on the mayor's commitment to ending crime on our streets."

"Sure...they only see a man comes home from a war alive only to be murdered in Garfield Park of all places."

"And in vicious fashion." Grant then tried a bit of gallows humor. "Well, Garfield was shot while in office. See the irony?"

"Not really, sir. Wasn't he actually killed by his doctors who botched getting the bullet out of him?"

"By gosh, you're right about that."

She now realized she was here to agree and bolster his ego. But she wanted a concession, so she said, "But, sir, all I want is to remain on the case, and—and to do what I can to identify the horrible person who killed Corporal Dewalt."

"Commendable, so we work together as a team, as it should be."

"Yes, that sounds good, doable, as they say."

"But you're to never engage with the press. You give them nothing. Refer them to me or to our PR department as you have 'no comment,' understood?"

"Yes, of course, it's in my job description."

"It is? Oh, good. Well then, show me what you've pieced together so far."

Even as she shared all her facts and theories with Dr. Grant, Jude sensed that he'd throw her under the bus at any time it became expedient to do so. Still, he was the boss, and she wanted to be here, to do her job, and more than anything to bring Corporal Samuel 'Sammy' Dewalt's killer to justice. For these reasons, she stifled any misgivings about the working relationship and pushed forward. Before long, Dr. Grant, whose track record as a medical examiner in Chicago was beyond reproach, said, "Dr. Avery, Judith, this is excellent work. You've managed a huge leap forward from the moment you touched the dead man's hat."

Coming from Grant, this was high praise indeed. She stifled a blush that refused to die as it slowly overcame her will. "Just doing my job, sir."

"Exemplary work, really. Between you and me, Dr. Avery, it's your case. Consider me a titular talking head."

"And we'll keep that our little secret then. And thank you for your vote of confidence."

"This case...if you had family, if you have a boyfriend even, this case will put a hell of a strain on the relationship. Just know that sometimes that strain is too much for a relationship to bear, and everything comes unglued. Unravels."

She realized he was back to the divorce thoughts going on some-where in the far reaches of his mind. He quickly recovered to tell her to get out of his office and back to work. "We still have to do our damned-est. Can't expect those bungling detectives to solve this case without us."

She quickly left, anxious to part from Grant who seemed at times despondent. She was not great with depressed people and their de-spondency. She believed few people were any good at such matters. Perhaps if trained in social work or psychiatry, she could offer some kind words to Grant, a symbolic gesture, but she knew not to offer a shoulder to cry on. That could lead to more complications in her life than she ever wished to have again, becoming involved with a married man as she had during her graduate years at the university.

The same day across the city

Mitch Goodwin loaded the video on as an attachment and was ready to forward it to Keith's contact in LA. Chicago to Los Angeles in a whisper-net second. Then, boom! And his best pal, his only pal, Keith Kiley would be *the man!* The video showed the murder of the vet in Chicago, the whining bastard everyone called Sammy. They'd labeled the video *Sammy's Last Complaint* as just before the crack of the sec-ond blow to his head, Sammy complained in a dying voice, "Why're you doing this to me?" and "I don't wanna die!"

Certainly Sammy had nothing the young men had wanted other than his life. Mitch had added what he thought was a bit of colorful commentary spliced in, mocking the veteran for being such a crybaby and a whiner, on public assistance, going around begging. "Conduct unbecoming a solider, soldier!" Mitch had said as Samuel Evan Dewalt was bleeding to death.

"Nailed him, Keith. KK! You really did, man!" Keith used KKboy as his profile name on social media.

Mitch was about to send the video attachment to Keith's LA bud-dy, who was more heavily invested in the murder game than anyone Mitch knew except for KK. But he hesitated. Put it on hold. He lifted his phone and hit KKboy's name when it came up on his contacts screen. When Keith came on, Mitch explained, "Video editing's done."

"I'm at work, Mitch, so what?"

"So it's ready to go to LA, but…"

"But what?"

"Are you absolutely sure you can trust this guy to keep the video private? This gets out and we're both in for life."

"Damn it, Mitch, just do it. Oh wait, you get my blackened hands on the ball bat? Some nigger's gonna fry for this, and who knows, if it goes viral, hell, we might be the two guys who get the race war up and going. Manson couldn't do it, Trump ain't done shit with it."

"I ain't so sure it's such a good idea. Sharing it with people in LA, I mean."

"LA only shares with me and a handful of others across the country. Send the damn video. I want to win this thing."

"Kind of like deadly Pokemon Go, isn't it?" asked Mitch.

"I got no response to that. Got no clue how you could put those two together. Damn it, Mitch, we killed two guys now, former soldier boys. It's no game, not anymore."

"He's just going to do you one better out there is LA, isn't he?"

"Maybe, maybe not."

"Suppose he does a nun, like he's been saying? Then what? Or two nuns! Just to be sure he outdistances you, eh?"

"Nature of the game. Then I see his two nuns, and I raise him maybe three little girls, real princesses, young enough to be virgins. Maybe from straight-laced suburban go-to-church families."

"You're a sick man," Mitch said. "I'd do a priest before I'd do a child."

"Bullshit. You couldn't do either. You haven't got the balls for this game."

"Like I said, you're a sick sonofabitch, KK, but I guess you don't need me to point that out."

"I am quite aware of my finer qualities. Now, you just send it, fat boy!"

"No need to get nasty."

"Do it."

"All right, all right, but if it gets out, goes viral, we're up a shit creek—both of us, and suppose your pal in LA wants to win more than he wants to see you safe from the law?"

"We all signed a pact, and—"

"I know, but a pact, a treaty is only as good as the weakest link in that pact."

"You worry too damn much. Getting on my nerves."

Mitch almost said but stopped the thought from being vocalized. *What, you going to off me next?* He instead said, "KK, seriously, how're you ever going to top two murdered vets, and the one, according to the news, a decorated vet?"

"There's always a way."

Mitch felt a child's memory of fear spike along a skittering walkway known as the spinal cord. The fear moved along his spine on spidery limbs. "So you got not one iota of regret over Sammy the vet?" Mitch pressed.

"Regrets are for losers, and remorse for morons. I am neither."

Mitch contemplated the rules of the game. There was a winner each month, and that was determined by a group called the Council of Elders of Chaos or CEC, all of whom held an equal vote. To become a member of the council, a guy like Keith had to kill someone, film it, and the murder must make headline news in a major venue like the Chicago Tribune. It must also have a racial component. After all, the ultimate aim of Chaos was a race war.

After a video was submitted to the Council, the *wave* it caused, the level of fear and confusion generated was put to a vote. It was late September in Chicago, and Keith believed it was going to be his lucky September given what he'd accomplished. Mitch felt somewhat confident as well. *Someone has to win,* he thought, *so why not KKboy and me?*

Mitch hit send and the video was on its way to LA and the head guy, the Elder of the elders, the man who'd started the game.

From all that Mitch could decipher, the game was cobbled together from several harmless video games that the Elder in LA had combined and fused and made real. He started the whole thing a year ago when he made his first *kill for real* video. Something about a little old lady in her home, a break-in that he'd filmed. Mitch had seen the film. Bad quality, really, shaky as can be. The guy did it alone, trying to do the deed and film at the same time. Really dragged out the beating the old woman took. Mitch flinched more than once at her obvious pain. She didn't go fast the way Keith had dispatched Sammy the slumber-bum vet.

As soon as Mitch had sent the video, he called Keith back to let him know it was done.

"I assumed so when I hung up. You can't keep calling me at work. You need to get out of your mom's basement and find a job just for something to do with your days, man."

"I don't do well in interviews. I get panic attacks."

"Apply for something online then, for...for online work, but whatever you do, quit calling me so much here."

"Okay, okay, okay."

Keith hung up, and Mitch just once wished Kiley would say thanks, but he sensed KKboy never would. KK might've at least asked Mitch how the dog bite was healing. Typical of KK, giving Mitch's pain not a single thought.

3

The same day, Jude, still pulling together all the evidence in the Dewalt caser, working like an orchestra conductor, met Pongo the dog. Human DNA had been pulled from the dog's saliva. Tests were being run on it. Once it was fully processed, it'd be run through the local and the national databases to determine a match to anyone in the system. It was a long shot.

Meeting with Assistant ME Dr. Sybil Shanley, Jude had urged the other assistant ME to make the case top drawer. "Dr. Grant wants it that way," she'd told Dr. Shanley. The older woman had listened politely on their first meeting over the dead man's clothing and hat, a kind of Mona Lisa smile and a slight blush of pink seemingly dying along her throat. Judith was unsure what Sybil's smile portended, but it wasn't congeniality, nor was it frivolity; no it was something entirely mysterious. Possibly to set Jude to questioning everything.

As much as Jude hated petty office protocols, and especially office politics, she knew it was the reality she lived in. For this reason, she had pasted on her own best smile for Shanley, who no doubt was at this moment trying to cipher any hidden meanings behind Avery's smile.

Does Sybil know something I don't, Jude thought, provoked by Shanley's smile. Of course, Shanley had been working for Grant for years. She definitely knew more about him and how things at the Chicago ME's office worked and didn't work. For this reason, Judith braced herself for a lecture on some aspect of the workplace, possibly an insight into Grant and how he worked. Judith was surprised, however, when Shanley simply nodded at everything Judith said, adding nothing.

"I don't mean to come off like some shrew, but I have been put in charge of this case, and it's my first *big* case since coming on, so I want to get it right and get it fast. For Dr. Grant, of course."

"I understand," Shanley finally said. "We are all here to please Dean, after all."

"He is rather larger than life, isn't he?"

"You could say that, sure."

"I was hoping to give him an addendum to my prelim report, but I can't do that without your report."

"That'd be a good way to go, Dr. Avery, if I hadn't already given my report to Dean."

"Oh...oh, I see. I was unaware. This morning?"

"This morning."

"He had it on his desk this AM?"

"Yes. I was told to make it top priority by Grant last evening. I came in after hours, did a second shift for the clothing and that hat you sent to me."

"Dr. Grant failed to...well, he didn't tell me any of that when I met with him. Seems strange."

"That's Dean. Best get used to it."

"He assured me that I was by all accounts in charge of the case, so I thought…"

"Yeah, I know the feeling. You think you know something, but you don't. Kind of like a missing battery in the flashlight or the essential ingredient in a recipe."

"But he told me I was in charge of the flashlight."

Shanley smiled at this. "Overseer on the case. You understood what Grant wanted you to understand."

"What would that be?"

Sybil was a petite blonde-headed woman a few years older than Judith, and she looked like someone who'd be far more comfortable weaving rugs or baskets than working around a forensics lab. She had small but clever hands, like a seamstress's, and while she looked demure and even timid if judged badly, the truth was just the opposite. Shanley was a fireball of energy and if angered, she let people know it.

Aside from that, and the fact Sybil drank far too much coffee, this was all that Jude knew of the only other woman in the ME's office.

"You go by Judith, right?" asked Shanley, looking her in the eye.

"Yes, Judith or Jude."

"Not Judy?"

"No, never Judy! I prefer Jude, thanks."

"Call me Sybil. We're all pretty informal around here, and I think we gals need to stick together."

"All right, no problem with informal. I prefer it myself except around certain males."

"Luther Noble, I suspect you mean."

Jude's grimace answered Sybil.

"You know, Judith, *ahh* Jude, you should have written Lisa up the other night."

"What? I mean how do you know about what happened last night? At the time, you weren't even here."

Sybil laughed at this. It was a laugh a person uses to say to another just how naive can you be? "Darlin'...Jude, a medical environment is always a petri dish for gossip and talk. The story is all over the building, on every floor." She laughed again as Dr. Avery blushed.

"You think my reporting Lisa would've made a better story?" she asked, a bit miffed.

"Not a better story for the hallways, no, but a better story for Grant. He's got to have heard the story by now as well."

"You think so?"

"He's holding it over your head right now and you don't even know it."

"You think he's upset with me for not writing Lisa up?"

"Angry, upset, doesn't really matter if he can *use* it to have you beholden to him."

"I don't like that word, beholden. How do you mean it?"

"He has a habit of getting what he wants, anyway he wants. He's not going to ask you to compromise yourself, not in any sexual sense or any ethical sense, but he will find a way to use your 'mistake' against you."

"I don't see how my being empathetic to Lisa's situation could possibly be used in some sort of office *blackmail*."

"Oh it will be far too subtle to be called blackmail or harassment. He's a smart man and happily married. Well, he was that for most of his adult life."

"Can we get back to the case?"

"Oh, but dear, we've been talking about the case all along."

Judith stared into the other woman's eyes to see if she was serious, and Shanley's eyes assured her that she was being absolutely serious.

"Why haven't you provided me with the report on the dog saliva and the clothing? I mean at least a copy of what you provided Grant?"

"I have. It's in your in-box, Dr. Avery...Jude."

Jude bit her lower lip before asking, "Are you familiar with the band *Tool*, Sybil?"

"*Tool*...yeah, heavy rock, right? Kind of like *Def Jam*."

"Tool hasn't put out a physical record for ten years."

"Really? I didn't know that."

"In-fighting with their own record label."

"Damn!"

"Even so, they've found a way to remain relevant."

"Are you saying that you're a *tool*?" joked Sybil.

"I am saying, like Tool, there are more ways than one to skin a cat."

Jude realized just how much confusion within had collided with frustration from without. It felt like a nine car pile up in her mind. What kind of end run was Dr. Grant pulling on her, and how did Sybil know so damn much?

"Sweetie," began Sybil, placing fingers over Jude's hand.

"Don't call me sweetie. I am no one's *sweetie*."

"Judith, Jude, listen, I've been through the wringer with Dean, and somehow I am still standing. If you ever need to talk, any advice about this place or Dean or Noble or a certain form needing to be filled out, I am here for you."

Jude studied Sybil for a moment. For all I know, Jude thought, she's being friendly toward me for her own ulterior motives.

"Judith, stop your dark thoughts about me."

"I have none, truly."

Shanley was quick to have picked up on Jude's internal monologue, and this impressed Jude. Sybil then said, "Dean's having an affair, yes, but it's not with me."

"I had no such thoughts."

"I am way too smart to shit where I eat. Another bit of advice for you."

"I think I am going to find those reports you left for me in my, what? In basket?"

"Your mailbox."

"I have a mailbox?"

"Online, dear, online."

"Oh, yes, of course." Jude rushed for the door, feeling foolish. From behind, she heard Sybil say, "If, in the future, you'd prefer hard copy, I can arrange that."

Before Dr. Avery got back to her own office, her iPhone went off, lighting up her lab coat pocket. She lifted it while still in the hallway. It was Dean calling her. The entire time she'd been sitting across from him earlier this morning, he had withheld information from her. Vital information on the case, yes, but also his knowledge of the incident with Lisa and Luther. She thought now that he should have shared it all then and there. Why hadn't he leveled with me, she wondered. The entire time he let me believe that we were on the same page, and that I had convinced him that the Dewalt case should remain mine.

But if Shanley could be believed, the report on the clothing, the hat, and the dog saliva had been in Grant's hands the whole time, along with the thrice-told tale of the confrontation she'd had with Luther and Lisa.

She decided not to speak of it over the phone; perhaps the next time they were face to face. "Yes, Dr. Grant?"

"News of our case and Dewalt's identity has gotten out as you know, I am sure. No surprise there. We have to keep some facts in-house, most being forensic findings. The battle ax thing for instance, no keeping a detail like that secret, but the dog bite, yes, and Wilson's identity, for now."

"I completely understand, sir. The detectives need some details to use against a future suspect, information no one else has. I get that."

"Exactly. Keep close wraps on all forensic info and reports."

"Of course. You can count on me, sir."

She was just on the edge of feeling good, that she and the top ME in the city were in a give and take about the most important case in Chicago at this moment. She felt like a star.

Then Grant said, "Lionel's been contacted by the parents."

"The parents?"

"Dewalt's folks, yeah, and I want you to meet with them. Mom, Pop, brother, and a sister. They're on their way across town now from the train station."

"You want me to talk to the four of them, alone, me?"

"I think you can handle it, yeah. They're a farm family in from Decatur, Illinois."

"Dr. Grant, don't we have people to do that sort of thing? Talk to the folks like you say? I mean, shouldn't *you* or even better the *detectives* on the case talk to the parents? For background information?"

"The detectives are trying to wrap up six other murder cases, Dr. Avery, and you might imagine the demands on my time."

"But I've had no experience interviewing bereft relatives."

"Then it's time you got some experience at it, and it's not an interview or an interrogation. They just want to know the facts surrounding the death of their loved one, but do not provide details we need to keep in house. The bat, the nails, okay, but nothing more."

"Nothing more like what?"

He hesitated, and she could almost feel his face turning red with anger through the phone. "Like the hat, the dog saliva, the last meal, for instance. Get down to interrogation room thirteen on the main floor."

"I thought it wasn't an interrogation."

"It's not."

"Just in an interrogation room, eh?"

"You meet them there and walk them to the morgue where they can formally ID Dewalt's corpse."

"You could get Sybil to do the job. I am sure she's had more experience at—"

"I'm asking you to take care of it, Dr. Avery. You're in charge of the case, remember?"

She really did not want to do this chore. She didn't answer him.

He took this as the end of the conversation and hung up.

It was a stiff, awkward Dr. Avery who met with the parents, who were elderly in their late fifties—bent, beaten from fighting to keep their farmland, fending off fracking overtures from oil companies while all the neighbors had sold out. They were ruddy-complexioned, white burnt to umber from hours in the sun, including the women. The father and mother were gray-haired last hold-outs. Stern, strong, old world backbone, grit, last vestiges of the old phrase *salt-of-the-earth*.

She was soon impressed with the Dewalts, as anyone would be, Jude imagined. And the younger brother and sister who'd remained on the farm to help their parents, also impressive people, grown ups with their own families and lives but still very much Sammy's siblings.

They each had a story about Sammy. They showed his photos as a happy-go-lucky kid. In each shot, a young tow-headed Tom Sawyer-looking boy in torn straw hat playing out back of the barn and riding onboard a tractor or a horse; fishing, boating, and swimming in the pond; loving life. Each photo had Sammy caught in a busy moment, stuffing his mom's pancakes in his mouth, in a wash tub as a four-year-old, or asleep in his bed.

Part of Jude cringed within as Sammy's family passed her each photo. The pictures hardly squared with the scraggly bearded, broken, and destroyed man she'd autopsied. The corpse that awaited the family two floors below and down the hall.

Sammy's childhood photos made her ill, in a way. She could feel it coming on with each little bright boy picture. It begged the question of how any child could become so homeless and so lost and so broken as Samuel Evan Dewalt had become in life. It raised the specter of everyone's having contributed in a way to his death. It raised the question of how no one seemed capable of reaching him, and how it was that he could not find the kind of strength inherent in his genes to save himself from running away from the safety and strength of home and family. What I'd give to have my family back, she told herself at one point. Why run from those who loved you so much, Sammy?

Questions assaulted her as she listened to the litany of stories of their loved one: Why could he not, on returning from the war, throw himself back into the life of the farm and home? Why Sammy Boy, as your dad called you, why were you unable to abide home and family in Decatur? And why did you feel it necessary to instead disappear? To become the prodigal son, the proverbial invisible man?

Ralph had prepped Dewalt's body for the viewing earlier. She'd inspected it before coming to meet the folks, and she'd ordered Ralph to carefully use a partial sheet to cover the cranium separate from the full sheet covering the corpse. The family could clearly see Sammy's features but not the awful head wounds. They could also see his tattoos, his destroyed foot. They need not see the fatal blows to Samuel's cranium.

While Dr. Avery did not wish to sound accusatory in the least, she did ask, "You had no idea where he was? That he was here, in Chicago?"

"Not until we got the call from your office, no," said the sister, Laurie, who seemed the designated spokesperson for the family. "Someone named Lionel."

"Yes, one of our assistants here." Dr. Avery realized that Lionel had continued to connect the dots to determine who Sammy was, and who might be his next of kin. Lionel needed to be congratulated, she mentally noted. He'd done the work of changing Street Sammy to be buried at the city's expense in a Potter's Field to Corporal Samuel Dewalt going home with family to be buried ceremoniously, as befitted a veteran. A proper funeral. Dr. Avery felt relieved over this fact.

After spending an hour with the family in the meeting room, Dr. Avery guided the foursome out and over to the elevator bank for the grim ride down to the below-ground morgue. As they made their way down, and then along a concrete corridor thickly painted with institutional gray and green, Judith felt she knew Sammy far better than ever, and she struggled with this new knowledge of the man.

It was a double-edged sword to know the personal life of the victim. On the one hand, it could be invaluably helpful, and it often did help explain an untimely death and any and all contributing factors such as living on the streets of Chicago. That certainly contributed to Sammy's death. The homeless were always vulnerable targets. Add to this his depression and carelessness with his own circumstances. Anyone who understood anything about depression knew that the depressive person was an uncaring soul who failed to observe the life and dangers surrounding him or her.

Samuel was like so many returning vets, despondent, so depressed in fact that he'd left home and the ones who loved him to spare them his deepening, dark sadness—like a sinkhole of the soul.

His motives may have been conflicted and mixed; he may well have had to find a place where no one knew him in order to get better. He may have felt being home on the farm, that any enjoyment he got from life, even the smallest calf licking his palm, was unfair to those in his unit who had been killed.

As they reached the morgue's viewing area, a small room with a curtained window, Dr. Avery considered the other edge of the sword of *knowing* the details of the victim's life. This side of the sword was just as sharp as the cold, clinical evidence she was responsible for.

She swallowed hard as the family around her collapsed into one another's arms on seeing Sammy's features on the other side of the glass. Tears and wailing followed. Knowing so much about Sammy caught her up emotionally, and a medical examiner could hardly do her best work if she was caught up emotionally, but the floodgates burst open, despite her calm exterior.

Jude had been changed from the cool-headed clinician to what she knew of herself now, since this meeting of 'the folks'; those left behind. Now that she knew his parents and his family life, she realized how it had already influenced her perceptions and any further examination of the corpse, or any new evidence uncovered in the case. In fact, she realized this must be how the lead detectives on the case felt.

The moment she pulled the curtain, Sammy's mother had burst into loud crying, moaning, and was instantly held up by her strong son, James, who had all he could do to keep his own knees from buckling. Meanwhile, Laurie held onto her father, Evander, who stoically looked into the dead face of his son and said, "Yes...it's him, our Sammy. God help me, it's my boy." He then broke into tears, and was helped to the seat he'd risen from. During the whole of the viewing, Ralph stood statue-like on the other side of the glass. He'd done well covering the gashes to the skull, keeping them from view. Dr. Avery nodded toward him and Ralph quietly pulled the curtain back.

Mrs. Dewalt, Martha, began insisting that she be allowed inside to hug her boy one final time, to be with him and to pray for his eternal soul.

Jude said, "I'm sorry but that's impossible."

"Impossible? Why?"

"It's just not a good idea, not here like this."

Then Evander joined his wife in insisting they be allowed to hold their boy,

Jude explained, "It's against protocol in a murder investigation."

Then the brother took up the cause, followed by the sister. Four against one. Protocol or grace seemed to be in dubious battle. The family wanted grace for their son, and all she could counter with were rules. Jude felt the anguish that welled up among the four farmers from Decatur.

She also thought of the last rule around here that she'd broken, and how it had gotten back to Dr. Grant. She really wanted to follow this rule, but she had always put people first, rules second, and she believed that perhaps this was one such moment.

Four sets of eyes drilled into her, all questioning. She finally assented, buzzed Ralph to unlock the nearby door, and she invited them inside the inner sanctum, insisting they touch nothing, including the corpse. "We must maintain a sterile environment here as much as humanly possible, you understand," she said.

The body language of the family said they would willingly comply with Dr. Avery's request. "Just so we can be nearer to him," pleaded

Sammy's mother. Guided inside, the family gathered around the gurney that their loved one 'slept' on as they soon were using that term. "He's at peace" and "Looks that way" and "Out of all pain now" phrases filled the viewing area. Nearby, Ralph stood at the deceased man's head to keep that wound covered. It would not do for mom and pop to see it, not at all.

"How'd he die?" asked the sister, Laurie. "He looks healthier than when he left home."

"*Ahhh*...blunt instrument to the head, two or three blows." It was all Dr. Avery wished to say on the subject.

Father Dewalt began a prayer over Samuel, his eldest.

Jude and Ralph bowed their heads in unison with the family, and when the prayer was finished, Jude asked that the family now leave the area. "It's my turn to insist now, Mr. and Mrs. Dewalt."

Going for the door, the mother was the last in line, and with a sudden bolt no one saw coming, Mrs. Dewalt rushed back and threw herself across her son's body. The action caused the cover over Sammy's shattered and shaved head to slip in ghostly fashion, wafting to the floor to reveal the ugly wounds to the veteran's head. This caused Mrs. Dewalt to wail in terror at the sight. Her husband blanched white at the cruel wounds as well.

"Out now, all of you! Out," Dr. Avery was saying as she pulled Mrs. Dewalt from her son. The rest needed no second telling as Laurie propped up her father, and James secured and escorted his mother out.

Ralph shrugged when Dr. Avery gave him a look of disappointment. "It dropped so fast, Dr. Avery. Sorry."

She stepped from the area and into the corridor about to call out to the family, to apologize, but then she realized she had made the mistake here, breaking with protocol. She decided to let the family go without another word, to let them find their own way out. "God," she muttered to Ralph now beside her, "hardest thing I ever had to do."

"I know. Been through it so often, for me, it's normalized, as they say; hardly anything to it, like washing my hands or going for a taco, and feeling that way makes me feel bad, too. But if you've not done many of these, it's rough." He swallowed hard and patted her on the shoulder, adding, "Sorry about the head covering slipping like it did, but I thought they were on their way out."

"So did I. Not your fault, Ralph. Me...my fault."

"You got it, doc." Ralph stepped back inside to care for Sammy's remains, to return him to cold storage. She heard him shout over his shoulder, "It was nice to have someone to say a prayer over Sammy though."

She wondered if Ralph could possibly keep this breach of protocol between them but somehow she doubted it.

Sometimes she feared pulling this off—being a forensic examiner in such a large city and county. Cook was enormous, and if she got it wrong, it would be an epic public failure. She just wanted to get things right. She didn't want to prove things just to prove she was good or right or professional; she wanted to conquer this job, make Grant and Shanley and any of the others respect her. Her big goal was to be so good at her work that she and Grant could one day relate to one another as equals. Which thought had her hearing Sybil's laughter in her head.

Jude feared that the day she *could* call herself Grant's equal was a long way off, if it were ever to arrive at all. Given the obstacle course she and Grant found themselves plopped down into, thanks to higher-ups, she might never get there.

The future is promised to no one, she reminded herself of a favorite saying of her mother's, and for medical examiners, given the political realities and complexities of the job, being in the spotlight, being on call to testify at trials, regardless of the supposed fact that the ME's office was above reproach, that it was not a political appointment and answered to no one but Lady Justice, despite all that, there remained pressure from above. There remained time allotments, routine versus red ball cases, backlogged cases, budget constraints, and the ever present eye of the Fourth Estate glaring down Dean's neck.

Dr. Avery felt unsure if she ever wanted to be in Grant's shoes, to be at center stage and to have such a glaring light on herself. To be that kind of 'rock star' every day? Every moment being hounded for answers that only months-long testing might provide, if even then?

Then to have the governor's office, the mayor's office, Police Plaza One, and the press pressuring you for information, along with the badgering needs and wants and craziness of the state attorney's office? For these reasons, she could neither count on, nor assume, any sort of actual permanence in her life, at least not on the job. Not now. Perhaps not ever. The idea of taking a job in a smaller venue, a mid-sized town, a smaller county had its appeal. At the same time, she was finding Chicago and Cook County exhilarating for a medical examiner. Never any want for work here, she reminded herself.

Besides, given the encouragement she'd gotten from Dr. Grant to 'lead' the investigation, and thus far he'd not taken it out of her hands, she felt a pleasing wind in her sails. Despite Grant's 'pretending' he had taken the Samuel Evan Dewalt case into his own hands to oversee every smidgen of evidence, and to bring the murderer to justice, and while seemingly showing the world outside these offices that all was under control, who could argue? Not those pressuring Grant, and not her, Jude Avery, God forbid. So, superficially, the investigation was going swimmingly well, and an arrest was imminent according to the Chicago PD.

Sure it was. Jude had seen the floor to ceiling backlog of rape kits and murder cases in the ME's office first hand. She knew how easily Sammy's case could join the cold cases confronting Dean's Law Enforcement Circus here. The whole of it was a huge balancing act on a high wire.

She recalled an old professor named Holden Wakely who had repeatedly said, "Prove one thing and prove it well. Focus in on the singularity of cause of death." Wakely had been a remarkable teacher. He often told her, "There are no guarantees in forensics, except for the promises made from the top, which amount to hopes and prayers far more than promises."

Until now, she hadn't a clue as to what Wakely had meant by that. How to focus on the one thing now, to zero in on Sammy's killers—plural, as Thadeus Wilson and his dog, Pongo, attested to. Two attackers, one with a 'nasty' club, one with what Wilson thought might be a GoPro camera. Two evil, twisted young men like the angry young ones found in any *herd,* those wanting to take control in any fashion they could. Those who used mayhem to spit into the collective face of a community as in the recent spate of mall fights organized on social media for the express purpose of terrifying the public.

Wakely wanted her to focus in on the two sadistic killers living out their lives there in a city with a population of two-point-seven million citizens. Locating the killers looked like the proverbial needle in a haystack. The numbers were against the Detectives Marks and Stephens, against Dr. Grant, against Dr. Avery, and against the entire department for that matter. In fact, the statistics were staggering if she dared factor in Cook County as well as the city inside Cook. The population figure then jumped to well over five million.

Cook County registered as the most populated county in the entire nation. Forty percent of all residents in Illinois lived in Cook County with its largess deriving from the largest city in the state, Chicago. Little wonder so much backlog and so many cold cases had backed up in the ME's office; little wonder she'd been hired along with three other MEs to take up some of the slack. Little wonder that Dr. Grant must be careful on all levels regarding adherence to rules, regulations, and protocol. The sheer numbers stood against Grant's office ever catching up or calling it even. Not in his or my lifetime for sure, she thought.

4

Workmen and construction guys must lose their levels every day, Keith Kiley thought as he walked about the dingy old place where *Sampson Levels* were produced and sold, his place of work. How else do we stay in business, he wondered. He was the day shift manager and had worked his way up from the job he'd gotten as a teenaged graduate of Senn High School. Since then, he'd spent most of his youth in this run down, turn of the century, dangerous old factory in the heart of Chicago, located on Halsted at Augusta. Keith had worked his way up from scrap boy since he had first entered this dungeon-like environment, this Hades of noise and accidents. He'd explained to Mitch how, as a high-schooler needing money to pay for a prom date, he'd taken the job. He'd been desperate to make money as the big night was coming up fast. The night he meant to have Suzie Young all to himself. The prom, the date, it'd all turned into a nightmare when he forced himself on her, and her father found him the next day and beat him half to death. Only good thing, no police report was filed. Keith had gotten nowhere with the sex either, so it was all for nothing and a waste of his paltry wages to boot. The only thing permanent coming out of that time was this crummy job in this sweat shop.

Now six years after graduating from Senn High School, here he remained but no longer as *the scrap boy* carrying a couple of damned pickle barrels from work station to work station, picking up metal shavings in barrel one, wood scraps in barrel two. Someone else now schlepped those barrels from one end of the factory to the other for the workmen who actually made the levels. He'd learned the craft before long, and he'd taught himself every aspect of the business down to the books.

As for all the scrap, the boss took it someplace for recycling, and the penny-pinching Mr. Donald J. Sampson would pocket the proceeds.

The old man had died two years ago, and drastic measures had to be made by the family—none of whom knew a damn thing about the shop or even how to work a level, and so the sons of Sampson, all two of them, came in one day, took a liking to young Keith, learned his history and how he knew every job in the place, and how the old man had mentored him. It made sense for them to make Keith day manager. They also curtailed the hours the place operated by ending the night shift altogether, laying off an entire shift. This meant at a young age, Keith was in charge of the place and the man to answer to.

With that responsibility came a much heftier paycheck but also problems. Every worker in the place had difficulties, handicaps, burdens, problems, and issues to unload on Keith. After two years now as manager, and six years as an intern coming to this steam-saturated warehouse, Kiley knew that without the payoffs to the city inspector, the damned place would've been condemned long ago. He had no idea how the old inspector managed to cover it up at his end, but now that he was in charge, he had to slip the payoff to the wretched old bastard. Payoff or not, the ancient factory looked and felt like a living, waking junior version of Hades. Hell with a lowercase *h*.

It was relentlessly mundane, the work, the people, their tedious, boring conversations and concerns, not to mention the dull end product they put out—boxes and boxes of levels. Small kids' toy levels, levels used by pros for hard to get at places, medium-sized levels, large levels, and super-sized levels for major construction jobs. All hand-crafted, all made by men on machines, not machines without the hand of man involved.

That dumb ass Mitch asked him once why not go to 3-D printed levels. Mitch Goodwin would never understand an answer to that question.

The factory had never been large enough to earn any respect in the area, squat two-story red-brick exterior, squeezed as it was and dwarfed by two huge factories on either side of it. And the owners had no intention of ever making it larger. The workers were cramped by the space. They might just as well be in some remote place in China or Mexico for the way the workers were packed at the work benches here at Sampson's. Terribly unsafe conditions. They worked so closely to coiled metal and under such conditions, surrounded by stacks of wood with twenty lathes screeching in their ears at once. But they did have safety glasses, and each break was adhered to, and they each got a half hour for lunch while Keith had to steal time when and where he could find it overseeing the lot of them. And every damn one of them had a sob story to do with their lives, their history, their present, and their false hopes of a future, family, kids, bills, and excuses. There wasn't one among the lot who wasn't excuse-ridden and excuse-driven.

Keith was just like the rest, and he knew it and sometimes accepted it. He hated this place, and he was bored out of his skull working this job, keeping this mini-hell operating. Steam rose from each table where squatted the hot vats used to make the metal pliant. The sons of Sampson, called the sons of bitches by the workmen and Keith whenever they weren't around, which was always, had promised better conditions, starting with window fans that never materialized. A man had to get out of the place more often than three times a day, and Keith left it to the men as long as each made his quota of finished product for the day.

Keith was well-liked as a result and respected by the men for his caring and kindness toward them, and his famous ear, and for giving in when a man needed a short-term financial fix. The petty cash drawer was forever empty.

Mr. K. Kiley the nameplate on his desk read. He had a bare red light bulb just outside his office door which when on meant he was present, but when turned off meant he was himself taking a break and outside the building as he was now.

Keith stared down one end of the street and saw what he had seen for years now. Row upon row of small, ugly factory buildings. He lit up a Marlboro and looked down the other end of the street as he turned on his heels. Duplicate view. Factory after factory. This was one of Chicago's infamous factory rows. Not unlike Chicago's old Publisher's Row in appearance. Books, print media, newspapers, magazines, a dying breed, and now Publisher's Row was a tourist attraction and former factories renovated into a *Bar Louie* location. The old clock tower and train station were filled with shops.

Keith could not imagine a fate such as that for this crummy area. "Not this neighborhood. No way," he said to himself between puffs of his cigarillo.

One of his workers joined him, silently smoking away when the old-timer joked, saying, "These few blocks here are a chunk of the city's early days, Keith."

"Is that right?" Keith had heard it before. The old man had memory loss.

"Damn place was established when the Black Hawk Indians made war on the city before it was a city, when it was simply Fort Dearborn. History, son, is what you're lookin' at here."

Beside them was a cabinet factory, across from them a lamp factory, further on a Linoleum factory, and yes, Keith told his new workers, there was still a market for Linoleum. "They use it in government building in the bathrooms, in asylums, and factories like ours!" There was one factory down the way that made playing cards, another manufactured plastics of all sorts, while yet another crafted door knobs and cabinet fixtures and light fixtures. All of the manufacturers here had fallen on hard times, and Keith thought of the entire place like a forgotten western ghost town in many ways. The single word he used for the entire street as far as the eye could see was *desolation*.

How any of the small businesses had hung on to remain in business in 2016, Keith hadn't a clue, but he had come to the conclusion that he and his workmen were never going to see window air-conditioners installed in their lifetimes.

This was Keith's day job, his every day *sucky life*, as he called it. He bemoaned his situation to Mitch and anyone else who cared to listen outside and away from the place, for he made it a rule to go light on the cynicism, sarcasm, anger, and frustration with Sampson's Level operation. The men did not need him sounding like one of them. One day, he imagined as he took the last drag on his smoke now, one day his men were going to take it no more; one day, he imagined, they'd all stop work, stand, walk out together and cripple the sons of Sampson who never lifted a finger to help their father but who now owned the place. Hit them where it hurts, their pocket books. The old lady then would have to get involved if she was still walking or able, which was doubtful. Keith would have to deal with the sons, and the sons would have to deal with Keith, and together they'd have to deal with the workmen and the work stoppage.

While he could not be sure of it, he smelled it in the air, the disaffection of the workers. The men had no union, however, save what they might call an informal agreement. Still the surliness and anger among them was on the rise again.

Keith hated the place and the circumstances, but he had no prospects for anything else. No one was hiring elsewhere, and he had no skills other than running this damnable level-making shop. Tossing the cigarillo butt into the nearest sewer grate, he turned and started back for his office, hesitating at the door, that momentary wave of courage washing over him. He was a big fellow, a man now, and no longer a kid. He'd turned twenty-five, and while he still looked and felt like eighteen most of the time, sometimes he felt old and tired and sick to death of having accomplished zip in a quarter of a century. Twenty-five years on the planet, and he was just another invisible man out here in what he termed *Desolation City*.

But at night, in his evenings now, playing the game for real, taking it from the virtual to his Garfield Park neighborhood where he rented an apartment, and having convinced Mitch to record an actual murder—which had been no easy task—made him feel special. Especially as he had a place to send the results of his actions to the Elder Council. What a rush it had been—killing that useless, self-pitying so-called soldier in the manner he had dispatched Sammy Dewalt. It had taken his breath away, and it had made him feel like a kid again, alive again, like an eighteen-year old getting his first taste of sex and booze at the prom. Too much booze, he recalled now, which had contributed to spoiling the sex part.

A part of him so wanted to tell someone, anyone that this was not all there was to him, the scrap boy who became the day manager of hell. A part of him wanted someone to confide in. Someone other than Mitch Goodwin. Someone who might appreciate his act of bravado against that vet in the park. It took courage of a sort to do what he'd done, same as it had taken courage to break into the guy's ratty little apartment through a gabled window via a rooftop, research him, take time to get close.

But that pitiful guy, Sammy, didn't have the apartment anymore; couldn't keep up with the pittance it cost. Keith believed he did the guy a favor, a *solid*. By the time Keith had investigated his chosen prey, he'd gotten to know precisely who he was down to why everyone in the neighborhood said he was suicidal. It still took some guts, Keith believed, to carry through with murdering a man you'd stalked and staked out for murder. One thing to fantasize about it, one thing to plan it and to arrive at the moment of no return, but quite another damned thing to carry through with it as he had.

God, how I wanna share it with someone trustworthy, he thought, but the only witness to it, the only person who knows what I've done and what courage it took is Mitch Goodwin. Except for that bastard with the dog. He saw it from a distance, now didn't he?

I wonder if that creep who'd interrupted my fun would make a good next victim, him and his dog, too. Damn dog took a chunk out of Mitch.

He tried to divert his thoughts to something else but this thing nagged at him. Wish I could tell Darlene, he thought. Wish I could tell someone who'd love me just the same. Love me for this brave act, the biggest thing I've ever done in my entire miserable life.

But it didn't look promising that Darlene was the one. Knowing her, he thought, she'd most likely freak out. Most likely go to the cops even. If only I could meet someone, anyone in whom I could confide. Not Darlene, not if I wish to remain anonymous and free. He decided that should Darlene ever find out, he'd likely have to kill her, too.

Still it nagged at him. Perhaps when word came back from the Elder Council that he'd won the month's collection of snuff films, then perhaps he'd feel vindicated, that the others appreciated his sacrifice and understood the nature of his accomplishment in sending Corporal Dewalt off to a better place.

Keith stared at the heavy metal-framed door that would open onto his private hell. The door was four-inches thick, and it had been painted years ago to appear like an upright, standing Sampson level, but who could make it out now, as faded as it was? The paint was so peeled and worn away that people had to guess at it.

He hesitated going back inside. That brave nagging worry had again seeped into his thoughts. *Walk away. You don't need this shit. No one's going to miss you, and you are certainly not going to miss this crap. Walk away.*

Instead, he pushed through the door and stepped back into the darkness within. His mind felt a pressure descend from the low-hanging ceiling and the walls on all sides, closing in...as if alive, as if pushing his soul into a smaller and smaller coffin, until it became a cube. Then the cube turned into a single cell hidden in the deepest recesses of the labyrinth called brain matter. "God, I hate this place," he muttered, rushing to his office where he kept the Jack Daniels.

A trail of worker voices followed him, "Boss, boss! Hey Mr. Kiley! You, okay?"

His gum-smacking, Hispanic secretary didn't give him time for his shot of whiskey. She knocked on his door and stepped inside from her adjoining cubicle. "Boss, we got an order from Kreski's in Des... desMoines, Iowa." She pronounced DesMoines as *dese-moans*. Keith thought her cute, even if she was on the heavy side. Perhaps it was the cleavage, or the occasional belly button that would peek from beneath her blouse when she reached for something overhead. But Kiley knew he had to take care with Maria as her boyfriend was the size of a sumo wrestler. Till now, while he'd begun routinely and kiddingly flirting with Maria, he'd not openly hit on her. But today she was wearing those tight-fitting shorts again, the ones that left little to the imagination. He'd hired her and during the interview, they were both sweating profusely, and so he assured her that wearing casual clothing and even shorts in the workplace was okay. "Until we get in the air-conditioning units," he'd told her, knowing that was a lie.

"How big an order we talking, Babe?" He routinely called her Babe as if it were her name.

"*Big order*, dude." She'd tease back. They'd settled into the back and forth and give and take weeks ago. It'd all been smiles and chuckles to date. But even this little bit of attention from Maria had given Keith a reason to come to work to lord it over Maria and demonstrate his power over the workers.

"How *big* an *order* would-ja like, Maria?"

She gave him a glare at the question.

"Burritos, I mean…for lunch! Ha, what'd you think I meant?"

"Burritos—just one."

"From the taco truck on the corner? So how big? They got large and larger."

"Usual, I dunno. Regular?"

"I got extra large," he teased.

She shook her head and tried to smile at the way Keith had slumped into his chair, his legs spread wide. "Want to sit here and tell Papa all about it?" He indicated his crotch, having decided to hell with all the cat and mouse, that he'd go for it. Killing an Afghanistan soldier had emboldened him, and he knew it.

But Maria was unmoved and not coming nearer. "You know I ain't that *kinna* girl, dude. If you gotta fire me for it, go ahead."

"*Heyyy*, whoa now! No one's firing you, Babe, cutie. Just that a man gets, you know, bored around here."

"You mean horny, don't you?"

He stared at her now. "Yeah, sure, and seeing a pretty thing like you all day. I know it's not politically correct, me being your boss and all, but I'm a man, too."

She smiled at this, looked about the place, and said, "Yeah, you're the man in this shit hole. You know, boss, I can walk outta here anytime I want. Ricky, my boyfriend proposed to me, *marriage*, yeah, and he wants me to quit this place."

"You're boyfriend's smart."

"Smart, good-looking, strong, got a good job, and he's not gonna get into no more trouble."

Keith stood and moved toward her. "You think you've got me all figured out, don't you, Maria? That I'm just some boring guy with shit for a life except for this place, but hell if you only knew—" He paused, waving his hand to gesture this 'kingdom' was his. "Don't you? Don't you?" he finished.

"I don't see no room here for upward mobility."

"Upward mobility?" He laughed. "Where'd you look up that word? The English to Spanish dictionary?" He laughed at his own feeble joke.

"You think I'm some dumb-ass PR? I'm Mexican, not a PR." Her face had turned red, eyebrows twitching. "This place is not for me, or for you, Mr. Kiley. You could do better." The young secretary's words came out in a mocking tone finalized with a grim smile and a sharp glint of her coal black eyes.

"You don't know what I'm capable of, girl." He suddenly took hold of her wrist, the tight grip sending a sharp pain through her; enough sudden pain that she found herself kneeling before him. "If you knew what I was capable of, girl, you'd be on your knees and under my desk every damn day taking care of me! The things I've done. The people I've lit up."

She finally dug her teeth into the hand that was on the verge of breaking her wrist. Maria drew bright red blood, making him shout, "Ouch, damn you!" But he did back off, repeatedly apologizing, with sorry atop sorry, begging her forgiveness, adding, "I—I don't know what came over me. Maria. You're just so sexy, and—and, are you all right? It's this place; it's getting to me."

She didn't answer his question or his apology, instead escaping his office for her connected cubicle where she grabbed her purse and rushed out. The order from Kreski's floated down in her wake.

"*Shittin'damn*," Keith Kiley chastised himself and saw that at least a couple of the workmen had witnessed some part of he altercation through his dingy office window. Every one of the workers watched Maria Rodriguez storm out, cursing in Spanish as she did so. The word *pendejo* echoed through the place.

Keith momentarily worried about Maria's boyfriend, Ricky. The young man stood taller than he did. She'd once let it slip the guy had a criminal record and had spent time in Joliet. Ricky also had a good forty pounds on Keith. "But I got weapons," he said to his empty office.

Keith now felt the eyes of the men in the shop curiously staring at him through his office window. He'd been a fool not to have closed his blinds before he laid a hand on Maria. When he stepped out to the now silent workplace, he shouted, "Lil girl couldn't take the heat no more, fellas. She up and quit on me just like that! Sorry you had to see that."

Eddie Koontz shook his head and shouted what was on all their minds, "Shit, nothing now to look at around here but the *f'ing* walls."

No one laughed at Eddie's joke. Everyone liked Maria. Keith frowned, turned to go back into his office when he noticed an unfinished giant of a level that was in the discard bin. It had been ruined by one of the workmen, a gash from an errant blade had left a wide scar across it. A single slip that'd ruined the piece. He hefted it like a club. "Whose mistake? Who's wasting company materials?"

The new scrap boy, a slow kid named Lonnie, rushed toward him, hands flapping. "It's from Rob's table, but it was my fault. I startled him. Not on purpose, you see, but—"

"All right, forget about it." Then to the men, he shouted louder, "*Forgetaboutit.*"

Mr. Kiley, with the discarded, unfinished level in hand, returned to his office. Once the door closed, he admired the heft of the big level, and he said to himself, "In case Ricky boy comes looking for trouble!" He leaned the big level against the back wall right behind his chair for easy access. Once satisfied, he moved from his office to slip through to Maria's former office, and there he knelt to lift the order from Kreski's where it lay on the grimy floor.

From Maria's cubicle, a whiff of her perfume clinging to a sweater hung over a coat rack at his back, Keith clicked on the PA system and announced, "Men, we may be getting some overtime this week. Big orders've come to me today from DesMoines. They need levels in Iowa."

A smattering of cheers for the overtime in hell traveled about the workers like a crippled, fluttering bird until the sound of the lathes again drowned out all else. And as the factory cacophony returned to normal, Mr. Kiley's phone rang. He reentered his own office to take the call. It was good old Mitch Goodwin with a new response from their contact in LA. "What's he say, Mitch? Give it to me straight?"

"Second place. You lost out to a g'damn pregnant mother's murder."

"That's wrong. Shit! I'd stack up my soldier and my method of dispatching my victim against anything anyone else did."

"That's just it. The winner used a car engine."

"A car engine how?"

"With engine running, the guy forced her head under the hood. Rotating blades, belts, pulleys. She's supposedly got it all until it tore her head clean off."

"Have you seen it, the video?"

"No, it's not readied for release to the cartel just yet. Just talk of it's coming. You know, like coming attractions."

"This is bullshit. How come we're just hearing about this now? It's the bloody end of the month. How do we know this guy got it in under the wire?"

"Guess there's really no way to know. Not for sure, but we gotta take the Elders's word for it."

"This so pisses me off. A pregnant woman. How's she going to put up a fight? The rules say there has to be some resistance, some fight in the victim."

"Don't ask me. I'm just along for the ride."

Keith felt a ball of choking frustration rise to his throat along with a growing anger toward Mitch. "Just be mad with me, damn you. Can you do that for me?" Keith slammed the phone down. Another disappointment in a day of disappointments.

Just outside his office, he could hear the drone of the lathes, the noise seeping in like a grimacing creature mocking him. "I had it. I was so close." He went to the blinds and closed out the sight of the factory and the workmen at their benches. He did not want them to see him crying.

5

Jude awoke to a new day and looked about her new home. A roomy flat, a third floor walk-up that guaranteed exercise. She'd only just begun shopping for furniture, and she wanted the place to look airy and light, but thus far there'd been no dining table or sofa to match her mood. If all went well, and if she ever got comfortable in the city, she might move to a pricier location, but for now this more modest setting suited her just fine. She had managed to find time to put up photos of her parents, some with herself between mom and dad at various stages of her life.

She'd been the only child of a military family, and had spent more of her life on military bases than anywhere else. After that, it was dorm life at colleges and universities. So having a place to actually call her own was a new experience, and one she was relishing on the one hand, but it was bitter sweet on the other. She'd always hoped to serve a meal to her parents in her own place some day, and that was never going to happen.

Her tall, dark-haired mother was a model military mom with her own career as a botanist, and her equally tall, dark-featured dad had been a medical genius who trained other medical doctors in the *do's-and-don'ts* of working in war zones with Doctors Without Borders. He had also been an accomplished ME. A much, much admired man. Jude had his drive, determination, and intellect coupled with her mother's good nature and love of life, along with her good looks.

The cooperation between military doctors and private doctors in war zones had become crucial over the years. It meant she saw little of her father, but what time they did have, he always somehow made magical. This meant the bond between Jude and her parents was special. In fact, the bond she shared with her mother and father proved the strongest element on Earth as far as Jude knew when a child, and it only grew stronger when she became a young woman.

When her mother began showing signs of illness, Judith's father resigned from his duties and the service to devote all his time to caring for the patient—his wife, Judith's mother, who'd developed cancer. Her father, Gene Avery, loved her mother, Elizabeth, so much so that when she succumbed to the disease, he simply fell apart. He was never the same, and Jude, by then an adult and in her medical studies, had a broken man on her hands, not unlike Samuel Dewalt in many ways.

Toward the end for her father, she'd become the caregiver, and the role came quite near to destroying her. She still felt a horrid guilt at the center of her being, not only for having to place her father in a home, but for not having been with him when he passed away from a heart attack. Now she had all this family history on Dewalt that she hadn't wanted the burden of knowing.

Tearing up at the flood of memories of her own, she called out to her pet parakeet, Boomer, "Hey, you're gonna have to fend for yourself for awhile. I gotta get outta here."

Having breakfast at the Up & Down Diner just down the street from her apartment along a residential block that skirted the Garfield Park district of the city, Jude sat alone at a table in a room filled with couples and families. Dining alone was no one's idea of fun, but she'd gotten used to it. The waitress had become her best friend in the same neighborhood where Sammy had become a familiar face. A neighborhood fixture, so to speak. Yet she had never seen Sammy, while the waitress here, Emelda, a Hispanic lady with an open smile and attitude, said, "Yeah, I knew Sammy." She shrugged and added, "Not well...as well as anyone got to know Sammy. I'd slip him leftovers when he come by."

"What was he like?"

She sat in the booth, glanced over her shoulder at the manager, and said, "He was like that book I read in high school once, about the Mockingbird."

"Ah yeah, *To Kill a Mockingbird*. I had to read it in school, too, and I saw the movie many times."

"There's a movie?"

"Yeah, older...black and white. Gregory Peck."

"I don't like black and white movies."

"So Sammy was like Boo Radley, eh?"

"Who? Oh, yeah, the guy in the story, yeah. That's the way he was. I couldn't get hardly a word out of him."

"Why then would anyone want to attack Sammy and kill him?"

"Why did that hateful drunk attack the little kids on Halloween?"

"Jem and Scout," said Judith, and seeing Emelda's confusion, added, "the kids in the novel."

"Oh, yeah...I forgot the names, but now hearing them again, wow. I can picture the whole story just from remembering the names."

"Atticus Finch bring back any memories?" Jude smiled at Emelda.

"He was such a good father and man."

"We could use more like him nowadays, that's for sure."

Emelda flinched on hearing her boss call out in a tone of irritation. "Back to work," she whispered to Jude.

"Me, too."

"What kind of work do you do, Dr. Avery?"

"I'm investigating Sammy's murder, forensically speaking."

"Get out of town. Really?"

"Emelda, did you ever see anyone heckling or harassing Sammy?"

"I don't think so. Nothing serious."

"What do you mean by nothing serious."

"Well...I just remembered but I gotta get back to the orders."

Jude handed her a business card with a background of Van Gogh's *The Starry Night*. "Call me when you can talk. I want to hear that story. It could be important."

Emelda tucked the card into her apron pocket and slipped from the booth in one fluid, practiced motion, going back to work. Judith finished her fruit cup, toast, and coffee. She left Emelda twice the amount of the normal tip she'd leave and a second business card. Leaving the diner, and this untold story about Sammy, behind her worried Jude.

What might come of it? Most likely nothing, but just suppose Emelda had unknowingly laid eyes on Sammy's killer?

As she made her way to Dean's world, Jude kept thinking of her own ties to the military. She had not joined up, but was born into it—a military brat. She recalled playing games and riding bikes on the military bases that formed the backdrop of her childhood; meeting other children, who, like herself, by the time adolescence kicked in, sorely *hated* the life, the restrictions, the *regs* as her parents called them. She recalled how awful she'd acted toward her mother when her father was not around to enforce those regs, and she felt the guilt well up anew with her memories of those teen years. She was unsure why her talk with Emelda had so vividly brought up those years of angst and acrimony, but it opened a floodgate of remorse and a concoction of regret.

Still, even counting her worst days as an angry teen, she imagined her own sadness and guilt born out of childhood a mere splinter of depression compared to the cross Sammy had carried. She could not fully comprehend what he'd felt over the death of his buddies, who'd died while he had lived. She was sure no one who hadn't experienced that kind of guilt firsthand could truly *ever* understand the debilitating depression it brought on in a sensitive soul. Who could mine that deep? In the mining of such emotions, there was danger to one's own psyche. The sheer layers of sorrow and horror one would have to dig down to could in the act alone, in the act of caring for another's wounds, paralyze the concerned person. There but for the grace of God go I, again rose in her thoughts. She could well understand why so many people around Sammy in his last days turned a blind eye; so much pain was wrapped up in a person's giving a damn.

Then there was the scum of the earth who'd killed Sammy with ruthless abandon and heartless glee. Human nature proved a complicated mess indeed.

The previous night at Mitch Goodwin's home

"They like humor, Keith. What can I tell you. Have a drink."

"Humor? There was nothing said about humor before."

"Yeah, well there is now."

"What kind of humor?"

"I dunno, the usual shit. No, dark. Very dark humor's what they seem to crave. Like she was 'belted' by his hot engine block."

"What's funny about that?"

Mitch shrugged and handed his only friend a mixed drink. "I guess a little sarcasm, facetiousness, laughs, ha-ha, you know."

"Laughs, huh? Fine, I got just the thing for 'em then, I do, and you're going to film it."

"A barrel of laughs. Let's do it. What is it?"

"Something the Elders have to freak out over. I got beat by a pregnant mom, eh? Something funny in that, eh? Well what if I literally 'leveled' the playing field with two nuns?" Keith lifted the large, discarded level from his workplace. "See ya mom and raise ya two nuns?"

"Holy shit! Look at that thing," replied Mitch, admiring the level, his eyes fixed on the glass tube with the green bubbles jostling inside it. "That's the ticket, buddy!"

"And I know. It just came to me."

"Inspiration is great, isn't it, KK?"

"And I know just where I can find plenty of nuns to choose from." He brandished the big level like a sword now.

"That's right. You went to St. Agatha's before Senn, didn't you?"

"Hated those nuns and that damn school."

"Kill all that pent up anger and win the contest in one fell swoop, buddy," urged Mitch. "When do we do it?"

"Tonight, get into St. Agatha's before they lock out the world for the night." Kevin lifted the huge scarred level he'd brought from work. He'd kept it close, still fearing Maria's boyfriend could show up anytime. Besides, the more he handled the near finished but discarded level, the more he thought of using it as a hammer to crush Ricky's skull. On the drive home with the new 'bat' on the seat beside him, another idea had begun to take shape. An idea involving nuns.

When Mitch explained that the Elders wanted more laughs and a comic element, everything fell into place with the 'leveling' punch line. Keith had sat down this time and insisted Mitch learn some lines and state them word for word for the filming of the murders of two and perhaps three nuns with his level.

In a way, Keith felt that for once he'd see to it that a Sampson level would be put to damn good use. It almost made his attitude toward the company soften.

◆ ◆ ◆

When Dr. Avery arrived at her lab, she was confronted with a 'matching set' of new murder victims wheeled into the autopsy room and a phone call from Dr. Grant that he and Shanley would perform one of the autopsies while she would start on the second simultaneously. A third murdered *sister*, still in her bloodied white habit and killed at St. Agatha's, awaited attention after that. It was an instant red ball case due to the victims, the innocent threesome of nuns on the ME slabs this morning. Thus far, the wounds appeared similar to one another in intensity and brutality.

The victims had been attacked by a pair of rampaging young men whose faces were covered in ski masks and their hands in gloves, according to the only witness, a priest who'd locked himself and others at the church into an office in back of the rectory—too late for the three sisters at the church. Their heads had been bashed in by something like a ball bat but not quite rounded as a bat, as the contours of the various impacts were sharply squared off. Doctors Shanley and Grant had independently come to the same conclusion in a separate autopsy room. The three of them had several conference calls between the two rooms. The trio had also determined that the murder weapon was wooden with a lacquered surface, and embedded in some of the wounds they'd found glass fragments coated with an alcohol-fluorescein solution, of all things. Microscopic wood fragments and fluorescein deeply embedded in the wounds, yet the bodies were in a clean church foyer, and there were no broken windows or glass of any sort about the bodies. So where did the glass come from and what did the unusual chemical mean? These elements were part and parcel of the deadly weapon. But what did they scream? What did they prove?

It did not occur to Shanley or Grant that the twisted killings at St. Agatha's had anything to do with the murder of Corporal Dewalt, but Jude thought it a bit coincidental that the geography of these killings fit into the realm of Garfield Park. A tumbler in her brain turned and she wondered if there could be a connection that they were simply not at this time privy to.

Evidence from the crime scene itself proved scant. The killers had left little to nothing of themselves, and there'd been no brave Wilson or Pongo to the rescue. Still, the condition of the bodies spoke volumes, and so did the priest who'd 'wisely and bravely'—or so said the police report—gotten others to safety. This priest had given his statement between tormented sobs to Stephens and Marks, which Jude later learned.

In the videotaped witness report, which Grant and Shanley hadn't bothered with but which Jude had taken time to see, the priest said it was only one man who wielded what looked like 'a piece of a wooden cross'—"The cross of Jesus," as he'd put it. "Using it in evil, evil fashion. A madman, crazed! Laughing the entire time, speaking words into the camera."

"Camera? What camera?" Stephens had pressed Father Thomas in the interrogation video.

"The other man was filming the rampage!"

"Sound familiar?" Stephens asked Jude when he had shared the video with her.

"Do you think it could be Dewalt's killers?" Jude asked.

"If not, what's worse? Two crazies doing this or four?" Not awaiting an answer, Stephens asked, "We get anything at all back on the dog bite, the saliva?"

Jude lifted a report. "White male, likely between twenty and thirty. No matches in NDIS or the state database, but we're checking with other databases—public workers, military."

"We need to catch a break. These monsters are loose out there, and we have to put an end to them yesterday." Stephens was visibly shaken. "Nuns, veterans...who's next, some little kids?"

Jude pounded the wall there in the viewing room. "Damn, that may be it, detective."

"What may be it?"

"They're escalating—number of victims, yes, but also the level of outrage they seem to be wanting to engender in us."

"In us?" asked Marks, who had joined them.

"Exactly. Us, we the people, society. I get that."

"You think this is some sort of game to these killers?" asked Stephens.

"Think about it," began Jude. "Filming it, for what reason?"

"And the killer laughing and playing to the camera, all for what cause?"

"In an effort to create chaos?" said Jude, shrugging.

Captain Mendes had also come in during the conversation and the others fell silent. "What've you learned about these horrendous nun murders?"

"I'm afraid not much, captain, but it's early." Stephens frowned and ran a hand through his sandy blond hair.

"What were you talking about when I came in? Something about chaos?"

The detective was reluctant to jump to any conclusions, but Jude was not. She spoke directly to the captain, explaining where their thoughts were drifting and why.

Captain Mendes rubbed his chin, stared through the glass at the priest, still in the interview room with his head in his hands, and then the captain said, "Chaos, the old *Helter-Skelter* crap brought to you by Charlie Manson, to push us toward their dream of a race war in America maybe? Been tried now many times. Who knows? Maybe our sick murderers do have an agenda other than pure insanity. Otherwise... why nuns, why vets? And like your Dr. Grant has said, 'Who'll they come after next?'"

They looked from one to the other as yet another question hung in the air. What had the priest meant when he'd said the killer was wielding a piece of the cross? Jude ruminated on what that could mean. A piece of a cross? A two-by-four? But a fluorescein solution and glass fragments? The questions hung in the air while Jude added, "The geography of the killings is again the Garfield Park area."

Captain Mendes paced the room like a caged bear, and then he said, "All I know is that my city is awash in a mix of horror, fear, and revulsion, and every news outlet is reporting on the horrible crime even as politicians are politicizing it. They've got the CPD under a microscope and *so* want to find blame." Mendes went to the one-way window and pulled the blinds to shut out the sight of the sobbing priest, who he'd kept hearing through the mic. He shut the mic down as well to give the priest a modicum of privacy. The three police officers exchanged looks, shoulders seemingly slumped forward on all of them. For Jude, it was hard to imagine the bustling life just outside the building up and down Michigan Avenue here at Police Plaza One.

Mendes returned his attention to his men and Jude. "No half-way intelligent person would kill this way in an area close to home. We have to assume the killers aren't in the Garfield Park area but rather using it as a killing ground."

"If that's the case, they'd have to be using a vehicle to come and go," said Marks.

"Not necessarily. The CTA runs trains and buses through the area," Jude said. "It's how I usually get around the city."

Stephens added, "Yeah, they could as well be using public transportation."

"No, no. They'd be concerned about the cameras on the CTA," said the captain. "No...a car, no doubt. Need to check with traffic cops in the area—meter maids—any tickets issued on the night of the Dewalt attack and the nuns. If there is a connection, a parking ticket could be an answer."

"I'll get on it," Stephens said.

"No, no! I know some people in traffic division," the captain replied. Jude imagined he wanted to do something, anything, even if it was a long shot. Mendes added, "I'll reach out."

"And if they're shitting where they eat?" asked Jude. "Crime makes people stupid, I've heard."

"Just can't imagine anyone being so half-brained as to commit such vicious murders so close to home." Captain Mendes left abruptly, on a mission. Stephens gave Jude a glance and a shrug.

Jude said, "He's grasping at straws."

"Yeah. Like the rest of us."

"Big city out there," added Marks.

"As for criminals being some sort of master-minds," Jude said, going for machine coffee, "that's more in the movies than in our line of work."

"Some truth to both." Stephens joined her, leaving the viewing area for a nearby lounge. "Some cases I've had, you get some sociopath doctor who thinks he is above everyone and smarter than police science, smarter than forensics, and they almost get away with murder, and in some cases they do."

"On the other hand?" she asked as they entered the lounge, leaving Marks behind.

"On the other hand, we wind up with some spineless, ugly little man as our offender."

"Most of my cases, we wind up with some sniveling, jelly-fish-brained sonofabitch that's downright stupid, yeah, if you're talking statistically."

Stephens bought her coffee for her. "Odds are these two are hardly the brightest bulbs in the chandelier."

"If they live in or around Garfield Park, and they are using the park as their hunting grounds, why suddenly move the mayhem then to St. Agatha's?"

"The church is on the line between Garfield Park and Chicago proper, but what if...what if one or both our perps, relatively young men according to Wilson and the DNA you took from Pongo? What if they're graduates of St. Agatha's?"

"Payback to the nuns?"

"Catholic school nuns can be tough and mean, or so I've heard."

"A well-earned reputation, yes."

With a cup in both hands now, Wayne Stephens guided her to a table with a view of Michigan Avenue. Below them, people swarmed about. It was lunch hour in downtown Chicago and the street was packed.

"Suppose the motive is revenge, in which case the killers will have had some history with the school at St. Agatha's." Stephens appeared in a sharing mood or wanted a sounding board, she thought, or was he showing off his detecting skills? "Captain's going for an inside straight, while I'm going for a surer bet."

"Why didn't you and your partner share your suspicions with Captain Mendes then?"

"A detective keeps his process to himself and his partner. Just the way it is."

"But he's your captain, and you're sharing with me?" She stared into his eyes, realizing for the first time how terribly azure they were.

"Well it's not entirely a sure bet as of now," he said, sipping his coffee and complaining how bad it was. "Only problem with our thinking on the school roster is that the St. Agatha only takes the kids through junior high, eighth grade. If the perps went there and came back for vengeance, and they're adult males as reported, that's at least four to eight years. Quite a lull in anger."

Jude considered this. "What do they say about revenge being served up cold?"

This had Stephens lifting his coffee for a toast and saying, "Touché, doctor, touché!"

When news of the nun murders had first brought them all back to work, Sybil and Jude had exchanged a sad look for what their boss, Dr. Grant, was faced with. If yesterday was bad news, today was far worse news. News from Hell.

Jude knew this new affront in a city with a history of godawful affronts affected Grant. It was as much a blow to his sensibilities as to her own and to Sybil's. She realized just how much pressure was on Dean and this office, along with the CPD, to stop this madness, to solve the Dewalt case and now the piled-on, added pressure to solve the murder of three Catholic nuns, and how the latter had become greater than the soldier cases. The pressure came from on top, and it had trickled down or rather struck like lightning through the ME's office as well as the CPD Homicide Bureau.

"We've got to tread lightly with the press, doctors," Grant said as he had, that morning, turned to face the women working for him. "We have to minimize leaks that are sure to come from this office. This is priority one for us now. It's all to do with the horror of nuns being brutally beaten to death inside a supposed sanctuary, a place believed free from evil. Perfect fodder for the press."

Sybil swallowed hard and added, "The crime scene photos are stark, the black and white of the nuns' habits contrasting horribly with the enormous pool of blood surrounding the women."

"Possibly part of his...their game," said Jude, shrugging. "The level of shock as a factor."

"Well *they* damn sure managed to do that," Sybil replied.

"Seems as if we're missing something," he said to Sybil. "That witness with the dog, Wilson, he said one of the killers was filming the kill. That's significant. That way they can revisit the moment, a thing murderers are prone to do. Return to the scene of the crime, and with technology now a simple click gets the bastards there."

"So callous," muttered Sybil.

"Are you sure that this mob filmed the murder of the nuns?" asked Grant, his forehead creasing into a map.

"The priest saw the camera," Jude said. "But then he was running; said he was trying to protect the others with him."

"Any cameras in the church?"

"It's not a bank."

Sybil then shrugged. "Isn't a church kind of a depository of the soul?"

"Very poetic but no, no cameras."

6

Jude decided to get back to her autopsy of the third nun. The first two had died, unquestionably, by the same tormenting blunt instrument, one that created not deep nail-gashes as with Dewalt, but deep, angular, sharp-edged bruises to the skull and faces of the victims. While Dr. Avery worked over victim number three from St. Agatha's, she soon pinpointed the findings in both autopsies she had conducted as the result of the exact *same* blunt object as well as the object used on the victims that Grant and Shanley had autopsied.

"Whatever the object is remains a mystery," she said for the recorder, "but embedded in the wounds, minute fragments of glass and traces of fluorescein consistent with findings from Sister Ursula and Sister Aurelia autopsied earlier and deceased at the same scene. Finding for all three victims killed with the same murder weapon."

According to Father Thomas, the first attack was on Sister Ursula, and then Aurelia and Sister Janette when they tried to intervene. Each was given a single blow, incapacitating them, and then the monster whaled on each woman's prone form.

This was all that Jude had gotten from the detectives who were quite unsatisfied with Father Thomas and his memory. They'd talked the father into going under hypnosis to determine what they could from the man's subconscious.

Earlier on the phone, she'd asked Detective Stephens if hypnosis was admissible in a court of law, to which Stephens firmly replied, "No, but it can be useful in an investigation."

"I'd like to sit in on that," she'd replied.

"Sorry, no can do. No one but our shrink, Dr. Wingate."

"All right but keep us apprised. We want to know if the men who attacked the nuns could be the same as attacked Corporal Dewalt. If there's any sure memory of one of the men taping, that is filming the attack, it would go a long way to designate a connection."

"We're hoping for a full description. Will let you know when we know if it's successful or not."

"Thanks, detective."

That's where they'd left it.

Jude had completed the autopsy on the third victim, Sister Janette. The entire time, she gave thought to the woman's bravery in trying to stop the attack on Sister Ursula, and then Sister Aurelia. Having seen two others of her habit given crushing blows to the head, she stepped in just the same, no doubt pleading and praying for the killer to stop before he should take the lives of her fellow nuns.

The autopsies Jude had performed this day had taken a great deal out of her both physically and mentally, for obvious reasons. The killers had chosen a place of love, peace, comfort, and faith to do the ugliest acts mankind was capable of. If they did so while filming, as they had with Dewalt in the park, then their depravity was multiplied tenfold.

When finished with the autopsy, her gloves, mask, and surgical garb were tossed into a bin, and she took advantage of the lab showers. Showers had been installed for the MEs, something Grant had seen to. Certainly a luxury as not every coroner's office or ME's office was equipped with showers for the doctors of death.

After showering and dressing to leave for home, Jude had her hand on the door and one foot out it when her desk phone rang. She hoped it was Detective Stephens with news of Father Thomas's hypnosis session. She anticipated this, but on the other end was a female voice, someone who'd been patched through from police headquarters, saying, "I lost your card, but I have to talk to you, Dr. Avery."

"Emelda?"

"Yes, from the diner."

"Yes, I know."

"I remembered something...something about Sammy. You said if I remembered—"

"Yes, I'm listening."

"There was one time when Sammy, he came into the diner. Someone had given him a twenty, and he wanted steak and eggs."

"How long ago?"

"Almost a month ago. I get so many customers in here. I'm sorry."

"Why did...how come you remembered it now?"

"I saw the two white boys who harassed Sammy that day. Nasty boys."

"You saw two young men harassing him?"

"Yes."

"And they dropped in today?"

"Yes, for breakfast. They was laughing and giggling, disturbing others. Early, very early."

"Why'd you wait so late to call me?"

"I looked high and low for your card. I was embarrassed."

"All right, okay, did they pay with a credit card?"

"No...cash."

"Damn. All right, can you come down to Police Plaza One and sit with a sketch artist to help get a sketch of the two?"

"I can, sure, if it helps for Sammy."

"It can help Sammy, yes. And, Emelda, what about surveillance cameras in the diner? Any chance these two were caught on camera?"

"The boss, he wouldn't give you no video without you get a warrant. I can assure you."

"Sounds like you've already talked to your boss about it."

"Yes, I did. Mr. Wright, he's got the wrong name; name should be Mr. Wrong."

Jude smiled at this. "I'll get an order for the video. Not to worry. But as it may take some time getting a judge to sign off on it, please come down to Michigan Avenue to sit with one of our sketch artists."

Jude wondered if Emelda and Father Thomas might not come up with the same features of the killers.If so, they'd be onto something big. The video at the diner could clinch it as well.

Maybe the killers did indeed live and work in the area. Perhaps they were more ignorant than they were master-minds of terror and crime.

"Tell no one else of your suspicions. I understand you've mentioned all this to Mr. Wright, but no one else is to know, not even your family, understood? I don't want those two suspects getting word that we're interested in the least."

"Bueno, yes, I understand. Hush-hush, like *Law and Order*."

"That's right."

They hung up after Jude gave her directions to Police Plaza One via the el train and a few blocks walk.

She then dialed Stephens's number and told him of this development and that he needed to see to a warrant for Mr. Wright's diner in Garfield Park. Stephens sounded skeptical but took down the information. "Don't hold your breath," he said when she asked how soon he could get an order for the video.

"Emelda said he tapes over. First of the month like clockwork. That gives you only forty-eight hours before the tape's erased."

"Not really. It would take twenty-eight days for the tape to catch up to this morning, but we'll do what we can."

"Anything new on Father Thomas?"

"Arranged for the session, but he didn't show up. I think the good father is having a crisis of faith or identity or lack of balls."

"Shit. It could be helpful, what's hidden away inside his head."

"Every one of those sisters had more guts in their pinky fingers than—"

"If that's your attitude taken with the priest, maybe you should have someone else looking in on him."

"Don't presume to tell me how to do my job, Dr. Avery. That man's clammed up out of fear. The short and simple of it."

"Sorry, detective. Did not mean to step on your toes. Just so frustrating. This whole matter."

"Understood, believe me." Stephens hung up, as abrupt as Grant.

Stephens and Marks did not have great hope for the camera footage in Wright's Up and Down diner, and they assumed the new ME in Grant's office was just showboating in sending them on this wild goose chase, but their own captain, on having gotten a call from Grant about following every lead, no matter how small, saw it differently. The captain himself had gotten the court order pushed through and had sent his detectives to go fetch.

The detectives did so with reluctance and a good bit of ill-will building up for this faceless waitress and Dr. Avery. They were, however, surprised when the owner, Malcolm Wright, handed them a second video. "Held onto this one that day Sammy came in and sat right there, center counter, when a couple of punks started in on him. I chased those bastards out with a hot cast iron skillet after I saw what they did to Sammy, after Sammy'd left."

"Is that right?" said Stephens, taken by surprise.

"Why'd you hold onto it?" asked Marks.

Wright shrugged. "I did a stint during Desert Storm."

"Good of you, sir, and thanks for your service," said Marks.

"I—I was always hoping Sammy would work out his inner demons, you know. Had this crazy notion, kinda superstitious notion, that if I filmed over what those punks did, one day it'd come back to haunt me that I erased that insult."

"That's good. Real good."

"In my book, an insult to a vet is a forever thing that needs to be called out. Silly of me, but I always thought if Sammy ever came in again and was clean and sober and doing well that I'd give him that video."

"Really? Why?"

"To remind him to never go back to that life again where he pretty much turned over his life decisions to others, including punks like those two."

"But you let those two cretins come back in and order?" asked Stephens.

"Hey, business is damn slow." Wright shrugged. "Business is business, and their money's as green as anyone else."

"You have any idea their names or where they live around here?"

"*Nah*...not on speaking terms with turds."

They thanked Wright, and Marks thanked him for his service to his country, to which Wright frowned and replied, "I didn't do much. Sammy now, he was a hero. I hope you get the mopes who killed that boy and fry their asses."

"We're on it," Stephens called over his shoulder as they left.

Wright shouted back, "Tell Emelda she's fired!"

This stopped Stephens in his tracks. He walked back to the counter and met Wright's eyes. "That lady is downtown doing her civic duty, you asshole. If I hear you fired her for doing the right thing, vet or no vet, you and me, we're going to dance out back."

"All right, all right, I was just foolin'. She's a hard worker and I don't wanna lose her."

"That's better." Stephens turned and, with Marks slapping him on the back, the detectives left.

7

Stephens and Marks each took a tape and in separate rooms began going through each to identify the two suspects Emelda and Wright had spoken of. Stephens insisted on taking the older tape, the one with Sammy at the center of an altercation; Marks took the recent tape in which the supposed same pair of young men had come in for breakfast only hours after the attack at St. Agatha's had taken place.

Stephens, out of a sense of professional courtesy and a twinge of liking for Jude's passion for catching Sammy's killers, had called her on her cell phone to let her know that they had retrieved not one but two videos from Wright's diner. He explained the second tape, and Jude, on hearing this, pleaded to be allowed in on the viewing of the tape.

"If you can get down here, fine, but I'm running it now and not waiting for anyone."

"I'll get a cab and be there in fifteen."

True to her word, Jude arrived after Stephens was some twenty minutes into the tape. She quietly slipped into the viewing room and into a seat beside Stephens. She'd brought two cups of coffee with her, handing the black one to him. He took it gratefully and offered her a half empty bag of cashews which she took. The offerings to one another cut a lot of ice.

Together they awaited on the film to introduce Sammy's entrance to the diner, and in ten more minutes they were watching a shy, retiring Sammy enter and sit at the counter. "Smack center just like Wright said," Stephens said.

They watched a boring several minutes as Sammy gave his order to Emelda, who was all smiles behind the counter. More time passed. Nothing happening. Boring. Finally, Emelda returned in the frame with a full plate of steak and eggs to go along with a refill on Sammy's coffee.

"For once somehow enough money to pay for his meal," said Jude.

In the gray, grainy video Emelda engaged Sammy in small talk or so it appeared. Sammy's pride and momentary happiness is then suddenly dashed when a jerk from a nearby booth got up and said something in Sammy's ear that had Emelda looking shocked and angry.

"Stop it there. Freeze it," she said and Stephens did so, asking, "What?"

"Wish there was audio. Wish we had some idea what's being said."

"There is none, so we're stuck with what we have." He started the video up again.

"We need to get Emelda in here, jog her memory as to what she heard go on between them."

"Among them, you mean—here's the other jerk with his camera rolling."

Sure enough, a second man at Sammy's back was filming him. Both men's faces were unclear, their backs to the surveillance camera. There was only one angle being shot.

"Maybe get Emelda fired while we're at it," Stephens muttered as he watched the first jerk harassing Dewalt at the counter now put out a cigarette in Sammy's coffee, and then they left when Wright came out of the kitchen, that cast iron skillet held overhead like a weapon.

The skinnier of the two jerks was trailed by an overweight pal who'd shoved Sammy's back as he moved by him. The tape then ended abruptly as if it'd snapped.

"Emelda said Sammy got up and rushed out after this. Said he was embarrassed. Said the jerks were talking trash about how he'd let his buddies die. Said she told him to pay no attention to those assholes, but Sammy bolted. Left his twenty on the counter and his food only half eaten."

"Didn't get a clear shot of their faces," Stephens complained. "I had hope, but we still don't know shit."

"Marks is next door with the other tape, right?" she asked.

"Right."

"Maybe the more recent tape shows more."

"Maybe, maybe not."

"Do you always have to be so pessimistic, Stephens?"

"The nature of the beast—detective."

"Let's go see how Marks has made out before you cut your throat."

Stephens rewound the tape before them to the section of keenest importance. "Captain's going to want to see this."

"Grant, too, no doubt."

Stephens pushed his chair back and the wheels screeched, whistled, and went silent. Jude stood from her chair, an exact duplicate office chair, without a sound. Together, they went next door to see how Marks was fairing.

Marks was glad to see his partner, but not so sure of Avery coming in behind him; however, he kept any concerns to himself. Stephens asked if he'd gotten anywhere.

"Matter of fact, yes. We have a pretty fair look at our boys, and they are whooping it up, quite lively for six-twenty-two AM. "Have a look."

The two animated young men entering were the same size and build as the two who'd harassed Sammy in the other tape. They took a booth, one's face away from the camera, while the other's was on camera, clear and definitive. "Hold that frame. Get a photo pulled off from it." Stephens was animated now. "This is good, real good."

"If it turns out these are out guys," Marks said. "We don't know."

"Sure looks like the same pair who hassled Sammy in this vid, man." Stephens held up the first tape. "We need to get the experts on both tapes to see if they match physically."

"It's them," said Jude. "I'd stake my reputation on it."

Marks looked from her to his partner. "Guess I'd best have a look at what you've got there, partner."

Stephens handed it over, and Marks replaced his tape with Stephens's and again they watched as Sammy, minding his own business at the counter, was hassled and filmed by these same two men.

"That's our guys, but this doesn't prove they killed Sammy or the nuns," Marks said.

"It's a start, a direction," Jude replied. "And I suspect one that will lead us down to the snake pit where these two live."

◆   ◆   ◆

Grant, on first having heard of the *Emelda* lead developed by Jude, was beyond skeptical. Coincidence never sat well with Dean in any case, but the notion that Dr. Avery's waitress at some diner she frequented, the notion that it was also frequented by Dewalt, and his killers? No, did not wash.

Not at first.

At first he'd put it down to her naiveté and newness to Chicago. "This city isn't like a military base, kiddo," he'd said to her. He had put her little fishing expedition in the Garfield Park district down as use-less *anecdotal* information, and while he'd not told her to her face just how cute and how foolish it sounded, he had certainly thought it so.

"You just happen to have a conversation with a waitress who cracks the case wide open," he had said, voicing that thought with a disap-proving shake of his head.

"But, sir—"

"Our work will sometimes pull us from the labs and the slabs, Dr. Avery, but we're not in the habit of doing the CPD's work out there." He'd pointed to his window overlooking Harrison Street. "Out there it is un-safe for one thing. You don't carry a gun, and you're not trained in dealing with the public, and believe me, Chicago can be an unforgiving bitch."

"To be perfectly honest, Dr. Grant, I do carry a weapon, a lady Smith & Wesson, at all times, and I have taken training to use it, and I have no difficulty dealing with people, sir."

Grant smiled at this. "Well now, you are full of surprises, Dr. Av-ery. All of which doesn't change the fact that your duties are here, not questioning would-be witnesses in a diner or an interrogation room."

"I understand my duties and have performed them to the best of my abilities."

"I have been impressed with your clinical work. It's superb. It's why I hired you."

"That and the fact I have no family to hinder me, as I recall."

"A fact which does not diminish your work here or our working relationship."

Grant had played back the scene in his head a second time now. He'd also heard from Stephens and Marks about how they had traced Corporal Dewalt's movement about the neighborhood, how he'd created relationships of his own with people at the Red Lion Inn and other food and drink establishments from a liquor store to a diner—the same diner that, coincidentally, Dr. Avery frequented.

"Uncanny," he'd said to himself on learning of this thread. "Okay, maybe coincidence is real." But he'd only said so to his empty office. As to Avery's hunches and this lead involving the waitress, he thought a *bit* better of it. After giving it a moment's more consideration, he decided no clue was too small to follow in this case, especially if the Dewalt murder could actually be connected to the killings at St. Agatha's Catholic School—which hadn't been absolutely established. While there were similarities, there were enough differences to drive a Mack truck through. By now, however, he'd decided, along with Sybil, his more trusted Assistant ME, that the glass and fluorescein embedded in the wounds of the three nuns had come from the murder weapon—a heavy, large, squared-off level.

As a result of their findings and their discussions, Grant had pulled rank on a number of people to see that any and all leads, no matter how irregular or outrageous, be pursued. "For now," he'd shouted at anyone within shouting distance, "It's brainstorming time. Throw every theory against the wall, see what sticks. Leave nothing out; consider every angle."

It was not exactly behind Jude's back, but he had been the one who had ordered Stephens and Marks to keep an open mind and check out the waitress' story. He'd caught a glimpse of the plump little waitress while she was leaving the interrogation room. She looked like such a fish out of water, stumbling about the place, unable to find her way out, and finally escorted by a police woman who took pity on her. Still, the videos had backed up her story surrounding Dewalt's being harassed in that diner just as she'd said.

Grant got on the phone to Judge Huey Daplemeyer with whom he had a long and enduring relationship. Huey did not mince words or suffer fools, thieves, murderers, rapists, or any form of lower humanity—as he called people who came before his court. Grant need only call Huey, give him the briefest outline of a case being worked, and Huey would be quite ready to sign off on a search warrant.

"Should we nail these two suspected in the nun murders and the vet murders—"

Before Dean could finish his sentence, Judge Daplemeyer interrupted. "You got it, Dean. Whatever you're onto, you have my support. Your office is the best I've ever worked with in all my days."

"Thanks again then, Huey."

"You up for the annual Illinois Law Enforcement tournament?"

"You know plum well golf's not my game."

"Sure wish they'd figure a way to make a charity cause using Texas Hold'em."

"Now that I'd be up for. See you Saturday night at Long's cabin."

"Got my poker face on already. Thanks for all the cleaning up you and your team do for this city."

"Stephens or Marks will contact you if things go as planned."

"Then you guy's are onto this monster? Great."

"Might be two monsters in this instance."

"Damn...such depravity makes me want to renounce being in the humanity club."

"I know," Dean said. "Same here."

"We'll get to the bottom of it."

"That's for sure."

"So how's that new girl working out for you? Dr. Avery is it?"

"A misstep here and there, but as you always say, judge," replied Grant, and together both men said, "Worth straightenin' out!"

◆　◆　◆

Setting up surveillance at Wright's Up & Down diner, Detectives Stephens and Marks, dressing the part of counter man and waiter in the undercover operation, quickly learned that, as Stephens put it, "*Working* for a living is a great deal harder than *detecting* for a living." Stephens took orders at the counter, while Marks unsteadily carried orders to the tables. The owner, Wright, continued as normal in the kitchen, while Emelda helped out at the tables. It was all in hopes that one or both of the suspects seen in the videos would again turn up, and when and if they should, take them into custody on suspicion of murder or as persons of interest. Once in custody, the detectives meant to grill them, each separately, shake them to whatever human core that they might have left after what they'd done—presuming their guilt. There would be no pussy-footing around with these punks. Stephens and Marks had perfected their interrogation techniques over many years. If the young men in the video had indeed murdered the two vets or the three nuns or all five of these human beings, it would come clear by the time their interrogations were completed. But the first order of business was to find these two yokels and get them under the lights.

"Almost closing time," Wright shouted from the kitchen window that looked out over his diner, when one lone customer rang the entry bell, sauntered in and took a place at the counter. He ordered a cup of cocoa and a piece of custard pie before Stephens recognized the face. It was the heavier-set man in the video of the two men they'd been hoping to see since breakfast was served, and here it was nearing midnight.

"Sure, coming right up," Stephens said as he lifted his gold shield to the man's doughy face. "Chicago PD. Got a few questions for you."

Mitch Goodwin leapt from his seat, turned, and hoped to flee but standing in his way was Marks, holding up his gold badge. "We just want a few words with ya, son. That's all. Now we can do it here or at the station. Your call."

"Whataya want with me? I done nothing."

"You got a friend you hang with that maybe done something?" Stephens said.

Mitch's mouth hung open and his eyes screamed guilty. When Marks asked, "You like to video tape murdering nuns? How 'bout vets?" Mitch's first thought was, those bastards in LA put the video out for the world to see.

"It wasn't my idea. I hadda go along with KK or he'd've killed *me*! Don't ya see? It was never my idea."

"Hands behind your back, now!" ordered Stephens, who then slapped the cuffs on Goodwin while Marks asked him his name and if he had anything sharp in his pockets.

"Mitch...Mitchell Goodwin, and I tell you, I was forced to do what I done. I was in fear for my life."

Marks lifted his wallet, found his ID and an address. "Sounds like you want to cooperate fully with law enforcement, Mitchell. You giving us permission to search your house, your car?"

"I...I don't own a car."

"Your house then?"

"Sure...sure, go right ahead."

"You got that on tape, Stephens?" asked Marks.

"I do indeed. Suspect is being cooperative and gave consent to search his premises."

"Who is this KK fellow?" asked Marks.

Mitch hesitated but finally said, "Keith Kiley. He did all the killing. Not me. I didn't swing no club or level."

"Level?"

"Yeah, what he used on the nuns. KK thought it'd be funny if we, you know, leveled some nuns."

"Funny, eh?"

"Well I never said it or thought it funny. I tell you, it was all KK's doing."

"Save your story for downtown. You can put it in a five-hundred word report at the station."

"Maybe I should ask for a lawyer," Mitch said.

"Stephens, what do you think? You think Mitch here needs a lawyer?" asked Marks.

"Eventually, sure, but for now it'd just hinder things. You understand that, Mr. Goodwin?"

"What Detective Stephens means, Mitch, is that if you've got nothing to hide, and if you were coerced via bodily harm by this KK character, that you were in fear for your own life, the Stockholm Syndrome and all at work, your best bet is to follow your first gut instinct, which was to work with us because right now, we're all the friends you got."

"That's the best legal advice you'll get right now, Mitch," added Stephens.

"All right, but I still want a lawyer.

"All right, Detective Marks, read the man his rights."

As soon as Marks began reading Mitch's Miranda rights, Mitch caved again. "All right, all right, I wave my rights. I just want to do what's right. I feel awful about those vets and those nuns that Keith killed, but you gotta understand, he made me film the killings, and if I didn't, I just know he'd have lost it and killed me. He's stone cold that way once he's crossed."

"How did Dewalt cross him?" asked Stephens, urging Mitch to have a seat at the counter. The handcuffed suspect eased into the stool, hands at his back.

"It was seeing a soldier going around like he was—homeless, pitiful. Shaming the uniform."

"Really, and this Kiley fellow, was he in the military?"

"Well…no, but he tried to enlist but—but they wouldn't take him."

"Low IQ?" asked Marks.

"Spurs. Bone spurs. Said he'd never make it through basic."

"Had a lot of anger pent up over that, eh?" asked Stephens.

"And the nuns?" asked Marks.

"He went to their school. Knew one of the ones he killed, Sister Ursula. The old one. Said she was a sadistic, mean old witch."

"This Keith, we want you to call him, ask him to meet you here at the diner." Stephens had gotten into Mitch's face, staring directly into his eyes.

"Now? You mean right now?"

"No time like the present."

Mitch shakily took his phone, handed to him by Marks, who'd emptied Mitch's pockets and had laid the contents onto the counter.

"It's late. He may not come this late," Mitch told the detectives.

"But he might if you told him it was urgent," coached Stephens.

"Tell him you're worried someone's fingered him for the killings.

That ought to light a fire under him." Marks smiled at his own brilliance.

"What if he thinks it's me, my doing somehow?"

Stephens and Marks exchanged a look that said Mitch was hardly reliable. "Do your best," Stephens said. "If he shows up, believe me, he won't have a chance to harm you."

Mitch nervously agreed and dialed, apologizing over the phone immediately. "Sorry, sorry I woke you man. Yeah, I know you've got work tomorrow, but something's come up now and you need to meet me at Up & Down." Mitch fell silent and the shouting from the other end was loud enough for the detectives to hear. Kiley was not about to show up.

Mitch hung up, saying, "It's no good. He's not interested."

"Where does he live?" asked Stephens.

"An address, now," added Marks.

"We'll drag his sorry ass out of there and down every step!"

"With his nuts and his skull bumping all the way."

Marks had earlier called for a black and white to transport the suspect downtown, and no one but Mitch was surprised to see the pair of uniformed officers enter, exchange a few niceties with the detectives and take the cuffed man into custody. Marks handed the transport officer in charge now of Goodwin an evidence bag containing all of Mitch's belongings save his keys. "Witness the keys, also, Office Walker, as the suspect has agreed to a search of his home. Thusly, the keys will remain with Detective Stephens and I until we make that search and seizure."

Officer Walker and his partner escorted Goodwin out and Marks held up Goodwin's keys. "Shall we seek out that video camera, partner?"

"Funny how most of these creeps crumple like a folding chair once caught, isn't it?"

The two detectives bid Wright and Emelda a good night, adding, "You can close up now." It was past closing time by an hour.

At Mitch Goodwin's apartment—a first floor flat in a low-rent district on the outskirts of Garfield Park, trees looking on, hanging low over the rooftops—the detectives found what most would expect from a man living alone. The kitchen was a spawning ground for flies and roaches. Discarded fast-food containers and pizza boxes covered every counter top and table. The electricity was off and unpaid bills were stacked high. "We got his phone, but where do you suppose Mitch would keep his cameras?"

"The witness to Dewalt's murder thought it was a GoPro. Keep looking." Stephens went for the rear room at the end of a hallway that passed the bathroom. "Smells like dog shit in here but obviously, he's got no dog, so go figure."

Marks searched about the small living room. "Nothing here. Damn it."

"Hit the Mother Lode here! Appears he sleeps with his cameras."

Marks joined Stephens and found his partner hefting not one but two cameras. "We should confiscate his computer as well," said Marks, pointing to a small pressed-board desk in one corner with a computer atop it. "We should call in forensics. Maybe get some ETs in here. It's just possible some DNA from the nuns could have gotten on his clothes. Anything of that nature from Dewalt would be degraded by now, but there's a chance with the nuns."

"I doubt it, their being in those habits. Not much chance of skin flakes dropping out."

"Is that supposed to be funny, Marks?"

"No, just stating the obvious. Why so sore?"

"I got a sister in training for the church."

"Really?"

"Really, yes. So no nun jokes, please. Heard 'em all."

"Learn something new every day."

"I try to."

Stephens called Dr. Avery as he'd promised, bringing her up to date. "I want to be on hand," she immediately told Stephens. "Don't touch anything."

"Well...sure, nothing more. We've handled the cameras but we want a team to scan the place for possible DNA evidence and to take control of the computer and the cameras. Bag and tag by the book."

"So the diner sting paid off. I'm so glad."

"We've got one in custody and a call in for a search warrant to take to the home of the other one who appears to be the leader."

"I'm getting two teams prepared for both locations. Once you guys are out of the way."

8

Jude felt heartened to hear that one suspect was in custody and that the detectives had their eye on the second man. Laymen were often dazzled when police, in a city as large and as diverse as Chicago, could close in on suspects as quickly as they did. But every crime scene left something of the perpetrators in such cases as this. The basics of detection hadn't changed since Nancy Drew and Hardy Boys. While the science of crime detection had flourished since Nancy Drew, the basics remained. You follow the clues, the crumb trail, and many such trails would lead to a dead end, but you follow them anyway.

Jude knew that the CPD detectives had a great deal of help. Her own small team had made the discovery of the fluorescein and glass embedded in the head wounds of the three nuns, which required modern forensics. After this, she'd had Lionel do his magic to pinpoint how many actual companies in the state, then the city, then the Garfield Park area manufactured large, heavy levels. There remained only a handful in the immediate vicinity in and around the park. Jude had turned the list over to the detectives who had arranged to get help in visiting each such shop. It made more sense to begin with the close-in shops than those far away.

Nonetheless, a small army of uniformed officers had spent hours canvassing the city, visiting firms that manufactured levels. Thus far, no murder weapon in any such company had been located. Nor had an iota of further information come of the visitations. Nor had anyone interviewed at the targeted businesses showed any sign of erratic behavior, although some managers and owners had complaints about 'certain' employees showing signs of disaffection with their work or work schedules.

Late in the day, however, an officer Pryor, a veteran himself, had reported back to his captain in the Mid-town Precinct that a place called Sampson's Level Company had a 'hinky' manager who seemed to run a 'loose' shop. When pressed on the words 'hinky and loose,' Officer Ben Pryor said the man was a 'nervous sort' and that his shop amounted to a total hazard zone despite their logo—*Sampson's Level Best*. He added in his report: "The place was a dungeon from the entryway to the very back wall."

On learning of Pryor's concerns, Stephens put a pin in a map. Sampson's proved to be the closest such place to the Garfield Park area. When Stephens shared this information with Jude, the proximity alone had her curious about the place. Had Sampson's been the place that had sold the killer the level that'd killed three nuns? Could a bill of sale be the killers' downfall? Jude thought Nancy Drew would be proud of her if it came to pass.

When she and Stephens had contacted Officer Pryor directly, he had said in a booming voice over the phone, "I think the place oughta be condemned or at least shut down. And whoever's inspecting the place has gotta be paid off."

Captain Theopolis Mendes, a half Spanish, half Greek man who'd only recently taken on duties as Captain of Precinct One, Chicago, looked like a stand-in for the actor Anthony Quinn. Mendes had a visit from Officer Pryor to gain assurances that Mendes would look into what was going on at Sampson's with regard to fines and levies for safety violations—or the lack thereof.

While Stephens was called away regarding another case, Jude, overhearing Pryor's voice and recognizing it, cornered Pryor when she learned that he was in-house. "Take me to this Sampson's place," she'd said to Officer Pryor.

"Whatever for, Dr. Avery?"

"I want to get microscopic samples from the wood they use and the chemicals they use."

"Guy at the place told me they don't use dangerous chemicals in their levels any more."

"Guy at the place told you that, did he?"

"Yes, he did."

"Boss told you that?"

"Yeah, well the day manager. They were just opening the doors to let the workmen in when my partner and I pulled up."

"Ever occur to you that everybody lies?"

"He seemed quite forthcoming. Went out of his way to show us around. But honestly, only safe place to step was in the confines of his office."

"Did you get his name?"

"In my report—Kiley."

"I'd still like you and your partner to escort me and my black bag over to this place."

Pryor shrugged. "Fine but I think you're barking up the wrong tree, doc."

"I'll be the judge of that."

"Like I told Captain Mendes, this place is a hazard hole. Wouldn't want you getting hurt."

"I'll take my chances." She had a hunch, an itch, and she wanted to impress Dean with her instinct for following a lead.

Pryor tried once more to dissuade her. "I swear there's metal shavings, big ones, sharp as any sword lying around and propped up everywhere. Look here." He held up his elbow to show where his uniform shirt had been sliced. A thin white swath of skin showed through.

"I've been warned. Now let's go. Meet me in the parking garage. Gotta get my kit."

As Jude was preparing to leave, Sybil cornered her, asking, "What's up?"

Jude confessed to her plan to check out Sampson's Level company for any forensic evidence that might be found there.

"You want company?"

"If you're up for it, sure. Officer Pryor warns, however, that the place is some kind of obstacle course from hell."

"Been in a few of those. Give me a minute to get my kit and let my team know I'll be in the field."

"You think we ought to tell Dean about this?" Jude asked.

"What he doesn't know won't get in his way today. Let's keep this between us girls, eh?" Sybil smiled and rushed off.

When the two lady medical examiners found Pryor and his female partner, Officer Joan McAffy, waiting with their unit, the two officers were arguing. All that Jude made out before they fell silent was McAffy declaring, "I'm not going back inside that damn place. You can!"

Jude wondered how bad could it be as she and Sybil slipped into the rear of the police car. In a matter of minutes, the foursome were out of downtown Chicago and on the Eisenhower, making their way to the industrial district where Sampson's, a stunted, old brick building, stood between two towering factories. In fact, both sides of the street here were lined with one belching factory after another. It recalled to Jude's mind a photo she'd once seen of 1800's Birmingham, England.

Jude hesitated a moment, studying the peeled 'level' painted on the door. At one time, it might have been cute, the door as level. She then pushed through the door ahead of Sybil and Pryor, while Mcaffy, true to her word, leaned against the unit she'd driven here.

The door opened onto a frightful darkness within, and once the ladies stood in the small foyer, their eyes worked to adjust to the lack of light in the place. At the same time, their ears adjusted to the piercing noise of multiple lathes operating at once, sending sparks flying. Men worked at benches like something out of a Dickens novel, each work-bench equipped with a small lamp on a swivel arm.

"Positively medieval in here," Jude said. "You didn't exaggerate," she added for Pryor, who repeatedly said, "Watch your step, and don't lean against any walls. Office to the right. Best get the manager's okay first since we've got no warrant."

Sybil had been muttering under her breath the whole time. Jude made out one phrase. "Any rats in here?" She then said in Jude's ear, "I can take a corpse apart, but rats go right through me."

"Live ones, you mean?"

"Live, dead, pregnant, any of 'em." Sybil shivered as she spoke.

Once inside the office, which bore a name plate reading, Keith Kiley, Mgr., the three of them realized it was empty. "Maybe he's on the floor," suggested Pryor.

"Maybe next door?" Sybil pointed to a second, adjoining but smaller office. Jude stuck her head around the partition. "No one home," she announced. "PA system in there. Could call him to his office," she suggested. "Without consent from someone in charge, we can't do our job."

"And we don't have enough viable cause to get a warrant," Sybil said and frowned.

Pryor went for the PA, prepared to ask Mr. Kiley to return to his office, when an elderly-looking, hard-drink-looking fellow with sagging eyes and a red nose and cheeks stepped in, saying, "Boss stepped out for a smoke. Likely just outside."

"We saw no one when we came in," said Pryor to the man, who pointed at Pryor and said, "You I saw earlier today. What's going on, officer?"

"Who are you, sir?"

"I'm Harold *Nobody*, just one of the peons working on the next order. At my age, they still let me work. Likely the longest worker this place has ever had."

And you look it, Jude thought but did not say. "What's your full name, sir?"

"Daniels, Harry Daniels."

"What's your interest here?" Sybil asked.

"Get my age, you get curious 'bout cops coming in not once but twice the same damn day. Now you tell me, young'un, what's up? All the men out there elected me spokesperson, so to speak."

"We're taking samples from every level-making manufacturer in Chicago," Sybil lied. "Starting at Sampson's."

"Samples?"

"We need wood, metal, and glass samples—and chemicals as well," said Jude.

"Mr. Kiley said you use some kind of safe chemical nowadays," said Pryor to the old man.

"Well yeah, that's right. They take stuff they call alcohol-fluorescein solution."

"Tell me, sir, Mr. *ahhh*..." began Jude when the man coughed out his name again as Daniels.

"Mr. Daniels, tell me, do we have your permission to take one of these display items with us? Take it back to the lab where we can study it under our high-powered microscopes?"

"I got no problem with it, but why?"

"It's part of an ongoing investigation, sir, and so we aren't at liberty to discuss the details, you understand."

"Understand? Sure, sure I understand."

"Mr. Daniels, have you noticed anything unusual from any of the men working here lately? Any undue absence, irritation, erratic behavior, or oddness in anyone?"

Daniels burst out with a huge belly laugh at Jude's question. When he collected himself, he said, "Look out at the workbenches out there if you want odd. People who work here are better'n any fun house freak show. Odd." He laughed more.

Jude ventured out of Kiley's office for a closer look at the working environment. It looked like something more fitting to a sweat shop in a third world country. She studied the faces of the men working at each bench, and a more motley looking crew she could not ever recall seeing anywhere at any time. Any one of them, if she should judge by the hard glares piercing into her, could be her killer. They had all stopped work, awaiting word from old Daniels about the police presence. She turned abruptly to Daniels, close to his face, and asked, "What did Mr. Kiley tell you about this morning's visit by Officer Pryor and Officer McAffy?"

"Told us it was all some sort of mistake. He was vague about it."

"Did something happen to Maria?" shouted one of the men from his bench.

"Naw, not that I know of," replied Daniels.

The man asking nodded. "Thank God for small favors."

"Who's Maria?" asked Jude of Daniels.

Thompson explained and went into some detail about the 'blow up' between Maria and Mr. Kiley the day before. That's when Mr. Kiley took that discard home with him."

"Discard?"

Daniels pointed to a large round barrel filled with unfinished pieces. "It had a bad gouge in it that Rob caused when he hurt his hand the other day."

"Mr. Kiley took a discard home with him? Would it have had the fluorescein in it?"

"Was damn near finished when the accident happened."

"How long has your boss been on that smoke break?" asked Sybil, joining them.

"Ouch!" Jude cried out, having been cut on her ankle by a metal strip among others leaning against the wall where she'd been standing. While the cut wasn't deep, it was long and it had drawn blood. She had to staunch it with a handkerchief while Daniels began pleading for her to accept his apology, thinking that he was somehow to blame.

"If you'd just get us that display sample you promised, Mr. Daniels," Jude said, assuring him. "Then we can get out of here to leave you folks to your work."

"We got a big order out of Iowa we're trying to fill. Can't believe all the goings-on. Nothing ever happens around here and now Maria gets fired or quit, nobody knows which, and now youz guyz show up not once but twice. I'll get that display model for you."

"Largest, sturdiest one you have, Mr. Daniels, please."

"Sure thing. Likely some big band aids in the secretary's office, detective," Daniels said to Jude, assuming her a police detective, as he went for the sample level.

Jude, who now had a good working relationship with Stephens—and Marks to a lesser degree—telephoned Stephens back to inform him of the possibility of the Sampson Level company as a possible if not probable lead. As she excitedly told him of the lead provided by Officer Pryor, Stephens authoritatively stopped her from saying another word when he said, "That's all right, Dr. Avery. No need to go on any further."

"Oh? Why's that?"

"I'm holding a baseball bat studded with nails in one gloved hand and—"

"You've located the murder weapon? The bat!" She could not contain her excitement.

"And a huge, broken, still bloody level with a logo on it reading, get this—Sampson's Level Best."

"You've found both murder weapons?"

"Yes, both are in our possession."

"You've found the murder weapons," she repeated. "Wow."

"Marks and I have, yes. We're in the home of the man whose pal calls him KK, bills are made out to Keith Kiley."

"He's the manager here at Sampson's. Damn, and it appears he's escaped."

"You just be damn careful, Dr. Avery. He's as mean a monster as they come."

Marks's voice in the background came through loud and clear. "He's a sure winner for the prize as to who wielded these weapons."

"Same guy for sure; we have paycheck stubs from the Sampson Level company."

"Now we just have to locate the sonofabitch, eh?"

"We've put out a BOLO on him," Marks shouted then. "Won't be lost for long."

Stephen's calmly said, "We suspect he may've been scared off, on the run. Not sure if he smelled us coming after him, you know. We attempted to get him to the diner for a meeting with his cameraman."

"You guys have done miraculous work, detective. Very good work."

"So, apparently, have you guys. And hey, call me Wayne."

"I can send a team over to the apartment. Gotta get some ETs down here, too. Canvas his office. Get all the goods we can on the bastard."

"Do that. Meantime, I'm bagging the guy's kill toys."

"Human caused mayhem," she replied with a sigh, not expecting any further reply.

"Ain't it always the way?"

"Too often the case, yes. They're saying the fires that devastated North Georgia and South Tennessee were arson again."

"Yeah, saw that on the news. Awful what people do to one another. Course in our line of work, we see the worst."

"And the best of people, like the Dewalts."

"And people like Emelda, and even that crusty old Wright." Stephens let out a laugh.

"The good, the bad, the ugly, as they say."

"Say, doc, you ever eat?"

"When I can, sure."

"I mean other than brown bagging it in your lab?"

"Sometimes, sure."

"I'd like to buy you diner some time."

"Some time is pretty wide open," she replied. "Can you be more, *ahhh,* specific?"

"Tonight? Say seven-ish?"

"With two crime scenes to process? Not likely."

Stephens fell silent save for a hem and a haw.

"How about tomorrow night? Much more likely I'm free."

"Good then, it's a go."

As soon as she hung up, a smile creasing her features, she started the work of getting a field team together for each location, Kiley's home and Kiley's place of work.

As for the one in custody, Mitch Goodwin, police detectives were pleased to have him in their grasp, and first order of business with him was to take a DNA swab which Dr. Grant had seen to personally with the hope to match Goodwin with that found on Pongo's saliva. If it matched, they had definite physical evidence that Goodwin was at the Dewalt murder scene. Of course, a defense lawyer would argue that the dog could easily have bitten the wrong man. Still, when faced with the evidence during his incarceration, the fact could help get a confession, so Dean put it on the front burner.

Goodwin looked to be the weaker of the two monsters, the link to break, the branch to shake, as it were. Grant and others in law enforcement had seen killer couples time and again, and no matter their sex or sexual orientation, one of the two led the other by the nose, while that other did as told like a puppet on a string. It was a form of dependence, what Oprah or Judge Judy railed against on their TV shows for years—the mental slavery that occurs when one person gives over his or her will to another so completely as to do anything the stronger personality wishes.

From all that Grant was hearing, however, that bond had been broken the moment Mitch was uncovered as the second man in the killings, and that he was so cooperative that now a clearer and clearer picture of Keith Kiley, aka KKboy, was forming.

When Grant had left with his swab, he turned back to the one-way glass to watch Stephens and Marks continue their interrogation. Marks was playing tough cop, pissed, angry cop, while Stephens had brought in a cold drink and a hamburger for Goodwin. At the moment, Mitch was struggling with one hand cuffed to the table and the other with a hamburger falling apart. At the same time, Goodwin's eyes went wide on seeing the killing tools that Marks began pulling from a huge evidence bag he'd held in abeyance at his feet. They were the supposed murder weapons used by Kiley, the spiked baseball bat and the broken, super-sized level.

"Where's my court-appointed lawyer," Goodwin immediately asked on seeing the damning evidence.

"On his way, I'm sure, Mitch. Meantime, do you recognize these instruments of death as the murder weapons used by your friend Kiley?"

"They are," he said, readily admitting. "You see why I was so afraid of him? He threatened me with those things, too. I swear it."

"He's still on the loose, Mitch, so we need to know where he'd go to hide. Does he have family, friends who'd harbor him? What do you know along those lines?"

"He's got no friends, nor family that I know of."

"Who'd take money to hide him then, Mitch? Come on, help us out here before he kills again."

"He won't kill again." Mitch took a final bite of what was left of his burger and washed it down with his Dr. Pepper.

"What's that supposed to mean," Stephens asked, pressing.

"He only does it for the camera and—"

"You mean you!" shouted Marks.

"He only does it for the camera," Goodwin repeated.

"And he's got no cameraman now, eh?" asked Stephens.

"Yeah, 'cause you guys *saved* me from that maniac."

"Help us to understand that, Mitch. Did he ever explain why he wanted to star in a snuff film?"

"Sorry, you guys have been real good to me, but I am not talking anymore to anyone but my lawyer. I want a lawyer now."

Captain of Detectives Mendes stood alongside Dr. Grant just outside the glass, and on hearing Goodwin call for a lawyer, he rapped loudly on the glass, signaling an end to the interrogation. Marks re-bagged the damning evidence, and he and his partner made their way to the door when Goodwin shouted at them, "I'm sorry, but I feel like I'm digging this hole I'm in deeper and deeper, and the sand's cavin' in on me."

"You got that much right," Stephens replied as he closed the door behind himself.

Outside they found Captain Mendes, frowning. "The weaker link, eh? The follower to this guy Kiley, is he?"

"True, captain."

"You think he has any conscience at all?" asked Jude who had just joined them. She stared in at Goodwin.

"I doubt it," said Marks.

"What about you, Detective Stephens?" she pressed.

"What's it matter? He's *lawyered* up now."

"Matters if we pipe this into the room." She held up a small black square, a camera SD card for a GoPro. "You got the camera, we found the video. Something you overlooked at this creep's place. The murder on film of each of their victims. While Mitch in there did not wield the weapons, he encouraged and egged the other monster on. He's guilty as hell of something."

The interrogation room was equipped with the necessary connections to import the video from a remote device using the card. "Just because he's waiting on a lawyer," began Dr. Grant with a wink to Jude, "seems to me we ought to give him something to keep him entertained."

"No law against showing the accused what we have on him," added Stephens.

Marks asked, "Can I be the one?"

To this, Jude handed over the card, and Marks reentered the room, saying to Mitch. "Got something here for your viewing pleasure, Mitch."

Mitch shuffled uncomfortably in his seat. "Where's my lawyer?"

"On his way, I'm sure. These court-appointed fellas are a little jaded, you know. Seen it all. Meanwhile, something here for you to see. Our forensics folks found it under boards in your home."

"Now I told you all that I only filmed the killings b—because Mitch threatened my life."

"Sure, sure, we get that, Mitch."

"I—I was in fear for my life. That's stand your ground law, right?"

The video came up with the screaming of several nuns who were cowering in the church. The cameraman's laughter competed with the screams, and Mitch's voice-over repeatedly said, "Level the bitches, KKboy, level their brains." This as blood flew, smearing the camera lens and discoloring white robes.

Marks, sickened by the film, still managed to calmly ask, "Mitch, that sounds a lot like you telling KKboy to do it again and again."

"I told ya! He'd've killed me if I didn't...wasn't playing the part, you see? You gotta see that!"

"That's enough!" came a shout from the door that'd been thrown open. "I will speak privately with my client now, detective." It was a lady from the Public Defender's Office that Marks and Stephens had sparred with many times before.

"Hello, Darlene. He's all yours, but the video evidence is all ours."

"The defense request copies of all incriminating evidence at this time, formally, understood?"

"We'll get right on that. Your client here video-tapped five murders that we know of. Two vets, three nuns. Good luck with that defense, Darlene."

The pleats in Darlene Austin's starched suit seemed to stiffen as Detective Marks turned off the video just as more screams rose. Marks then sauntered out to allow Goodwin privacy with his lawyer. On his way out, Captain Mendes, complying with the law, shut down the looking glass and announced this fact to Goodwin and his attorney.

Marks stormed past the others, angry and sullen. Stephens shouted after his partner, "Where ya going, man?"

"Getting a drink! I need a drink."

"I need a shower," said Jude.

"I need to get back to my lab," said Grant. "Dr. Avery, I've got a DNA swab from the cretin. Going to rush it through, see if Pongo and Mitch in there met or not."

"Good, good, sir."

Captain Mendes, a large man who stood a head taller than Grant, lamented aloud, "We gotta follow these stupid rules while creeps like this and his buddy play by no rules whatsoever."

"A crime in itself, I'd say," Grant replied, shook Mendes's hand and said, "Jude, shall we?"

She felt a bit strange being escorted back to the ME's Office by Dr. Grant himself. Along the way, he said, "I'll see to the DNA match with the dog. You've got more than a handful to deal with."

She smiled and nodded, but her thought was at odds with the agreement: That dog will play well on the six o'clock news.

Meanwhile, the manhunt for Keith Kiley was in full APB, red alert. Every cop in the city had his photo. Every CPD blue knight was on the lookout and every CPD unit on the prowl for KKboy, Keith Kiley. All transportation out of the city had been instantly blocked, bus and train stations combed by police armed with photos of Kiley taken off the videos his accomplice Goodwin had taken. The airport was overrun with police and security, checking every face in the crowds. Every teller at every airline was given Kiley's name and photo to alert police should he show up to buy a ticket out of Chicago. Even the el trains that took passengers to suburbs like Elgin were on the alert. Finally, area-wide car dealerships and rental agencies were alerted to be on the lookout and report anyone who even resembled the photo now circulated to all media outlets.

KKboy's photos had been shared on social media as well, causing a tweet storm of sightings. Everywhere in the city, sirens roared as police units raced to scene after scene where the suspect had been 'seen' but thus far they had all come up bogus or empty. Fake 'sightings' soon popped up so regularly that they began to impede any progress.

No one seemed to know where Kiley had gotten off to, but speculation ran rampant. "This is getting so out of hand," Stephens complained to Jude over dinner. It had been almost forty-eight hours and still no Kiley to be found.

"How does a man like that just disappear?" she asked.

"He's got some connection to LA, according to his computer and same with Goodwin. It's just possible he got out of the city, went over state lines, talked some private pilot into flying him to LA."

"Do you have a fix on who in LA he'd run to for help?"

"No, but we've got the IP numbers on both the computers we have in our possession—Goodwin's and Kiley's," Stephens said proudly. "Got our geniuses working with your man Lionel on it."

"What about the IP address at the other end?"

"The one they send to in LA? Sorry, no way. Getting no cooperation from the internet service provider."

"Lionel's like a bull terrier. He'll keep trying."

"Absolutely. We're working on a court order, but you know how hard it is to get ISPs to help out?"

"I've heard, yes."

Stephens then added, "I had Lionel email the Elders."

"You did? With what results?"

"Using Kiley's identity, of course. Prior to that, Goodwin's."

"Anything back?"

He shook his head. "Afraid not."

"No response at all to either of them?"

"It's almost as if they smell a rat somehow."

Jude lifted her glass of wine and sipped at it. "It's been over twenty-four hours since anyone's seen the bastard."

Stephens took a phone call. It was his captain calling to chew him out. Stephens covered his phone in his large hand, cupped it, and whispered clearly, "We are still attempting to make contact with the Elders. We've had no cooperation via email to whomever is at the other end, and, thus far, the ISP's unwilling to give us the information. We need that warrant."

After Stephens endured more shouting over his iPhone, he finally got off and turned back to Jude. "Sorry about that. Mendes."

"No need to apologize. I have my own Mendes—Dean Grant."

The two smiled across at one another and drank more wine. She said after a moment, "Look, if Kiley's got such a head start on us, maybe someone ought to be in LA for us."

Their meals arrived and with their wine glasses refreshed, the couple fell silent while eating, each further contemplating the case. Each contemplated one another as well.

"You look lovely tonight, Dr. Avery," he said to her.

"Why thank you. It's hard to look one's best in a lab coat all day long."

"I think it's more than that," he said. "I think you enjoy my company."

"Well of course I do!"

"I'd like to get things off my mind long enough to breathe, but truth be told, I keep picturing that disgusting SOB in a cushy Cessna, descending into LA about now."

"I kind of pictured the maniac hiding up in the rafters of that now condemned level factory. Are you sure he hasn't been inside there this whole time?"

"It's been thoroughly searched."

"So what if he wasn't there at the time, but returned? Even boarded up, he'd have keys. He was managing the place. He'd also know every nook and cranny in the place."

"You proposing you and I go case the place again? We don't have keys."

"But the Sampson family does."

"You think they'd turn 'em over without a court order?"

She shrugged. "Maybe, if they thought cooperating with law enforcement would help them get out from under some of the fines they're facing."

"Finish your steak, Jude, and we'll just find out how cooperative they can be."

After finishing up at *Redondo's* Spanish Restaurant on Lincoln near Belmont, the detective and the ME drove out to the mansion home of the Sampsons in Lake Forest that nearly skirted the outdoor theater Ravenia Park. As they approached, it occurred to Stephens that perhaps they should have considered Kiley's coming here, and he said to Jude, "This would make a helluva hideout. Kind of like a Bogey and Edward G. Robinson hideout."

"You don't really think he's here, do you?"

"Not sure; I mean anything's possible. Tell you what, you go to the door, flash your badge, ask for keys to the factory while I slip about the side widows for a peek inside."

"You sure?"

"I'm sure...but be careful. Try to get a read on whoever answers the door. Any strange behavior. If they welcome you inside or keep you out, all that."

"All right, if you're sure."

"You carrying?"

"On a date? No."

"Here, take my spare."

She took the heavy .38 in hand. "Where am I to put it?"

"In your purse."

She had to dump some things on the seat to accommodate the weapon. "Maybe we're being foolish."

"Better foolish than dead."

"I suppose you're just thinking like a killer, eh?"

"Absolutely. He had, according to Mitch Goodwin, no place to go. Knew no one. Hadn't a friend save Mitch, so who would he turn to if not the Sampsons?"

"Co-workers did say he started with the company as a boy."

"Family. For what it's worth."

"Look at the way they live here and how they let that factory deteriorate around the heads of their workforce. It's a sinful, sinful thing."

"The filthy rich make their own rules."

Stephens slipped out of his seat and tucked his head back inside to say, "Give me a minute to get around the side.

She did so. In a moment, she found herself standing at the large ornate door. She lifted the knocker and let it fall. Once was enough as the noise resounded through the stout, wooden door.

She practiced in her mind what she wanted to say to these people. Some words she knew she must stifle. When the door slowly opened, she felt a sense of peril rising. Could that horrid murderer be on the other side, a gun or a poker pointed at the head of the elderly lady who stood like a guard before Jude now and asking, "Can I help you, young lady?"

"I am Dr. Judith Avery, ma'am, with the Chicago Medical Examiner's Office." Jude held up her police shield and ID. "And I've come to ask you for the use of keys to the Sampson Level Company, to gain access once more. There're some areas my evidence technicians failed to cover, you see, and it's important for us to be thorough, you see."

"Keys? Really? Just hand them over to you here and now? I think not. I have a better suggestion."

"Oh, and that would be?"

"Young Joseph is within and he can follow you down, let you in, await your plodding about the place, and then lock up after you. Is that acceptable?"

"Well...yes, I suppose so, Mrs. Sampson, I presume?"

"Oh, my heavens, do forgive me my manners. Yes, I am Mrs. Harold Sampson. Harold's no longer with us, and my sons run the business nowadays."

Jude imagined that she had last word on the business and not the sons. "Joseph is your son?"

"Grandson. Has more sense than any of my sons."

"I see. Well, I'll wait in the car."

"Oh, haven't you a moment for late tea?" asked the lady, warming to Jude, it seemed.

"I just had a meal and really am too full, but thank you for your kindness, Mrs. Sampson. Perhaps another time."

"Yes, of course."

Jude rushed back to Wayne's waiting vehicle in the driveway. Moments later, he slipped back behind the wheel. "How'd they act at the door?"

"Perfectly normal, even invited me in for tea. You see anything unusual, Mr. Peeping Tom?"

"Their alarm system is down. That much was proven. I suspect they've fallen on hard times, despite the palatial surroundings."

"Well...now we have to wait for Joseph."

"Joseph?"

"Man with the warehouse keys."

"Oh, I see."

"He's to follow us down to the factory. Apparently, Mother Sampson does not trust us with the keys."

"Or inside there alone."

"Sending her grandson. Said something about his being sharper than all her sons put together."

"Said that, did she?"

"Something to that effect, yes."

One of the three garage doors opened and a Bentley pulled out. Joseph, no doubt. He pulled around Stephens's car in the double-wide driveway and led the way back to Chicago. He took the winding Sheridan Road, eschewing the highway. They were soon passing directly through the campus of Northwestern University and Evanston, Illinois, following the Ravenswood CTA train route now, cutting across to Chicago, still on Sheridan. After a time, Joseph cut west on Irving Park, heading for the factory district where Sampson's Level manufacturing had gone on for generations. The squat red-brick factory rested now, its door darkened by a city condemnation notice.

Two streets over from the place, they saw a blaze. Something was on fire, something huge. Fire truck alarms came up all around them as if from nowhere, and Joseph pulled over as did Stephens, to allow the fire trucks to safely go by them.

"Can't be," Jude said, staring at Wayne. "You don't suppose that damned level factory is on fire, do you?"

"Leveled, you mean?"

"Not funny."

"Well if it is afire," began Wayne, "and our killer's been hiding inside with some makeshift campfire stove, he's flushed out now."

"Get to the warehouse, now."

Joseph sped off ahead of them, falling behind the fire trucks; Stephens followed suit. Once they turned onto the dingy little factory street that housed the small Level factory, it became obvious that Jude's worst fear was realized. The Sampson Level factory was a torrent of flame. Combustibles within began exploding, and it was obvious the firemen could do nothing but contain it as best they could from afar as no one knew what new explosion might come.

"What if he was hiding in there and got out?" she asked Stephens.

Wayne had already gotten on his radio, calling for any and all units in the area to converge and be on the alert for any sign of Keith Kiley.

"Where the hell can that monster be?" she wondered aloud. "If he's lying dead within the inferno, it's too good for him to escape justice this way."

"Won't know if he's inside until morning at the earliest and possibly not for days, depending...judging from your description of the place."

"You know, young Joseph over there," she pointed to the well-dressed young Sampson, "he sure took us on the longest route here. You don't suppose this fire's an inside job, do you?"

"The Sampson clan stands to win. Fire will get out from under a lot of litigation."

"Makes one wonder."

"Litigation and dead weight when Grandson Joseph hires a professional to clean up the family mess?"

"It's been known to happen."

"And maybe Baby Joseph also knew that KKboy was hiding inside?"

"Take care of *all* loose ends, eh?"

"Grandma seemed to believe in the boy..."

"You gathered all that from a porch visit?"

She frowned at him. "What little I could pick up off that porch, yeah. Call me observant."

"Dr. Observant. Still it'd be the devil to prove."

"Fire inspectors might disagree with you, Wayne."

"One thing to prove arson, another to prove the trail leads back to Lake Forest."

"Might be hard to prove," she conceded. "I'll hold judgment."

"I'm sure."

"What's that supposed to mean?" she asked, pressing him.

He shrugged. "Means I am sure you'll do your level best, Jude. But for now, the fire guys aren't getting inside anytime soon to determine anything."

"What do you propose we do then?"

"I propose to run you home where you can get rest. You'll need it if they find Kiley's inside there, burnt to a crisp."

"I imagine you're right, but frankly, I'm wide awake."

"Drinks?" he asked.

"I could use something stronger than dinner wine, sure."

"I know just the place; not far from here."

"I'll drink to that."

The next morning, Jude awoke in her own bed *beside* Wayne. She blinked a good deal and recalled their night of passion and lust. And she now knew why she'd failed to put any pictures of her parents up in this room. In her head, though, she heard a familiar phrase: Find it where you can. This she recalled was the attitude of her best friend during high school days on the army base. Kat Hearns was a wild one, and much of her had rubbed off on Jude when younger, but she hadn't indulged in a one-night stand in years. She wondered if this was a one-night stand or if something more permanent, *wondered* if something real could come from falling in love with Wayne Stephens, *wondered* if she was being girlishly silly.

Feeling a bit foolish, she even tried on the name: *Dr. Judith Stephens.* Then she corrected that to *Avery-Stephens.* Then she wondered if the sleeping man would object to *Stephens-Avery* if she pushed it. Then she mentally slapped herself for the silliness, got up, threw a waiting robe over her nude body and made for the kitchen.

There she made six cups of coffee in her old brewer, the one she'd never give up for any newfangled item. She then went in for a shower. She and Wayne had fallen asleep in one another's sweat, hearts pounding. The lovemaking had been sensual, sweet at times, the touch of his fingertips along the contours of her face, her lips, and her breasts had taken her breath away, and she almost suffocated on his kisses. But it was the good kind of suffocation, and she already knew she'd want more.

As she showered, she fantasized his waking up to the smell of the coffee and her—what lingered of her in the bed beside him. She imagined his skipping the coffee for her, coming in on her to share the shower. "God knows he needs it after the things I did to him," she told the stall, empty save for her, when, as if on magical cue, he in fact entered the shower to join her.

He didn't slip out the back, Jack, she thought as she wrapped her arms about him, and Stephens gently forced her against the warm tiles, kissing and caressing her with abandon. "How're we going to keep this between us, Dr. Avery?" he asked between kisses.

"It wouldn't set well, I'm sure, with your boss or mine."

"Bloody protocol. Not sure it extends outside the squad room to the coroner's office, but frankly, Scarlett, the way I feel, I don't give a damn."

"You will if your job's in jeopardy," she replied, pulling away. "Mine as well."

"You think so?"

"I know men. Your job is your identity."

"And yours isn't?" he snapped back, a tinge of defensiveness filtering through.

"Are we having our first fight in my shower?" A smile came over her features.

"Ha, I guess so."

"Well why don't we put it on hold?" She kissed him anew. "At least until we get some clothes on."

"That could be another hour." He turned off the shower, took her hand, and led her back to the bedroom where each enjoyed the slick, wet body of the other. "You're getting my bedsheets soaked again!"

"Is that a capital offense around here?"

She silenced him with a smothering kiss. He returned her kiss with his own.

A half hour later, the couple lay spent on the now chilled bedsheets. They showered anew while both their iPhones pinged. Once dressed and having coffee, sitting across from one another at her kitchenette table, they studied their phones to determine who was calling and which call to return first. "My partner, wondering where I am. Likely heard about the fire at Sampson's by now."

"Marks, he seems a bit distracted lately."

"That's his usual way. He's got some bad debts, bad habits, and a bad liver from bad liquor."

"Sounds like a Tom Waits song."

"Who's after you?" He indicated the phone in her hand.

"Grant, of course. I'm late and I've never been late."

"Tell him you're at the fire scene. He'll understand. And by time we get there, hell, it won't be a lie."

"I like the way you think, Wayne."

"Is that all you like about me, my mind?"

She laughed at this. "You know better'n that."

He reached across the table and took her hands in his. "You know, I don't want to push my luck or move too fast with this, but, hey, Jude…I am hoping we're not going to let others dictate our relationship."

She was a bit surprised where he'd taken that remark. She'd thought he was going to say something entirely different. Something about how he'd like to see her again and again. "I—I perfectly agree. You and I, we should make a pact to that effect. We decide. Not some bureaucracy or anyone else, neither partners nor bosses."

"Good…good," he replied, squeezing her hands harder. "I like you, Jude; like you like…well, like I've not liked anyone, ever, in a long, long time."

She thought in response to this: Do go on. But he didn't. He merely stared into her green eyes. She said, "Long long time? How long? A week ago? Two?"

"No, no, sweetheart, I'm talking about my first love ever."

"*Hmmm*…good answer, cowboy."

Along the way to what remained of Sampson's Level factory, the two of them made their return calls, with her complaining that he shouldn't be on the phone while driving. He ignored her and told Marks where he was heading. Marks was in fact on the scene already, and he said, "I've made excuses for you with the captain, so get here quick, pal. And hey, they're all trying to locate Dr. Avery as well. You got any idea why she's not answering her phone?"

"None, but I just picked her up at her place, and we're headed your way."

"No rush, really. Fire guys are still picking through the rubble. It's too dangerous to go inside just yet."

"Do they know how the fire in a supposed empty building started?" Stephens asked as they came in view of the fire trucks.

"Still determining. May take all day, if not longer."

"Then why'd they call us in, Dennis?"

"They have a body inside, and they won't move it out until someone from Grant's office and ours gives them the thumbs up."

Jude worked to make out the one-sided conversation when Wayne said, "Well, Dr. Avery's right here now, and I'm sure she can give them the green light." He dropped the call and explained the situation to Jude.

"Then it's true maybe..."

"What's that?" he asked, pulling onto the curb so as to be out of the way of the fire trucks.

"That KKboy, Kiley was inside. He likely caused the fire as well."

"Assuming the Sampsons had nothing to do with it."

They exited the vehicle and walked toward the smoldering embers of the gutted factory. Only one half a wall on the backside and another on the west side stood. Everything else was gone. Smoke and cinders, a few embers taking flight like glowing butterflies. Small clouds of pure smoke rose in spots like leftover campfires.

Jude had returned her calls as well. Grant yelled at her for not having answered her phone earlier. "When I call, you pick up. Simple as that, Dr. Avery."

She'd apologized, claiming she had overslept and did not hear the phone.

"Get a land line, too. I thought you had a land line."

"Sorry, and yes, will do."

"I managed to get Sybil down there. I think you should join her."

She'd seen a call from Shanley as well on her call list, but after speaking with Grant, she had decided to simply find Shanley at the site of the fire.

She now saw Sybil, in a white lab coat amid the charred, blackened remains of the factory, and she felt a twinge of pain where that metal strip had cut her in passing the day before. She also felt a tinge of worry for Sybil amid all that rubble, but Ralph was standing over her, watchful of loose pipes and wiring hanging about. Sybil was hunched over a charred body.

An evidence tech van rocked nearby with people going in and out for supplies. Jude saw Luther rushing a small oxygen tank from the van to Dr. Shanley, whose lab coat was smeared, like a Jackson Pollock painting, with creosote and ash.

Jude found what she needed from the van with Lisa Coombs's help, slipping on booties, gloves, and a lab coat. Lisa placed an all-purpose medical valise in her hand as well, and she heard Lisa shout to be careful, which slowed Jude from rushing in with abandon—a thing she wanted to do badly at this point. Instead she tip-toed her way through the morass of debris and smoldering ash. Each step felt like a mine field.

Jude saw cadaver dogs, trained to seek out bodies, amid the rubble, and even they were being cautious and nimble with their four feet. She wondered if one or more of the dogs was a bomb-sniffing canine, and if a third was a drug-sniffer. Hard to tell. Meanwhile, numbers of firemen were shouldering and walking out with possible combustibles that could re-ignite the fire. The fact they were allowing Dr. Shanley, Ralph, and her into the still dangerous ground told her that the fire marshal or whomever was in control here had been pressured to do so. No doubt Dr. Grant's influence.

Everyone wanted this to be the end of the nun murders. The newspapers, TV news, cable, and social media had been eating up the Chicago authorities from top to bottom since the triple murder event at St. Agatha's.

Suddenly, Jude realized someone had come up behind her, shadowing her steps. She thought at first it'd be Wayne being overprotective of her, but a glance back and she saw that it was Lisa. "What're you doing, Lisa?"

"Call it moral support, and should you need an extra pair of hands, I'm here for you."

"Well...all right, and thanks." Jude pointed to the coming and going firemen and asked, "Are they searching for more bodies?"

"Someone next door said one of the workmen acted as a night watchman."

"Really?"

Lisa continued between gasps as she picked her way along toward the one body they did have. "They say he had a little bed, TV, and stove at the rear. Otherwise homeless."

Jude flashed on the opulent home where the Sampsons lived in the northern suburbs. *Hmmm...while everyone's hoping it's Kiley.*

"Kiley, ma'am? Doctor?"

"The SOB we tagged for the vet and the nun murders, the manager of this hell hole."

"They're trying to determine if the watchman's stove was the cause."

"And if there's anyone else beneath the rubble," added Ralph who'd come toward them, extending a steady hand to Dr. Avery. "There were two stories."

"Both collapsed in on top of anything or anyone on the main floor," finished Lisa.

Jude pictured the elderly man who'd stepped into Kiley's office while she and the others had been searching for Kiley. She wondered if the charred body was this poor soul when the saw Marks and Stephens interviewing the same man. He stumbled forward, looking confused or hungover or both.

Jude needed to keep her focus on the job at hand for now. She'd ask Wayne later if he'd learned anything knew from the elderly fellow.

Stephens asked the old man to slow down and take a deep breath, fearful he was about to keel over with a heart attack, he was that agitated at seeing his place of work and makeshift home leveled by fire.

"They burnt her down. My only home. Damn them."

"Your home?" Stephens asked. "You're the guy who lived in the back room?"

"I got paid to watch the place; figured might as well make it as comfortable as home. Got evicted from my apartment a year ago."

"Then who's body are they picking over?" Dennis Marks asked the old man.

"If I *hafta* guess, I'd say it was Mr. Kiley."

"Why do you suspect that it's him, sir?"

"He run me out last night. Give me two fifty dollar bills and told me to check into a hotel."

"He did, did he?"

"But why would he burn it down? Damn, I've lost all my stuff... everything."

Marks repeated the question, "This Kiley fellow paid you to leave for the night?"

"Yeah, on my oath, he did."

"Then you knew he was hiding out inside, but you didn't call authorities?"

"He's always been a good boss to me. I never believed he was guilty of a thing." The old fellow shrugged. "I do unto others like, you know, they do unto me."

"Probably why you're down and out, old-timer, with an attitude like that." Marks shook his head.

Stephens was looking past Marks and the old man in the direction of Dr. Avery who was staring back at the detectives and their 'witness.' Marks caught the look between his partner and the new medical examiner, and he said, "She's a looker, eh, Wayne?"

Stephens stiffened almost imperceptibly and nodded. "Yeah, not bad."

"Seems more pleasant than Dr. Shanley, but who isn't?" Marks laughed at his own remark, but Stephens said, "God, I hope the corpse is that bastard Kiley. Old-timer, your congenial boss is a spree killer, responsible for the deaths of three nuns and two veterans."

"Don't make sense. I'm a vet, and he always respected my service, he did."

"*Schitzo* for sure," said Marks.

"Look, sir," Stephens said, looking deeply into the old eyes of the vet. "We may have some questions for you later. Where can we find you?"

"You can't. I got nowhere now."

"We can take you to a homeless shelter."

"Me in a homeless shelter?" A tear formed at the corner of the vet's eye. "A nightmare is what this is."

"What do you say? Want a ride and an introduction? It's a bed at night."

"I'll hafta find a new job."

"Marks and me, we'll keep our ears open and help you out there. What do you say, Mr. *ahhh…*"

"Daniels, Harry Daniels."

Daniels went along with the detective. Marks hung back, while Stephens guided the broken man to his car. With a final glance out to the area of the corpse in the rubble, Stephens studied the people there, finding that Jude had made it to the body. It looked like a gathering of mourners at a grave site as the gray clouds opened, and a light rain began to fall. A much needed rain to soften the lingering heat wave.

Jude had quietly, secretly watched Stephens take in the old-timer, imagining him taking the Sampson worker downtown for questioning. She'd then shook it off and finished her way toward Dr. Shanley with Ralph's help. When she got within speaking distance, Shanley had shouted for her to be careful where she stepped. She'd already put her foot down into smoldering ash twice by this time.

"Fire Marshall says this is safe enough for us, eh?" she called back to Sybil.

Sybil remained focused on the corpse. She'd taken some skin samples and had gotten general measurements of height and girth. She had also calculated the man's weight, skin tone, shoe size, length of torso.

"He's ready to bag, Dr. Avery," she called to Jude. "No need you come any further. You can have at him on your slab." As soon as this was said, an entire section of wall caved in some six feet from where Jude stood. It made Jude gasp and lurch to one side, but the scorched wall, fortunately fell away from her and not toward her. When Jude regained her composure, she tried to calmly go forward, asking Sybil, "Do you think it's our man Kiley?"

"I do…I do. But of course, that's yet to be absolutely determined."

"Awful nasty way to check out," Jude replied, standing close now to the remains, seeing the only thing remaining in the way of the face was a bald, charred, eyeless, skinless, red-blackened fleshy skull.

"Wouldn't be my first choice, no."

"His dental records'll be the only certain method to ID this as Keith Kiley."

In the distance, Jude saw a parked Bentley with a man and a woman inside, watching the goings-on. She recognized them as Joseph behind the wheel and his grandma in the passenger seat. Once again, she wondered if these two were capable of paying some arsonist off, to get out from under the factory with a profit. She also wondered if, in doing so, they had arranged to have one Keith Kiley present when the fire was set. She hated to be so prejudicial toward Grandma Sampson and young Joseph, but if she had one prejudice in life, it was her dislike for those she termed 'The Filthy Rich'—those wealthy without having worked for it and contemptible of all others who had. The wealthy without compunction to harm others. The wealthy without wisdom or without compassion or the simplest basic understanding of others less fortunate.

She felt a sense of anger rising in her directed at Grandma Sampson in particular, but there was plenty left over for Little Joey. She'd like nothing more than to prove this fire was intentionally set by the Sampson family owners.

As Sybil had called for Luther and Lisa to bag, tag, and transport the body with an end destination being Dr. Avery's slab without any stops along the way, Jude went in search of the fire marshal in charge. After asking one muscled up fireman after another, she found the man in charge, a former football defensive lineman, she imagined, named Phil Hart.

"I have a suspicion this was no accident, chief," she told him.

"You can tell that from just looking, can you?"

"Just a hunch given all the history of this place—especially recent history." She used her head to indicate the Bentley at the periphery of the safe zone. As she did so, Joseph pulled the car around in a fast three-point turn and peeled away.

"Damn nice vehicle," said the fire chief. "You can be sure, doc, our best fire investigators are on it. Too soon for any answers yet, but they're on it."

"As soon as you do have answers, I'd like—"

"Lady...doctor, your boss has been on my ass for hours. We're doing all we can as fast as we can, so if you please, I'm rather busy right now."

"Of course, of course. I'm sorry. Just a horrible series of events, such brutal killings, and we know it's connected to this place which should have been condemned years and years ago."

With that, Jude rushed to catch a ride with none other than the charred corpse. With Luther and Lisa in the cab, she'd have to buckle in with the corpse, knowing the odor was going to be extremely bad in a confined space.

She'd resigned herself to it, however, about to climb in behind the corpse when Ralph once again came to her rescue, suggesting she ride with him in his Volkswagen coupe. She looked at the huge medical assistant and the car he pointed out and asked, "Is there room in there for anyone but you, Ralph?"

He laughed, his grin infectious. She laughed, too, leapt down from the back of the death van, and joined Ralph. "You're a lifesaver, Ralph. Thanks."

"Not at all. Can't leave you with Ignoble."

"Is that what they call him?"

"That's what I call him."

"So, do you think we have our man, Kiley?"

"On the surface, same build, same appearance, but like you said, it'll take teeth to be damn sure."

Without any distinguishing marks such as the crushed foot of Corporal Dewalt, birthmarks, or any known scars, and little to no help from Mitch, who couldn't make bail, all that Jude had to work with were the fire victim's teeth. The victim proved to be the right height and weight of Kiley, and he'd had ID on him that indeed proclaimed him to be Keith Kiley. When the packet of materials taken off the body and from around the body was opened, there it was—Kiley's wallet. Sybil had said nothing about the man's ID being on him. She'd simply stashed it in the 'belongings' box. "Keith, he always wore a trinket round his neck—a shark's tooth," the old man named Harry Daniels had said. She had the transcript of Daniels's statement to Stephens in hand now. "Claims to have caught that shark deep sea fishing, but none of the men believed him."

While the bagged corpse was being placed into the ET van, Jude had halted Noble and Coombs to examine a charred shark's tooth around the dead man's neck tucked under the dead man's tee-shirt, which was burned into his flesh. She now wondered why the people Kiley supervised didn't believe him about how he'd gotten the shark's tooth. She'd removed the gold chain and tooth that Sybil had either overlooked at the scene or had left as a 'prize' for Jude to discover. Putting the trinket aside for now, Jude searched the transcript for an answer.

Detective Stephens had asked the same question, "Why didn't people believe him about the shark's tooth?"

"You go to Florida or anywhere on the eastern seaboard, you can buy a shark's tooth for a saw buck. Besides, the man was always boasting about *something*. Some said he was talking big about sleeping with Maria, the secretary...that he boasted 'bout that. But she never showed no sign of it that I could see."

Maria more and more sounds like someone I'd like to interview, Jude thought. She got on her phone and called Wayne to say, "Hope your day's going better'n mine."

"It's going kind of slow right now. I'm getting Old Man Daniels situated at the homeless shelter."

"I suppose the Sampsons will do right by him and all their employees, huh?" She gave out a derisive laugh.

"I'm kinda in the midst of filling out paperwork, Jude."

"Well, I called to ask, if...I mean, I suppose all the employee files went up in smoke too, right?"

Stephens shot back, saying, "No, actually, they were in files older than the damn building, pretty solid file cabinets that withstood the flames. Records are intact."

"Then I assume you have Kiley's information pulled?"

"In our murder book now, yes."

"Good, that can corroborate a lot, I'm sure. But there's another employee who might be helpful."

"Who's that?"

"Can you locate this Maria Rodriguez and get her in for questioning?"

"For you, Dr. Avery, sure."

"And Kiley's dental records?"

"They're not going to be in those file cabinets, doc," he joked.

"Well, no, didn't think so. But we need his dental X-rays like yesterday."

"We still have his place sealed," said Stephens. "We took a stack of his bills the other day. Likely a dental bill in there."

"Good. And as quickly as you can, get that information to us," she replied. "I'm back at my lab with everything Dr. Shanley bagged."

"All by your lonesome?"

"Except for Ralph and Lionel, yes."

"What happened to Dr. Shanley?"

"After processing the crime scene, she was exhausted, so I sent her home," Jude lied and pictured the last time she'd seen Sybil. Once out of her filthy lab coat, she'd said, "I'm going home for the day. It's all yours, Jude."

"You take care, Sybil," Jude had told her colleague. "Get some rest, and again, sorry I was so...hard to find."

Sybil had smiled at this and said, "Hey, if it was up to Dean, neither of us would have a life."

"I'm learning that." She thought of what Grant had said to her regarding his decision to hire her over others just as qualified, the fact she was single and 'unencumbered.' Whether there was some sort of code against her becoming involved with a detective in the department or not, she imagined Grant would make life hell for her if he knew of the newly kindled relationship that'd caught fire between Wayne and her.

"One more thing," she said, "I do think it best to keep our feelings for one another on the QT."

"I couldn't agree with you more, darlin.'"

"We do seem to find agreements everywhere, don't we?"

"How about we agree to see one another tonight."

"Agreed."

On her slab in the ME's laboratory, the supposed body of one Keith Kiley looked more like a used fire log than a human being, and other than the shark's tooth and the wallet, the corpse was giving up nothing. Jude fared no better in finding distinguishing marks than if she were dealing with a pure-as-driven-snow, lily-white corpse. Nothing identifying. Ralph and Lionel had done the *scut* work of cleaning the body as best as science knew how under such conditions, but still all that Jude could find in the way of distinguishing marks were a handful of scorched skin tags, old scars, even a missing toe or rather a deformed toe on the dead man's left foot.

While still awaiting the dental charts, she had decided to open the corpse up to seek answers from within as the without was so thoroughly tattered. Have a look inside where the fire had not had so much reach. With the Y-section cut made and the encrusted skin pulled back, breaking off in places, she found a series of shriveled organs awaiting her examination. The organs told a less than stellar story, detailing the life of a heavy smoker, according to the lungs. Tell-tale signs long before the man inhaled the fire's smoke proved this as the lungs were shredded with cavities, so many that when she lifted the lungs from their resting place, they began to pull apart like pizza dough. The odor alone was like being in a Friendly Smoker shop. The other organs told a similar tale. Despite the fire's having sucked out most of the moisture and juices of the internal organs, there remained unmistakable evidence of years upon years of heavy determined drinking.

Mitch, according to Detective Marks, failed to corroborate such findings in Kiley, lying about small matters, such as claiming that Keith Kiley didn't smoke and that he only occasionally drank. "When he was celebrating, which was not often," Marks had quoted Mitch. "Mitch said repeatedly that Kiley 'was a pothead but that's all.'"

Still, the early assumption that they had Kiley's corpse here was, for Jude Avery, feeling odd from the get-go. Other than the general size and weight of the body, measurements, and the skin pigmentation where the fire hadn't reached along a swath of the rear end, the corpse in Jude's opinion did not have the feel of a young man but an older man, at least in his forties, perhaps in his fifties. The internal organs alone proved this fact, that it could not be Keith Kelly's remains. On the surface, yes; below the surface, not a chance.

She had in the meantime heard that celebratory congratulations had been going around the police department and the ME crews that they had 'got the bastard.' Even Dr. Grant, who should know better, had joined in this premature chorus of congratulations, planning a news conference for the six o'clock news hour.

Being the new hire, she wasn't anxious to prove otherwise with the condition of the dead man's heart, lungs, and liver. Grant and Sybil surely would agree once she reported on her findings, but she wasn't jubilant like the others. Not likely they'd want to accept her findings. So she'd taken a late-late lunch break, getting out for air and sustenance at a nearby diner used by a mix of firemen, cops, and medical personnel. From there, she again called Wayne, asking after those dental records.

"I need them now more than ever."

"You sound harried. What's up?"

"The dead man pulled from the fire isn't Kiley."

"Oh, shit; don't tell me. Are you sure of that?"

"As sure as I am digesting a Reuben sandwich right now at *Gad-flies*."

"Shit, damn. I'd hoped it was over. Now you're telling me that SOB's still out there somewhere laughing at us."

"Not sure how much laughing he's doing, but he's out there, yes. I'd stake my reputation on it."

"Why haven't you told anyone? Other than me, I mean."

"No one's in a mood to hear the truth right now, but dental records can't be argued with."

"We've run down his dentist. Old guy's retired. Sent his records to another dentist, so it's taking time, but we're homing in on them."

"Before Dr. Grant makes a fool of himself, get those records to me. I'll try to get him to trust my judgment based on my findings so far."

"Good luck with it. Get there as soon as we can with the goods."

After hanging up, Jude walked back to the ME's office and returned to the lab where she awaited the dental records which would be conclusive and add to her compilation of proof that the dead man was *not* KKboy. That Kiley had found a stand-in for himself, had set up a dupe to be him long enough for Kiley to make his run for freedom. She feared waiting a moment later. She phoned Grant and asked him to come down to her lab to have a look at her findings, giving away no details despite his insistence that she tell him what was on her mind.

"Please, sir, just trust me. You hired me for my expertise."

"All right, okay, be right down in five. Ten."

She hung up wondering how far along he'd gotten in his written speech for the news hounds. When Grant arrived, he listened to her suspicions that they hadn't Kiley's corpse at all but that of a plant. He also examined the body, taking in the evidence of her position. It was staring Dean in the face. He knew his speech was only fit now for the trash can. He cursed to the sky and stormed out, leaving her to herself and unsure of her next step when she got a call from Marks.

"Maria Rodriguez is being brought in for an interview." Marks sounded extremely bored by the chore put on him.

"Don't let her get away before I can speak to her, please."

"I'll do what I can, doc."

Jude rushed back to HQ and she soon sat across from Maria. After introducing herself to the young woman, Jude said, "I wanted to get your take on Mr. Keith Kiley, your former boss."

"I done talked to the detectives. I want outta here."

Jude believed in the notion of 'A Jury of Her Peers' having seen the Susan Glasspell play first hand and having read the short story. So often women had a unique perspective, understanding clues missed by men, even men trained as detectives.

What she got from Maria was not a great deal of help, however, Maria had Kiley's 'number' down pat. "He is always bragging."

"How so, Maria?"

"I think he always thinks he is a big shot, a big man, and he thinks others ought to believe the same way."

This recalled to mind old Harry Daniels's take on Kiley. "Go on."

Maria sniffled. "Sorry, catching a cold." She wiped her nose with balled up tissues. "He was always talking 'bout special talents he had but I never wanted to see." She laughed at this. "But it was not just sexual stuff he wanted."

"What do you mean?" pressed Jude.

Maria shrugged. "He talked 'bout secrets he could not share with nobody, and how that was so sad for him 'cause 'bout how he wanted to share his true self."

"That's how he said it. Share himself?"

"With someone who loved him, you know, who wouldn't hold his worst secrets against him, he said."

"Did he ever share any of those secrets with you?" Jude asked.

Maria shook her head. "Not really. He'd get right to the edge, and he'd say he was far more than what I saw at that desk he sat behind. That kinda stuff."

"So he never said anything about attacking a soldier?"

"No, nothing like that. He would say he took care of somebody who pissed him off, like he beat them up. Stuff men say to brag."

"You were wise to get clear of him, Maria."

"I can't believe he done what they say he done."

"We believe he's killed repeatedly."

"Aye dios mio! Nuns at the church? You don't think he might come after me, do you?"

Maria obviously hadn't heard a word about the fire and the dead man in the rubble.

"Has he contacted you at all since you left Sampson?"

"No...no. I think he's afraid of Ricky."

"Ricky?"

"My boyfriend, fiancé."

"*Ahhh*, well congratulations."

"Should I tell Ricky about what happen' with Mr. Kiley? I was afraid."

"Do what your gut tells you."

"Okay. I don't tell him or nobody, not now."

"Thanks for coming in and sharing what you know of Kiley."

"Is he, Mr. Kiley, is he really a murderer?"

"We believe so, yes."

"I know you say so, but knowing someone, working in the same place all that time...it's hard to believe."

"Maria, if he tries in any way to contact you, call me immediately." Jude handed the young woman her card.

"I will. I don't want to be anywhere near that man ever again. Maybe I should tell Ricky what's going on."

"If you do, I am sure your boyfriend will understand."

"I lied to him why I quit that job."

Jude nodded, understanding. "Between us, I suspect Kiley is too busy on the run right now to come after you or Ricky."

"Good. I pray to God you're right."

"I can have a police car get you home."

She gasped at the notion. "Oh, no! That would not be good. Not in my neighborhood."

Jude nodded. "Understood. Look, do you have protection? A gun?"

"I do, yes. So you are worried he could come after me?"

"No, no. Just be cautious and keep a weapon close until we apprehend the bastard."

"You'll let me know then?"

"We will, yes." Jude watched the young woman, looking a bit dazed, walk off, confused as to how to get out of the building.

Marks stood at Jude's side now and said, "You think we ought to have a unit keep her under surveillance? Just in case?" He then indicated the viewing room and that he'd listened in on the conversation.

"Not sure, but to be on the safe side..."

"I'll see to it." Marks rushed off to arrange this.

Jude found herself alone again in a crowd. She turned and left for the safe confines of her lab.

Keith Kiley had fled the level factory after having hidden in a little known crawl space below the boards where decades of dust and wood mites had found refuge. It was an area for plumbers to get at the pipes. He'd holed up there for hours while a plan began to hatch in his fevered brain. Most of the day, as police and forensic people had picked about his office and the factory, he had tried to work out how they could have zeroed in on him so suddenly, swooping in as they had. His suspicion that they were onto him had their origins in Mitch's shaky voice of the night before, asking him to meet him at the Up & Down. He knew then that something bad was afoot for him.

He vacated his home in a hurry, and thank goodness because as he watched from another building foyer down the street and across, he saw the cops descend on his place. He'd rushed out so quickly he had no thought other than to flee. He realized how foolish he'd been not to dispose of the baseball bat and the level, and to not have taken his laptop with him. But he had panicked. Too late now to worry about such mistakes. Instead, he concentrated on a way out of the city, a way to get to LA, locate the Elders and beg them for assistance in disappearing for good.

His plan evolved, changed, morphed until he believed it foolproof, and that it would at least afford him a period of time when no one would be looking for him. All he needed was a corpse, a charred and unrecognizable corpse.

There was a homeless man, a guy who was always looking for a handout, named Toohey or Stewey, he could not recall, but he regularly came by the factory because some of the softhearted workmen would give the man enough to buy a burger and drink at the McDonald's half a block away. The man came around like clockwork at 1:45 most every day.

But first, Kiley had to be sure that old Daniels, who acted as a night watchman, living at the back of the factory had a reason to not be on hand when Kiley set the place ablaze. He liked Daniels. Had no reason to harm him in the bargain. He even admired the old man whose work ethic was strong despite having lost his apartment and was working day and night to get himself right with the world. But this homeless guy was just a bum. Not even homeless for good reason. He was an addict, pure and simple.

The world would not miss him for a moment.

Kiley crawled up out of the pipe chase, dusted what he could see off of his clothing, and, with debris hanging from him, he found old man Daniels in his back room. The factory had been on lock down, and it was shut down silent. A man's voice echoed within. It was Daniels talking to himself. Kiley didn't want to startle the old guy, so he called out his name and added, "It's me, Keith."

Daniels stuck his head through the back door on his quaint little room. "Mr. Kiley, I knew you'd show up! They got some fool notion that you're a killer. I told them that was nuts. You cleared it up, didn't you?"

"I did, Mr. Dan, I did."

"Thank gawd for that. I been worrying my head off, sir, and with the factory condemned, and us all losing our jobs just when—"

"I want to give you a bonus, Mr. D, for all your years of service. It ain't much but take this hundred and go buy yourself a steak and get a room at the Ajax for the night."

"That's mighty kind of you, sir."

"Not at all. I hope too those damn Sampsons'll provide something for all the men."

"Then we won't be ever reopening, sir?"

"Afraid not, old friend. Afraid not."

After escorting Daniels out the rear, he awaited the soon-to-be dead man. He knew where Daniels kept his stash of booze, and he also knew where a couple of cans of kerosene used for degreasing and cleaning the machinery awaited his use.

Now it was only a matter of time and patience. And once he got shed of the factory and the cops were hauling off his body to the morgue, he'd make his way to LA from Chicago using the dead man's wallet and ID. He believed his plan to be one born of genius. He believed it would work like a charm. A ticket on a Greyhound or a plane to LA had his new name on it.

10

D r. Grant pushed through the flapping, double-doors to Jude's operating theater with good news waving overhead, shouting, "The dog's going to be our chief witness!"

"Great news for Pongo!" Jude shouted back.

In typical style, Grant stomped up to Jude, demanding to know if she'd confirmed that the burned body wasn't, in fact, Keith Kiley. Jude held up both hands in the universal gesture of forfeit and acceptance only to calm him down. "Yes. Well...I received the dental records a few minutes ago. Ralph is developing the films on our well-done John Doe."

"I'm sorry to be abrupt with you, Jude. You've been doing a great job here and you're earning everyone's respect," he was saying as he focused on the folder of dental X-rays that she'd handed to him.

You could have fooled me, she thought but kept it to herself. Instead, she patiently waited for Ralph, who returned after seconds that felt like hours. Thanking the tech, she took the films and slid them onto a viewing box, flipping on the sputtering light. Dean stepped close and snapped the older X-rays onto an adjacent panel.

"Am I seeing what I think I am?" he asked as his eyes came away from the films and lighted on her.

"That's from our John Doe. They don't match. Our corpse is absolutely not Keith Kiley."

"Damn, damn, damn."

"I realize it is an un...a disquieting truth, but sir, it is irrefutable."

"Disquieting, Dr. Avery? You have a gift for understatement. This is not going to sit well with those I have to answer to."

"I tried to tell everyone to await the autopsy, but everyone so wanted it to be Kiley."

"Me included, and I should've known better."

"If you gave assurances to the mayor's office, I'm sure that—"

"You don't have a clue, doctor, how badly those jerks in the mayor's office would like to see me disgraced."

"Is it really that contentious, sir?"

"Welcome to the big time, Dr. Avery. It's Chicago, and Chicago means politics—dirty politics."

"In university, they taught us that the ME's office was above politics and could not be influenced."

"In a perfect world, in an academic world that might be true, but this is the real world. If the mayor could find a wedge, any excuse to throw me under the bus, well...I've been standing on this curb since he took office."

"What keeps you in the game if it's that...corrupt here?"

"I suppose there's enough pride in me and stubbornheadedness that I actually like the fight, like having enemies. Without them, where and how would I vent my spleen? Rant and rave?"

She smiled at this. "I go out to Lake Michigan, stand on the levee rocks and scream at the horizon."

"I'll have to try that before I inform the mayor and his henchmen that we don't have Kiley's body after all. *Damnitalltohell.*"

"Would you like for me or for Sybil to act as a go-between and make that call?"

"No, no, no! That would make it even worse."

She scrunched up her features, curious. "How would that make it worse, sir?"

"Well...it'd look like I was trying to dodge responsibility and chuck it in a lateral pass while I sat on the bench."

Football metaphors, she thought. What would men do without them? "That's your decision, sir, but perhaps a woman's touch would ease the message. Dr. Shanley is, I have observed, extremely diplomatic."

"And you're even more diplomatic than Sybil."

"I don't know about that."

"Well the fact that we have a John Doe instead of Kiley on your slab there—" Grant paused, pointed at the charred, now open remains on her stained stainless steel slab and continued, adding, "Well it changes the equation completely. Do we have any idea who the victim is and how he came to be inside that factory when the fire broke out?"

"I've theorized that, given his general measurements, that Kiley set him up in an attempt to buy himself time to escape. If the cops dropped their APB on him—as they did by the way—he'd have a far easier time getting out of the city to make his escape."

"How can you prove that theory?"

"Awaiting drug tests now. I believe we'll find some form of barbiturates. From the look of the organs, the man was a habitual user of alcohol, which often translates into addiction for other drugs. Kiley may well have enticed the man with drugs, got him *stoned*, and then set the place on fire."

"You sound pretty convinced." Grant appeared to be rolling this about in his head, likely wondering how it would play out in a rewritten statement to the press and a phone call to the mayor's office.

"I thought the fire might have been set by a professional arsonist hired by the owners, sir."

"You did? And now?"

"Fire marshal called and said that the fire was arson but hardly the work of a professional. Quite messy use of kerosene and a kicked over cook stove. I don't see the Sampsons taking such steps personally, and as it was not a purchased arson, I am left to believe it was Kiley, who reportedly paid the night man to vacate for the evening."

"Does add up to a pretty neat theory. We'll go with it. And hey, Jude, thanks for straightening me out. That'll go a long way to whitewash any previous problems you've had fitting in here."

"Problems fitting in?"

"The business with Noble and Coombs. I'll see to it that goes away."

"What do you mean?" she asked as he started off.

"They came to me with complaints, the two of them. Said you acted quite unprofessionally toward them."

"Really? Said that did they?"

"I'm sure it will go no further."

"I should have struck first," she countered.

"I suspect you should have, yes, from what I could gather from others."

"Others? There were no others involved. Lisa Coombs is like Noble's slave, and no one's lifted a finger to help her."

"That's your problem, Dr. Avery."

"Meaning?"

"You can't fix all the problems of everyone around you. Best get used to that. And as for Noble and Coombs, they need to work out their own difficulties."

"Then you know about their, ahhh, difficulties? Why do you put up with Noble?"

"We're short-handed as is, and as repugnant as I find him, he does his job."

"I don't think doing one's job is enough when it comes to a misogynist."

"That word's been waved around like a mallet since the primaries."

"If it fits!"

Grant quickly escaped without another word. He was well aware that Noble and Dr. Avery were like oil and water. She felt somewhat vindicated at having vented her feelings about the man.

Then she got an idea of how to get even with Mr. Noble.

After Stephens and Marks had arrived with the actual dental records, having taken steps to get them via proper channels, they had left temporarily to find and speak with Lionel. Now they returned to find Jude staring at the X-rays of teeth—Keith Kiley's and the dead man's. She was relieved that she no longer had to rely on what was under the dead man's charred skin for answers that could be refuted. Young men smoked gobs and drank tanks of alcohol, causing many to be carrying around old man organs, but dental patterns were irrefutable.

"I suspect if you go through the records of the workmen at Sampson's, you'll find a match to the dead man," she told the detectives.

"With the fire all over the news, it shouldn't be hard to find someone looking for a missing loved one. Putting two and two together."

"We know how to do our jobs, Dr. Avery," Stephens shot back, and she knew his curtness was for his partner's benefit, and for Ralph, who'd helped out with the X-rays.

"I was only trying to be helpful, detective."

"Why is it then every time you say the word *detective*, it sounds like an insult?" Stephens was laying it on thick.

"Maybe if you two had been better at detecting, *dee-tec-tive*, this poor schlep here could tell us something about Kiley."

"We brought in Maria Rodriguez," Marks said to Stephens, "and Dr. Avery here did a good job questioning her, but the girl Friday, she pretty much said she knows nothing."

"I'm sorry Detective Marks, but I got quite a lot out of that interview about how Kiley thinks."

"Come on. I watched the whole of it. The girl had nothing to offer."

"Just like a man," said Jude. "Look, it's been a tough day, detectives. I'm sorry if I sound abrupt."

"Abrupt? You pretty well put this guy's death on us." Stephens rushed out ahead of Marks.

Damn but he's good at this subterfuge, Jude thought. And if Wayne's this good a performer...how careful should I be with my heart?

◆ ◆ ◆

Jude had Ralph place the new John Doe into a compartment in the freezer wall with a hope he'd soon be identified by the detectives, given her profile of the man based on the age of his organs and the habits he kept according to those organs, along with the deformed toe he'd been born with. Funny what information lies waiting below a hat, inside a shoe, under a T-shirt, she thought as she entered the interrogation room. This time, it was the same room where she had met the Dewalt family.

When she entered the viewing room and had her second look at Maria Rodriguez, Jude thought she looked like many other young women in Chicago, wearing the latest trendy young-teen clothes off the rack at Target. But a bit too much makeup on her dark-eyed, dark-haired Spanish features contrasted with those youthful trendy tight jeans. Jude did not know precisely why, but she felt judgmental toward the young woman, not quite yet in her twenties, trying to look fourteen.

"Couldn't get much out of her," Stephens said to Jude. "She's terrified. Kiley called her on her cell phone and wanted her to leave the city with him."

"Maybe she'll open up to me again like she did before."

"That's why Marks insisted I call you in on this. Said you had good vibes with her."

"I'll do what I can. No promises, but..."

Jude entered the interrogation room.

Maria was immediately defensive. "I told those jerk cops like I told you before—I don't know nothing about Mr. Kiley's being a killer. A jerk, yeah, and I quit because he was all the time hitting on me, but I decided that I really, truly don't want my boyfriend to know on account of if he knew, he'd be hunting down Mr. Kiley worse than *youz guyz* are doing, and I don't want my man going back to jail never. I mean no more!"

That was quite a mouthful, Jude thought. "We need to know where Kiley called from, Maria. It's why they confiscated your phone."

"I can't help you cops. You know what people in my neighborhood do to snitches?"

"First, I am not a police woman, so right now you are not talking to a cop, Maria."

Maria's instinct antennae was a-twiddle at this. "Then who...what are you?"

"Forensics expert, a medical examiner."

"The card you gave me said police."

"No...you assumed so maybe? Did you read the card."

Maria frowned and snatched out the card still in her jeans. Staring at the card, she then made a face that clearly showed that this impressed her. "Wow...like on TV, ID channel, Criminal Minds, CSI right?" She shrugged it off, adding, "Whole time we were talkin' last time, I just thought you was a cop."

"Right, well given the surroundings," said Jude, eyes going about the sparsely furnished, institutional gray room.

"That's kinda cool, what you do," Maria began, relaxing somewhat. "When I was a little kid, I had a goofy dream that I wanted to be like that, a scientist, you know, but I never had no chance, not really."

"Maybe you should look into going back to school someday."

Maria's laugh sounded a hollow note. "Some day, sure."

"Maria, I talked with a Mr. Daniels at the Sampson factory the other day, and he—"

"Mr. Dan? He was always nice to me."

"And he told me that Mr. Kiley sort of 'armed himself' with a faulty but large level just after you stormed out of his office and quit. Said Mr. Kiley informed everyone that you had voluntarily quit."

"Said that did he?"

"Reportedly, yes. Said the other workmen were all sorry to see you go, too."

"Yeah? Well, I got 'long with everybody there. I did my job, too, and I did it good."

"But Kiley fired you anyway?"

"Hold on! I quit. I wasn't fired; I quit 'cause like I said before, he hit on me too much."

"Did he say anything to you that might be called threatening?"

She fell silent at this. "How'd you know that?"

Jude leaned in closer over the interrogation table. "Then he did threaten you? Can you recall his exact words?"

"*Ahhh*...no, I can't but he was like bragging that he had done stuff. I told you all that."

"Stuff?"

"Things."

"Things? What sort of *things*?"

"What're you deaf?" Maria shouted, then her face fell. "I'm sorry. Look, he never got 'round to saying exactly, but he was like bragging that he could surprise me with what he had done or what's that word... oh yeah, *accomplished*. I thought he was like talking about maybe high school. Bragged about being on the football team, stuff like that."

"High school?"

"Trophies, you know—like maybe he was on the track team or something like that. He was building up to being nasty with me again."

"But given what we know about Mr. Kiley now, Maria, does that change your conclusions about what he was talking about while in this *braggadocious* mood?"

"Bragga...braggadocious, ha! Hold on, you think he was talking about killing those nuns to impress me?"

"No, no. He hadn't yet, but by then he had killed two veterans, we suspect."

She deflated like a balloon. "My god, my god...he was, he was talkin' 'bout that all the...the whole time, and I—I didn't know. Just thought it was, you know, locker room big shot talk, but he never ever said he'd killed nobody. Did say he wasn't afraid of my boyfriend who's like three times his size. Oh...aye dios mio."

"Maria, would you be interested if I could put you together with a hypnotist to bring back your exact memories of that confrontation with Keith Kiley?"

She was already shaking her head before she said an emphatic, "*Nooo*! Don't want no kind of hoo-doo voodoo done on my head, lady, *ahhh*, Dr. Avery."

"Other than saliva from a dog, Maria, we don't have a lot of strong evidence to put Kiley away if and when he's caught, so your memories of that day, hours before the nuns were murdered could—"

"Why do these things happen to me?" Maria asked, not expecting an answer. "Why me, Lord? Oh my god. Then Mr. Kiley's still out there somewhere roaming free, and he knows I talked to you guyz..." Maria's gaze had turned to a soft reflection of her surroundings.

"Will you help us, Maria?" Jude pressed the girl.

"Hypnosis...aye dios mio. Can I call my mama? I have to talk to mama. Can I get my phone back?"

"Use mine," said Jude, handing her a phone.

"That won't work. I got mama on speed dial. I got no idea what her number is."

Stephens entered the room with Maria's Samsung phone.

"We've got what we wanted from it." Stephens had obviously been watching the interrogation from just outside.

Maria grasped her phone as if her life depended on it and pressed for her mother. "Let's give her some privacy," suggested Jude, stepping out with Stephens.

From outside, they watched Maria make the call. After a heart to heart with her mother, Maria called out for then to return.

Maria said, "Mama says I should do what you want, Dr. Avery."

"Hypnosis has no lasting effect, Maria, and could help us like I said, when and if we catch him and put him on trial for multiple murder."

"You think it would help, really? I got a lousy memory for stuff."

"It could help, yes."

Maria took another deep breath as a squeaky, final *yes* escaped with her exhalation.

Jude knew it was a long shot, but she thought it worth pursuing. When she exited the interrogation room, she asked Stephens if the departmental shrink who'd hypnotized Father Thomas might not be of help with Maria's memory.

"Dr. Davenport, yes. She's pretty good."

"Think you can get her on short notice?"

"I'll give her a call." Stephens got on his cell phone while Marks said, "This line of questioning is getting us nowhere. The girl told you she didn't hear a thing admissible in a court of law, and even if Kiley did let something slip, it'd be tossed out as hearsay."

"All the same, I think it's worth pursuing. Besides, right now we need every nail we can muster to put in the bastard's coffin."

Stephens nodded, turned and stepped away, going for a corner to talk to the shrink.

"Dr. Avery, this here is our territory—interrogations," Marks said. "And we don't normally see any of Grant's people doing our job, but like I told Wayne, you got some history with this girl."

"Well, thanks, detective, and please tell Detective Stephens thanks for understanding."

"He accused me of bending over backwards for you."

"He feels that way, does he?"

"Says you don't mind stepping on toes."

"I certainly don't mean to cause any trouble, detective."

"Oh, hell. Wayne's a hard ass at times."

Jude smiled inwardly at this. "I only want what we all want here."

"Like I said, Wayne'll be fine once he gets his head out of his ass," Marks said with a grin. "But frankly, I think that young woman in there's a dead end." Marks abruptly left her standing alone. She mentally scored a positive check mark next to Marks's name. He seemed to have a core of sensitivity under that outer crust, and he seemed to have his partner's best interest at heart, as well as hers, for some reason she could not fathom.

Had Wayne confided in him about their relations of the night before and this morning? Or was Marks a better detective than he looked to be? Or was she reading too much into his words?

She turned and glanced at the fidgeting young woman in the interrogation room and studied her through the one-way glass. Maybe Marks was right, that there was nothing inside that dark-haired skull of use to this case, but there was only one way to get beyond the assumptions.

At least that's what her scientific *intuition* kept screaming inside her head.

Dr. Grant went ahead with the scheduled news conference, making it clear from the beginning of his remarks that Keith Kiley was not in custody and was not the victim of the fire at the Sampson Level factory. He did this with the help of visuals—a life-size photo of Kiley, several closeups of the killer's face, and a splice of the most recent video tape they had showing Kiley with Goodwin at the diner. He dared not use the kill tapes. They were not for public consumption.

"Mr. Goodwin is cooperating with police and has been charged as an accomplice in the deaths of five people. The murder weapons used in these heinous crimes have been confiscated and are being tested as we speak. This case is coming together at a fast pace, and you can be certain that Mr. Kiley will soon be apprehended. He has no rat hole to hide in that the CPD cannot find him."

Jude and Sybil watched this unfold on the TV screen in Shanley's office. "Dean's in rare form," Sybil said. "Not easy making hay with what little we have."

"Seems in his element," ventured Jude, nursing a cup of coffee.

"Evening news! Grant lives for it; might call him a media whore. He loves being the center of attention and why not? After all, he's on the verge—again—of solving the case. Chicago press dubs him the Sherlock of Chicago." Sybil laughed lightly. "You may's well get used to it, Jude."

"His gamble to take full credit for the *capture* of Keith Kiley and his accomplice?"

"You're catching on fast, sister girl."

"We still know next to nothing of the motive, and the cameraman, Goodwin's holding back what he knows about it."

"Where're you getting your updates? From that gorgeous Detective Stephens?"

Jude fought back a blush. "You might say we've got a professional respect for one another and a pact."

"A pact, really? To share information? Or is there more being shared than that?"

"I admit I like Wayne."

"Wayne is it?"

"We're on first names, yes. You can get more with honey than vinegar."

"And just how much honey are you using, sweetheart?" Sybil giggled outright.

"Don't read into it anymore than there is."

"I wouldn't dare."

"You already have!"

"Hey, the flirtation for information thing, I've counted on it more than a few times myself."

"You read me like a book, girlfriend!"

"You know, I haven't had a conversation like this since I left the college dorm."

"Come to think of it, neither have I."

"Honestly, what do you think of Stephens? He's a hunk, isn't he?"

"Marks is more my type," she lied in an effort to throw Sybil off.

Sybil burst into laughter at this. "Marks? Marks, really? Come on. Joking right?"

"Well, I admit, he's not the hunk that Stephens is, but he's thorough and mannerly, and besides, I like the quiet, strong type."

"He's a bunion head."

"You mean onion head?"

"No, annoying. Like a bunion."

"He's been nothing of the sort to me." Jude continued the charade.

"On a more serious and somber note," began Sybil. "I've been comparing a number of separate but seemingly similar if not connected murders like ours in and around Los Angeles."

"Really? California's a long way from here."

"Not as far as the internet flies. Lionel's had time to go through a lot of what's on Kiley's and Goodwin's computers. There seems a definite connection among their two devices and someone in LA."

"That's intriguing. Could be where he's running to, perhaps?"

"It's a website devoted to snuff films like the ones Kiley and Goodwin were making, Jude."

"That is more than intriguing. Who's behind it?"

"Lionel's stumped at this point. He's got the IP address but the server isn't interested in serving us, and it'd take a mountain of time to move a Chicago judge to order it done or jail time for the CEO of the server."

"What do we do then?"

"We get on a plane, go to LA."

"We? You mean you and Grant?"

"No, I mean you and me."

"*Ahhh...uhhhh....*I don't know about that, Sybil. I'd have to find a sitter for Boomer."

"Boomer? You have a dog?"

"Parakeet. Boomer's a bird."

Sybil shook her head and gave Jude a disapproving look. "This is our chance to beat Dean at his own game."

"Is that how you see this? A game?"

"Come on, Jude. Aren't you sick and tired of doing all the work while the men take all the credit?"

"No...I mean, yes, but not like this. Going behind Dean's back."

"Did I say we'd do it behind Dean's back?"

"Well no, but—however else?"

"Trust me, I know how to get Dean to say yes to a request, even make it appear to be his idea. Once that's done, are you with me? A trip to LA?"

"If...I suppose if you can get it green-lighted by Dean, sure."

"That's the spirit."

Sybil then spread out the contents of a file before Jude. A series of grisly murders in LA that did have the level of twisted hatred and anger seen in the Kiley murders of vets and nuns. "About time we entered into our own pact—the pact of the sisterhood of the ME's office," Shanley said as Jude studied the series of bizarre murders in LA that might or might not be connected to those here in Chicago.

"All these murders have one thing in common," Jude said

"I know, but I wanted you to tell me."

"An element of the spectacle."

"That's right—entertainment."

"Sick entertainment."

"Any question now as to what motivated Goodwin and Kiley?"

"If this is their reasoning," Jude said, "how damn sick is that?"

"Hey, even Hitler rationalized the killing of millions of human beings."

"Yeah, I get it."

"We're going to need a lot more coffee. Lionel's continuing to work on the hard drive. Meantime, what do you say we take all this to dinner and grab a bite."

Jude thought of her promise to Stephens.

"Unless you have other plans, I mean," said Sybil, reading her hesitation.

"I can make arrangements. Where would you care to meet?"

"How about Berghoff's? I feel like steak."

"You do know our expense account doesn't support Berghoff's."

"This is on me," assured Sybil.

"Fine. In an hour. Meet you there."

◆　◆　◆

The APB and the BOLO on Keith Kiley had been fully reinstated based on the findings or lack of findings, actually, of Assistant Medical Examiner for Chicago, Dr. Judith Avery. Ironically, her picture was duplicated and republished across the city and beyond with the new story of what the CPD knew to be true in the case of the murdered nuns.

The heinous killing of the nuns had eclipsed the brutal murders of the two vets, including Dewalt's ugly demise. The story given out by Grant had taken an unexpected turn with Jude's photo. The newspapers and TV appeared to be competing over who could learn more about Jude, and few to no words were being devoted to Dean.

Sybil had a copy of the evening Tribune at her table at Berghoff's when Jude arrived. She had it folded on the story about Jude. "I worry about you, Jude."

As Jude sat across from Sybil, she asked, "Whatever are you talking about?"

"This!" she jabbed at the story in the *Trib.*

"What is it?" Jude snatched the paper from Sybil and stared at her photo first. "Where...how'd they get this years-old photo of me?"

"That's not the half of it, sweetheart. You're outshining Grant!"

"Oh no."

"Oh yes."

"This can't be good for my career."

"I tried to tell you to keep a low profile."

"I did nothing to provoke this."

"That's not going to save you from Dean's wrath."

"But I didn't invite this on myself."

"Regardless, it's on you, sister-girl."

Jude studied the byline. A Rachel DuChampe. "Do you know this reporter?"

"I...well, yes, I do."

'Is she someone you can talk to? Ask her to back off?"

"I have a confession to make, Jude."

"Oh this doesn't sound good."

The waiter interrupted to take their order. Sybil appeared to be getting her story together at the same time. Jude asked the waiter to come back in five minutes. The waiter did an about face and vacated the table.

"Don't tell me you had something to do with this. That you're sabotaging me behind my back."

"No, no! Nothing like that. Rachel...well, she's my girlfriend, my BFF, and she hears things."

"Hears things as in what kind of things?"

"She swore to me she wouldn't use our pillow talk."

"Hold on, this Tribune reporter is your lover?"

"Don't get upset, Jude, but she's here now, and she's got contacts in LA, and she can help us."

"Really?" Jude looked over her shoulder at the reporter who'd suddenly appeared at their table.

"Rachel," the young woman said, "Rachel DuChampe."

Jude scooted from her seat, standing, about to bolt when DuChampe put up a hand to her and said, "Please, this rendezvous was entirely my idea. Please stay, and forgive Sybil, please."

Jude stayed put, giving Rachel and Sybil the benefit of the doubt. She prepared herself to listen to the other two women.

Sybil began. "Rachel has been following a series of murders in the LA area and the methods used, and well they're quite similar to what we've been dealing with here in Chicago."

"We've come to the conclusion that the killings are strikingly similar in a number of ways," added Rachel, a short brunette with fuzzy hair, wire rims, and a shapely figure. "We're convinced now more than ever that what you guys have uncovered here is only part of the puzzle."

"I'm listening."

The way she said these two words, everyone at the table understood it to mean that Jude was listening with a skeptical mind. Sybil said, "I was skeptical before I saw all that Rachel's put together. Give her a chance."

"Well, sure, your two 'suspects' here in the Windy City could have taken a trip to LA," began Jude, "could have committed these other atrocities there, but I checked. They never left the city according to Detective Marks. There was nothing on their record to indicate that either one of them had done any traveling in the past year, and these murders in LA were committed over the past few months. I'll need a good deal more details to even begin to consider—"

"I've got plenty of details, Dr. Avery, trust me."

Rachel quickly whipped out a notepad and began flipping through its pages. Her movements seemed to say she feared Jude would bolt before she could go any further. She began speaking in rapid fire. "Right here, let's start with Delialah Morrisey, not only brutally killed but her unborn child left atop her bloody slashed open stomach in a mock Cesarian section. There were a series of unborn child murders done up in the same manner. Then...then..."

"Hold on, as gruesome as the crime scenes you describe, Rachel, I don't see anything similar among these murders and the vet killings or the nun killings."

"Oh, but there is a definite similarity," Rachel said.

"What might that be?"

"The single witness to one of the unborn child murders—she saw that it was two men, and one of them was filming the entire event."

Jude's eyes met Rachel's and then Sybil's. "How reliable is this witness?"

"We don't know. She disappeared from LA. Authorities there only have her on tape in interrogation. She was so unnerved by the...the thing she saw that she feared for her own life at that point and bolted. No one knows her whereabouts."

"Are they seeking her out?" asked Jude. "Do they believe her story?"

"The detective in charge says she was, in his words, terribly believable. Terribly and thoroughly believable." Rachel then launched into other notes and clippings she'd pulled now from her purse. Jude saw that she had clippings from the LA Times regarding—in bold news-print:

Unborn Child Murders

And slipping out alongside these were news clippings on what must be an unrelated case with headlines reading:

Animal Cruelty Case Beyond the Pale

But Rachel dug deeper for a third set of clippings that she turned over to Jude, who took in the headline:

Schoolyard Slayings Leave Police Baffled

A sub-title proclaimed:

Gutted School Children Left on Playground Carousels Posed by Killer

Rachel started to speak but Jude held up a hand to her. "Hold on. Are you telling me that more than one child was posed on a carousel in the park...playground...and posed for...for photographs?"

"Photographs perhaps, but even more likely, a film...a snuff film," replied Rachel.

Jude turned to Sybil. "How long have you known about this?"

"Couple of weeks now since Rachel started talking about it, but it took me awhile to come around to her thinking."

"Have you brought it to Dean's attention?"

"I tried but he shut me down."

Jude recalled the last discussion she'd had with Dean, and how she'd begun to count the number of times he'd interrupted or cut her off. "He's got to know. I mean if you and I go to LA, he's going to know at some point."

"Long holiday weekend coming up. He doesn't have to know until we're out there, and Rachel's contacts are all primed and ready for us.

The detectives in LA have been talking with Stephens and Marks about the possibilities, and now since Lionel's found a connection between our suspects in Chicago to some anonymous person or persons in LA, well..."

"What about Marks and Stephens? Are they taking a flight to LA?" Jude asked.

"No...their hands are full right now with trying to locate Kiley."

"Who may already be in LA with this contact of his," added Rachel.

Jude took in a deep breath and sighed with its release. She nervously bit on her lower lip. "I think we ought to let the detectives here know we're going."

"Great," said Rachel. "I've got us on a flight out of Midway—hope you don't mind sharing room with packages and animal crates."

Sybil explained, "It's a transport with UPS. Told ya, Rachel's got connections. Won't cost us or the ME's office a dime."

"Sybil, this case is shaping up to be something extremely, extremely ugly when from the get-go we thought it was the ugliest case either of us had ever seen."

"I know. The stuff of nightmares," said Rachel.

Sybil added, "And where's it come from? How do people get so bloody warped in the soul?"

"First you have to have a soul," replied Jude. "Does seem some people are born without that special ingredient."

"The soul gene, eh?" asked Rachel.

"The compassion gene, the empathy gene," added Sybil, sipping at her drink.

"Well...to be honest, an aggression gene has been discovered. Maybe they do have a soul and a pinch of empathy, but it's overpowered by this need to dominate others and play god." Jude swallowed hard. "But then again, if they had a worthwhile soul..."

"How soon can we leave, Rachel?" asked Sybil.

"We can't leave," Jude answered instead, "without our confronting Dean about this in no uncertain terms and get his blessings. If we do otherwise, you and I will be looking for a job next week."

Sybil studied Jude's features and using a French fry, she pointed at Jude as if it were a gun. "When you're right, Dr. Avery, you're right.

We together—the three of us, Rach—we all have to beat that man into submission."

Sybil's serious delivery and the words she'd chosen made Jude and Rachel burst into laughter, and Sybil joined them.

"But first," said Jude, "I'm going to need fortification." She dug into her prime rib dinner.

The other two women nodded at one another. They knew that in Jude they had a strong ally.

11

Dean was not pleased. He sat at his desk across from the three ladies who'd cornered him with their harebrained scheme to fly off to LA in search of some phantom killer or killers there, who might or might not have a connection with Keith Kiley and Mitch Goodwin, who may or may not be roaming LA with murder in their hearts and a camera to record it. "It's too dangerous," he said several times, adding, "and I can't afford to lose you two, Sybil, Judith."

The last time Sybil had broached the subject, she'd attempted it alone and Dean had unequivocally turned her down. It sounded outlandish, some newspaper reporter's dream of winning the scoop of the week, and on flimsy evidence, at best hearsay nonsense.

But now Sybil had brought that reporter and Jude in with her to again argue her contention, that there was a clear connection between the murders in both Chicago and LA. A real tale of two cities.

Rachel laid out the 'evidence' as she saw it in the same manner as she had with Jude. Grant at first would hardly glance at the facts, and he wanted badly to ignore the similarities until he heard of the notion that the killers had posed dead children on a carousel in a school playground and a witness had seen this atrocity being filmed by the killers.

Grant asked a series of questions. He wanted to know what Stephens and Marks thought of the so-called connection. He then wanted Jude's opinion. Wanted to hear it out of her mouth. Several times he asked Sybil to be quiet and let Jude speak.

"I'm convinced there's too much here to be called coincidence, sir, and I know you don't believe in coincidence in crime, so yes, I do believe there is enough here to warrant our time and energy to pursue."

"You have to take Stephens or Marks with you then," said Grant.

"We don't need a man, Dr. Grant," countered Sybil.

"You need a detective with a gun—preferably a Chicago detective with a gun."

"We'll be quite safe. LAPD detectives will be working hand-in-hand with us," Rachel assured Grant.

"Look, if Kiley has somehow gotten to LA, you're going to want a Chi-town guy with a badge on hand. Talk it over with Marks and Stephens. Get both if you can to go along with your...with the plan."

"We'll do that, sir," Jude assured him.

"This is going to put a strain on my friend at UPS," said Rachel.

"UPS?" asked Grant.

"Our flight to LA, Dr. Grant, will originate at Midway's UPS hangar," explained Rachel. "I told him it'd be me and Sybil, but she insisted on Dr. Avery, and now you're insisting on a detective."

"That's four instead of two. Talk to your friend. Our budget here is shot to hell." Grant then said, "Before y'all go, see if Marks and Stephens can get corroboration from Goodwin at Cook County that there is this nebulous connection and what he knows about it."

"Of course, yes, sir," Jude quickly agreed to this and urged the other ladies to exit quickly before Dean should have a change of heart.

◆   ◆   ◆

The flight to LA was actually quite comfortable as the UPS plane had a pleasant section for passengers. Aside from the reporter, the two MEs and Detective Stephens, there were a pair of UPS execs on their way to a conference in LA. The UPS execs, a man and woman, appeared more than collegial workplace friends, and they sat apart from the team of would-be truth-seekers in the Kiley murder case.

Stephens claimed to have won the LA trip fair and square from Marks on a coin toss, but Jude didn't believe him. She knew that he was on hand as much to protect his interests in her—his woman—as much as anything else. However, he had confided to Jude and to the other two ladies that Goodwin, while uncooperative and holding his 'ace in the hole,' as he called it, close to his chest since his lawyer had told him to keep his mouth shut no matter what the authorities came at him with until a deal could be cut, that it all spelled one thing: *the ladies were right.*

"When I put it to him outright, he flinched."

"Flinched," Jude asked.

"You read the 'body language' of the dead, Jude, but I read it in the living."

"So what does a flinch tell you?"

"Under the right circumstances, it's like a secret leaps right out of a guy's pores."

This made Jude laugh, and the other ladies smiled and cocked their ears closer.

"Of course fat Mitch denied it, but then I told him our computer guys knew better, and he flinched again, I knew it was true. There's a definite connection between our boy Kiley and someone in LA."

"How deep is the connection is the question," said Rachel, her reporter's mind ticking, rolling over this information.

"Well, Goodwin, he would not verbally admit to it. Still body language gave him away. As to the depth of the connection Kiley has with his counterparts in LA, Marks and me, we believe it's a competition. A sick competition but a competition just the same, but this one between murderers."

"That's what we've been kicking over," Jude told him.

"Too bad there wasn't more cooperation between CPD and LAPD," said Rachel. "No telling how many lives could've been saved."

"Hold on, don't put that on us, Ms. DuChampe. Murder happens every damn day and every police department in the country's been slashed. Write up *that* story, why don't you?"

"All right, cool down, cowboy," said Rachel. "I just wish after all these years, different agencies would cooperate with one another."

"You can talk to your LA friends about that once we get there," suggested Jude. "In the meantime, what're the chances that Keith Kiley's somewhere in LA?"

"Pretty damn good if he's seeking out his rival," said Stephens. "I sure would like to get my hands on him, if not the sight on my .38."

Just then, the pilot's voice came over the PA system, giving them a truncated weather report. Sybil erupted with, "Damn, and we thought it was hot in Chicago." The ground temperature at LAX was 101 degrees.

"Is there anything to that old notion that heat like we've had in Chicago and LA brings on more crime?" Rachel asked of Stephens.

"I think that's an old wives' tale brought about by instances of murder in the summertime, but we have to deal with killings year round, so no. Not been my experience."

"What about you two in the ME's office?" asked Rachel.

"Well, there's definitely more death thanks to the heat wave," Jude said, "but I gotta agree with Detective Stephens. Murder is a year-round affair."

Waiting just off the taxi strip at the UPS hangar at LAX were a pair of detectives from the LAPD who were on hand to greet the entourage from Chicago law enforcement. They were congenial as the introductions were made until they got around to Rachel. "A reporter? I thought the idea was to keep this on the QT," said Detective Joe Kilborn. His partner, Max Stiles did a little walk around in a circle of frustration.

"Hey, if it weren't for Rachel here," Jude said, "none of us would be onto this godawful connection between our cities and these heinous murders."

"Hear, hear!" agreed Sybil. "So keep your opinions to yourselves."

Wayne shrugged and raised his hands in rapid succession. "Let's all start over, shall we? We need to work as a team if anything's to come of this gathering."

Stiles and Kilborn glanced at one another and Kilborn reached out a hand to Rachel, took hers in his and shook. "But all's quiet on the Western Front, got that?"

"I just want the final chapter in a series I started in Chicago," Rachel said. "That's all."

Stiles remained cautious, a bit sullen, and offered no hand to Rachel. Jude imagined he'd been burned by reporters in the past.

"Where to first?" Stephens asked the detectives of LA.

"We'll get you settled at the Sunset," replied Kilborn.

"Sunset?" asked Sybil.

"Best we could do you for—" began Stiles. "Motel near the airport. Leastwise when you're all ready to leave back to Chicago, you'll be close to the airport."

"Easy quick cab ride."

"You sound as if you're anxious for us to leave, Detective Stiles," said Jude.

"Yeah, we only just stepped off the plane."

"We're not convinced there's anything to this so-called connection," Kilborn said in a near apologetic tone. "So your trip may just be a waste of your time."

"And yours as well, you think?" said Jude.

"Perhaps after we share what we have with you fellas," said Stephens, "then you might have more faith in our mission here."

"Always a possibility, eh, Max?" said Kilborn to his partner.

Revealing some body language of his own, Wayne took off his suit coat. "Damn hot here, gents."

"Got that right," said Stiles, turning and saying over his shoulder, "Got an SUV from the motor pool. Bring yourselves along."

The welcome was tepid at best. The group from Chicago followed Kilborn and Stiles to a roomy SUV, and soon they were deposited at a middle-of-the road motel with a beeping sign that was spitting out sparks that rained down, creating a firefly effect in the dusky sky. A nearby Texas Steak House beckoned and the LA detectives said they'd join the Chicago team for dinner once their bags were stowed.

"Over dinner, you can tell us precisely what you got," Kilborn said to Stephens as he stepped into the room they'd reserved for him.

"LAPD was nice to get us rooms," Stephens said to Kilborn.

"Don't count on it. The bean counters'll probably send the CPD a bill."

"Sounds familiar! Well...anyhow, thanks for making the arrangements."

Kilborn snorted and said, "It ain't much."

◆ ◆ ◆

The group later assembled to compare notes and talk over the possibilities in what morphed into a free for all of ideas. Not all of them meshed, and the Chicago people could not fully convince the LA people that Keith Kiley had made his way to LA. At one point, Sybil leaned into Jude and said in a whisper, "Grant may have stolen your case from under you, something you were warned about, but he only has Goodwin in custody." She then said loud for all to hear, "We, us'ns, folks, we have it in our power to put down this evil nexus of snuff films that go far beyond our two towns."

"We worked the case in Chicago to its bare bones," added Stephens. "And it led us here, gentlemen."

Joe Kilborn and Max Stiles listened better with beers set out before them. They'd passed on the steakhouse and opted for a place called the Five Seasons, the fifth being Drinking Season, Max jested. It was a place with a micro brewery where people could watch the brewers at work through a Plexiglas partition. The locals typically opted for the 'tour of the Seasons' which amounted to eight separate beers at once.

The ladies shared one of these orders, as did the LA detectives, while Stephens ordered a single beer.

Everyone was a good deal more relaxed than they'd been on first meeting. A phone rang and everyone but Stephens was checking to see if it was theirs. Stephens's phone had a distinctive ring, an instrumental of Bad to the Bone. Soon it was determined to be Jude's phone, a call from Ralph and Lionel, a conference call. "Hold on, hold on," she said. "I'm putting you on speaker for everyone to hear this, Ralph, Lionel. Okay, go ahead."

Lionel's voice came over loud and clear despite the noise of the restaurant. It was early evening yet, and the place was not filled. Lionel said, "Kiley and Goodwin were involved with a group in LA calling themselves The Elders."

"That doesn't give us a whole helluva lot to go on, son," said Stiles, slurring his words.

"It's a start," countered Rachel.

"They come up often on the hard drive, and there's a website for members only. I'm trying to join now, but they appear to have rigorous standards."

"What sort of standards?"

"Begins with question of animal mutilation. 'Have you ever mutilated one' it asks."

"Then what?"

"Well, it asks 'Have you ever filmed an animal mutilation.'"

"So do you have an IP address on these freaks?" asked Stephens.

"Wayne? That you?" asked Lionel.

"That's right. I'm here with Dr. Shanley and Dr. Avery."

"Oh...news to me. Ralph, why didn't you tell me?"

"Never mind that. What about an IP address?"

"Working on it, but these guys are six shades of gray if not more."

"All right, keep us apprised, and hey, send us what you have. Send it to Dr. Avery's computer. We'll take it from here."

"Elders. Never heard of them," said Kilborn. He looked to Stiles, who shook his head.

"Maybe we should check with gangs, vice, special victims," suggested Stephens.

"Yeah, sure, we could do that," Stiles said without enthusiasm.

"Homicide is limited in their knowledge even in Chicago," Stephens countered. "I'd assume the same is true here."

Kilborn nodded. "We'll ask around for sure."

"The Elders," muttered Rachel. "They sound like bad characters."

"Either that or some fat kid working out of his basement," Stiles said, the downed beers getting to him now. He laughed as if he'd told a joke worthy of Conan O'Brien.

"We'll turn over a few rocks, Detective Stephens," said Kilborn. "Count on it."

"We'd like to go over autopsy reports on the series of murders we spoke of," Jude said to Kilborn. "I'd like you to introduce us to your ME, Dr. Rudolph Hunsucker."

"That old ball of fur's not going to take kindly to you two poking around his findings," said Stiles.

"What Max means to say is for you ladies to not expect a kind welcome from Iron-assed Hunsucker."

"He's that bad, is he?" asked Jude.

"Former army surgeon or something like that and he still barks like a drill sergeant," said Kilborn, letting out a laugh. "Just want you to know what kind of horse you're bucking."

"Old army horse, eh?" Jude replied, curious if Hunsucker might have had any dealings with her father; if their paths ever crossed in the military. It might be helpful if it were so.

"Our boss, Dr. Grant, no doubt's had a chance to contact your ME by now," said Sybil. "He's got to be expecting us."

"We can find out right quick," said Stiles, now standing, a bit wobbly.

"Why don't you first go visit the little boy's room, Max," his partner suggested. "Freshen up as they say."

When Max nodded, turned, and stepped away from the table, Kilborn pointed and said, "Max's going through some things lately; a rough patch. Family thing."

"Sure."

"Understood."

"Got it," came the chorus of words and nods about the table.

"He's a good man, good detective," Kilborn assured them all.

"If you say so, detective," said Stephens without conviction.

"Had a great guy as a realtor once, affable, wonderful guy, like my dad," began Rachel, "but he couldn't sell my house. Kept making it to every showing late and pie-eyed."

"He could be a liability in this endeavor," Jude ventured to say.

"Max is no liability. Likes his beer is all. He'll be all right."

Stephens put it to Kilborn. "All right until he gets you killed, Joe?"

Kilborn glared at Stephens. "You got a partner you left back in Chicago?"

"Yeah, sure do."

"Then you know how it goes—through thick and thin, till death do us part."

"That's what I'm worried about," said Stephens, "that last part."

"I'm not about to throw Max under the bus, so the rest of you can just…" he stopped himself. "He's my problem, and I'm dealing with it."

The others decided silence was the best option at this point. Jude said, "I'd like to get those reports from Hunsucker's people before anything else."

Stiles returned to the table just in time to hear this, and he appeared to have sobered somewhat, his hair, eyes, and eyebrows still wet from a quick cleansing.

"We got this, Stephens," Stiles said as Wayne reached for his wallet. Stiles tossed two twenties on the table, and his partner took care of the rest along with the tip.

"We're on expense account," Kilborn said as everyone made for the door well after Max had.

From behind them, they heard the bartender shouting, "Come again, folks!"

Outside, they found Stiles hadn't gotten far. He was smoking and pacing. His partner conferred with him, and both overheard Rachel tell the others, "I'm catching a cab to the LA Times to meet with my contacts there."

"Pricks have been excoriating us in the press," Kilborn complained to Rachel.

"Them and the local TV anchors," added Stiles, his face turning sour. "Saying we're doing *nothing*."

"Yeah, we're just sitting on our thumbs while the Unborn Killer, as they've labeled him, is getting away with it with…with, what's that word, Max? Im…Im…"

"Impunity, Joe."

"Right, right, impunity."

"Your pals at the Times act as if we don't give a damn is how they're treating us while we bust our humps overtime, ignoring our own families in the bargain."

"*Heyyy*, Max, let's just get these folks over to the ME's and then you, me, and Stephens here can check in at headquarters. Wayne here's got some paperwork to sign if he's going to be on our mean streets."

Stiles gritted his teeth and started to say more but thought better of it. "Sure, sure."

With Rachel going in one direction and the police and medical people going in another, all was soon sorted out. At the state-of-the-art ME's office and labs, Jude and Sybil marveled at the equipment and the expanse of the place. "I thought Cook County was good but wow," Sybil confided to Jude.

They were met with a gruff, short, and stout Dr. Rudolph Hunsucker, whose mustache and eyebrows looked like three escaped hamsters. As he talked, introducing himself to them, the hamsters stirred, rose, fell, expanded, and contracted. "I am told, Dr. Shanley, you are a remarkable clinician, and you, Dr. Avery, I am told your father was in the military, and I recognized the name. I served for a time with your father—brilliant man. I hope you have half his capabilities."

"Why, thank you, Dr. Hunsucker."

"Why thank me?" he lightly joked. "Not at all. I am delighted to have two such talented women visiting me. Makes an old man feel quite excited as you might imagine. But Dr. Grant did not tell me how perfectly beautiful you two are. I should think we could put together a calendar of women in forensics. For a good cause, of course."

The little round man was doing his best to be congenial, and both Sybil and Jude realized it was fitfully difficult for him to do so. Socializing for most men in the profession was just not done, and understanding women remained a huge mystery for men like Jude's father, Grant, and now Hunsucker. Any one of them would prefer to be 'talking' to a dead woman rather than a live one.

"Dr. Hunsucker, we're hoping actually to simply go over the several murders involving unborn fetuses and mothers with their wombs cut open. That is only to compare and contrast against cases in Chicago."

"Yes, yes, that was explained to me by Dr. Grant—a fine man I've met at conferences. I was happy to take his call and so I have prepared copies of the autopsy reports so that you can take them with you."

It was done, Jude felt certain, to get the strangers out of his hair as quickly as possible. "Why, thank you, Dr. Hunsucker. How thoughtful and thorough of you."

"Why thank me?" he again jested. "I simply thought it best for your comfort, my dears."

Sybil intentionally crowded his personal space and said, "Do you really think we'd make good pin up girls for a calendar, Doctor, or were you just being sweet?"

This had Dr. Hunsucker babbling. "Oh, yes…I mean why it would be lovely, and we're getting so many young ladies coming into the profession these days."

"I'll suggest it to Dr. Grant when we get back," Sybil continued to tease the old man.

"I—I hope you took no offense at my suggestion, but as Mark Twain said, when you turn seventy, you can get away with saying anything. No one takes me seriously on such…such matters."

"The important thing is the autopsies you have devoted your life to, sir, not our sensitivities or political correctness."

"Yes, yes…that is how I see it. Thank you, Dr. Avery, Dr. Shanley. My assistant, Darlene through these doors, she has everything you need set out in a neat pile of folders. And as for me, I must get back to my work. We've just had another victim of this monster rolled into the morgue."

"Really?" asked Jude. "Another Unborn Child murder victim?"

"Yes, so I must be off."

"Dr. Hunsucker, I would be so honored to assist you," Jude quickly said, stopping Hunsucker from another step.

"Really, well…Dr. Avery, I suppose…why not? Yes, come along."

"I'll find a lounge and go over the files," Sybil said to Jude. Under her breath, she added, "Smart move."

"Who knows, we might just get that calendar going with a Kickstarter page," joked Dr. Avery, rushing off to catch up to Dr. Hunsucker.

Part of Jude was instantly kicking herself after she'd invited herself in on the cutting and had suited up for the autopsy. What changed her mind and passion for it was simple to understand as she found herself staring at two slabs—one with mother, one with child. It was a horror of horrors. The mother had been mutilated to get at the fetus, and the fetus had been mutilated for reasons unfathomable, for reasons unthinkable. It went so far beyond the worst of animal cruelty she'd ever seen, what this fiend had done to the helpless child, so small and as yet unformed.

Dr. Hunsucker asked her to attend to the mother while he, donning microscope glasses usually seen only in surgical procedures, autopsied the fetus. The man's hands shook over the mass of flesh that'd been carved into an unrecognizable bloody lump. The sheer number of rents, tears, cuts and brutal rips the killer had created had turned this life into something that resembled sushi stacked on a hibachi. Jude imagined a second man working with the knife-wielder, one doing the deed, another to film it, or did the killer wear a body cam to increase the sick entertainment value for the so-called Elders?

While Jude was busy with the most difficult autopsy of her career and thinking she'd had to come all the way to LA for this, Sybil had roosted in a lounge area corner with the autopsy reports on the earlier victims of the Unborn Child Killer. Her experience with the information was nearly as devastatingly torturous as Jude's actually being involved in an autopsy like those on the pages she purveyed.

◆　◆　◆

Keith Kiley had grown a thick beard the color of burnt orange, and still in the clothes he'd escaped Chicago in, wandered the unfamiliar streets of downtown LA until he found the seedier side of the city. Kiley knew Chicago streets like the back of his hand. Knew every neighborhood and back alley as he'd grown up in the city. He knew which el line to take to get from here to there, but LA was entirely a different story. Back in Chi-Town, he knew every crevice, crook and cranny, and where to go to hide, and who he could trust, but not so here in LA.

Here he felt like a stranger in a strange land. Nothing was working out as he'd imagined when he'd raced here headlong after setting Sampson's on fire, after planting 'his' body inside. The flight out of O'Hare

Airport was a breeze, but once he got into LA by cab from LAX, he became a stray dog without so much as a bone. He didn't even have Mitch anymore. No one.

A choking ball of sad loneliness had filled his mind and his gut. He had begun to think of Maria Rodriguez, and he'd made a call to tell her how much he was thinking of her. The call did not go well. The bitch had hung up on him before he got out half what he wished to say.

Now he was in this damnable city and knowing no one, nor where to go or how to find a connection to the Elders. Many of the people he asked questions of either ignored him or claimed they knew no 'Englez' as they called it. He stewed about how obvious illegals roamed the streets here, unable to speak the language. He felt some of the old rage rise in him over this. How he would like to kill some Mexicans, and it made him wonder if the Elders would like him for doing just that. Help out the cause of the race war. But for now, he was lost.

Finally, he located a computer cafe where he knew he could make a connection to the Elders. While Mitch had done most of the emails to the Elders and had forwarded the videos via private messaging on Facebook, Kiley knew the digital path needed to make contact. His only fear was that the police might well be tracking him digitally, so he'd need to set up a new FB presence, something that would not tip off the authorities in Chicago where, no doubt, they were monitoring any activity as KKboy.

Kiley bought a cup of coffee and a roll before settling in at one of the cafe's public computers. Out of habit, he almost logged in using his KKboy account even though he'd just minutes before told himself he mustn't flag where he was by using that identity. The Elders would know him well as KKboy when he declared it in the private messaging. After fifteen minutes of setting up his new online identity, Kiley contacted the Elders via the digital front they used on Facebook. He'd need more than 140 characters of a tweet to get their attention and help.

Help was his main message, that he needed their help. He needed a safe haven, protection from the authorities, possibly a ticket to Timbuktu. Help, he repeated in his message to the Elders. He didn't get an immediate response; he hardly expected an immediate response, so he ordered more coffee and an egg sandwich. He then returned to the computer he'd been using to find a swarthy, dark-haired Armenian man sitting at the computer he'd just vacated.

"Hey, that's my station," he said to the stranger.

"Nobody here. I take it," replied the man in broken English.

"The hell you say! I'm waiting for a message, and now you've cleared my screen, asshole!"

A burly, whiskered man from behind the counter had rushed over, with a huge ladle in hand, to referee. "That's enough, mister!" he said to Kiley. "We don't have any unpleasantness in here. We don't put up with it. Now you sit yourself down and wait for the next available computer or you let me bag your stuff up and you go!"

Kiley gritted his teeth, glared at the Armenian, and then at the counter man, but he wisely found an easy chair and a table to sit and enjoy his coffee and sandwich. Under his breath he said some threatening words, but he knew he could not make a scene.

Everyone went back to their corners. Kiley chomped down his sandwich, eyes boring a hole in the man who'd taken his seat at the computer he had been on. He glanced around to see if any of the other ten or so computers were available. So far, no. He cursed inwardly at the inconvenience and thought how poor these people in this place must be that they can't afford their own damn computers.

He fought with himself, his patience wearing thin, but what could he do? He must wait. The mounting fear that the law could be closing in began to work on him. He began to fidget. His fidgeting was soon drawing attention from others in the cafe, especially the owner behind the counter who'd gotten on his mobile phone.

Kiley wondered if the man was on the phone with some local cops he knew, maybe asking them to come by to have a look at Kiley, just to be on the safe side. Kiley stood, started for the door, thought better of it, turned, paced the room, his anxiety growing with each moment.

Being on the run had not been any kind of picnic. He'd had to hide out in Chicago all that time, hardly a thing to eat, feeling like a rat in Sampson's the whole time. Then the fear that filled him while escaping Chicago, looking over his shoulder the entire way. Even on the plane at 30,000 feet, he had wondered when someone would grab him and stick a gun in his ear.

And now here in this wretched little cafe in this dingy little neighborhood in LA, he worried that cops were right outside, surrounding the place right now. After all, his face—without the beard—was plastered everywhere, and before he'd even reached LA, that face had arrived ahead of him.

He wondered if the Elders could get some plastic surgeon out here in Lala Land to change his notorious face, so he could remain free and one of them.

A young Asian woman finally wrapped up what she was doing at a computer, and Kiley instantly claimed the station. He quickly returned to where he had been, hoping for a life line, a message from the Elders, how he could find them, where they could meet. He returned to the message box where his words stared back at him, his pleas for their help in his time of need. How he had earned their help; that he needed protection from the authorities, a way to disappear.

Still no message back. He stared at the blankness after his message. Nothing.

He could hardly believe it. He sighed heavily, unsure what to do. Write another plea? As he kicked over his options, looking over his shoulder from time to time at the owner of the place, he wanted to scream. He was building up to a scream when he saw the dancing dots on the screen—the sign that the Elders were responding. His heart fluttered at the sight. Safety was at hand, on its way.

The message read: Meet us at Second Avenue and Brentwell.

That's all it said.

Where the hell is Second and Brentwell, he wondered. Jotting down the two street names, he went to the counterman and asked after the address.

"Not far, maybe six, seven blocks. Short bus ride," said the owner. "Look, sorry about having to hassle you earlier, but I can't have my customers breaking out in fights here."

"Oh, I understand, and hey, thank you, sir. I'm new around here, so I need all the help I can get."

"Well then, welcome to the neighborhood."

"Thanks...thanks again. So I go which way when I go out the door, left or right?"

"Right. Westward, young man. Go west," joked the owner.

Kiley rushed out, turned right and went in search of Brentwell where it crossed Second, realizing that he was already on Second. This was promising, very promising. A smile creased Kiley's face. For the first time since arriving in LA, he began to feel some sense of success at truly eluding the police now in two cities.

12

The day and its events had worn Jude to what she called 'a frazzle,' so she begged off going for a bite with Sybil, who was anxious to reveal all she'd learned from the autopsy reports. "Later, please," she had said, and Sybil had given her an understanding look. "I've had to autopsy children and babies," Sybil replied. "It's the hardest part of the hardest job in creation."

As a result, Jude found herself alone at the motel and in the shower. It felt like no amount of showering could get the day off, no matter how hard she scrubbed.

She mused about her new home, the cozy, third-floor flat and her own bed. She worried about how Boomer was doing at that dog and cat shelter she'd left him at. The people there said they often had bird lovers leave their 'babies' with them, and that Boomer would be well cared for. She also thought of the expense. Then she began to focus on Wayne and wished he was in the shower with her right here, right now.

After toweling off and putting on a robe, her thoughts drifted back to the case they were following. She wanted to see Kiley and all his kind pay dearly for their godawful deeds.

After pacing the room, she plopped onto the bed where she got on her iPhone and called Sybil, asking her to come to her room with her notes and the copies of the reports that Dr. Hunsucker had provided for them. "I'll order a pizza or do you prefer Chinese?"

"Chinese would be better for my hips," replied Sybil. "Be right over."

They'd collared a uniform patrolman to drive them back to the motel, and neither of them had heard from either Stephens or Rachel

DuChampe, both of whom were following up on their own leads. Everyone felt that it would take a team, an unofficial task force like theirs to corner Kiley and his friends in LA.

Every small link in the chain, Jude thought, is important.

Sybil arrived ahead of the Chinese order. She started right in on all the parallels she had found in the Unborn Child Killer cases and the Chicago murders. In fact, she ticked them off with such sureness that Jude was immediately impressed. "Bottom line is the sensational nature of the crimes, and the choice of victims, of course. They rival veterans and nuns."

"Rival sounds like the nail we've been looking for, yes. Rivals in sensational murders, and then leaving tell-tale signs it's the work of dark-skinned people. Is that to throw off authorities or simply to rile up hatred for black and brown people? That Helter-Skelter thread we discussed as a possibility in Kiley's case?"

"Stands to reason in today's political climate," Sybil added when a knock came at the door.

"Food," said Sybil. "I'm famished."

When they opened the door, they found Rachel rather than their food order, and she had a fat lip where someone had smacked her. Jude stared at the other woman and asked, "What happened?"

At the same time, Sybil threw an arm around her lover and pulled her inside to sit in a chair at the table, asking repeatedly, "What happened, Rachel. What happened?"

"Asked one too many questions in one too many joints along Sunset Strip."

"Who's the sonofabitch?" asked Sybil. "Let me at him!"

"He's long gone by now. I was flashing Kiley's face around. They took me for a cop."

"Who are they?" insisted Sybil.

"Biker bunch that just so happened to be in the bar I chose."

"Why were you there alone?"

"I wasn't alone. My friends at the Times were with me, Joanne and Dave."

"And they didn't stop this thug before he broke your lip?"

"They tried, and they got roughed up, too."

"Seems to me you got a reaction out of these brutes," said Jude. "Don't suppose you got any photos?"

"Fact is, Jo anticipated trouble and she got some shots on her phone which she sent to me."

"You think they knew Kiley or knew of him?"

"His face is plastered all over the city, so in that sense, yes, of course."

"But you think they might know more? Beyond his features, do you?" pressed Jude. "If they know something useful, we need to get the detectives to haul their asses in for questioning."

"Could be a dead end."

"Or a road that needs taking," countered Jude. "Look, we can't leave one rock unturned."

They had left the door half open, and now a man stood blocking the light, and the suddenness of losing light to shadow had Jude reaching for her gun when the delivery boy shouted, "Ho Chin's! Ho Chin's! Don't shoot!" Jude replaced her gun in its holster on the bureau, while Sybil apologized to the delivery boy and was in the process of finding payment and taking in the grub, as she called it. At the same moment, Jude explained, "I've already paid for the food via Visa. Just tip the poor kid well, would you?"

"Well, take this fiver, anyway, young man," Sybil said to the baby-faced delivery man. "Not much for the year my friend took off your life."

"Thank you, thank you," the young man repeated, shaking all the way to his waiting vehicle.

"You two sure are jumpy," Rachel remarked. "Chinese, I love Chinese take-out. Perfect."

"You going to be able to eat with that fat lip?" asked Sybil.

"They leave enough chopsticks for three?" Rachel *scooched* her chair closer to the table and the food.

As the ladies feasted over moo goo gai pan, fried rice, and rangoon with a complement of sauces, they talked over the sheer outrage each felt toward this Unborn Child Killer. Each brought the others up to date on their findings, and each lady wondered at the growing evidence of a sure connection between Kiley and the LA killer or killers. They all felt certain there was a rivalry that surrounded the taping of the snuff videos.

Rachel finally silenced the other two when she said, "I had Joanne and Dave check Kiley's records for travel to see if at any time Kiley was in LA when these murders were committed, and he wasn't. Not once, so there is that."

"That does say a lot, Jude," said Sybil, nibbling at her last rangoon.

"I'm still pissed at those bikers you ran into," said Jude as if not hearing.

"They did react rather violently to our passing Kiley's picture around," said Rachel.

"Real outlaws, some jerks like to think of themselves," Jude added. "I dated a biker when I was too young to know better."

The others laughed at this. Sybil then said, "If that's true, Rachel, how come you couldn't get more cooperation out of those guys?"

"Yeah, badges! We don't need no stinkin' badges!" joked Rachel.

When their appetites were sated, Rachel held up a photo and said, "Here's the hairy werewolf who hit me. Racist SOB could well be a candidate for starting a race war, don't you think?"

It was obvious that Rachel was more interested in Sybil's opinion than Jude's.

"Looks like a guy I'd like to brain for what he did to Rach." Sybil got up and went to Rachel and put her arms around her, and the two women began a slow, sensual kiss.

"Hey, you two, get a room," said Jude.

"We got a room," replied Sybil, who then looked up at Jude and added, "If we're through here, I think we'll just go find my room. What do you say, Rach?"

Rachel stood and made for the door, Sybil following. Jude held up a hand, caught the couple before they should disappear, and said, "Before anything else, shenanigans or otherwise, Rachel, I think you need to send those biker bum photos to Stephens's phone."

"I don't have the connection."

"Well, I do. Leave your phone with me, and I'll see to it."

"I've got Wayne's number in my phone," countered Sybil. "We'll take care of it. You get some much-deserved rest."

"Sure, sure." Jude had wanted the excuse to contact Wayne, to determine where he was, what he was up to, and if there were any new leads. But she didn't want to appear too anxious to contact him in front of the other women. So she waved them off. "Have a good time. See you later."

"Don't count on it, dearie," Rachel called back.

Tough lady, Jude thought, and good with chopsticks. Jude had observed that Rachel had taken both her fortune cookie and her chopsticks with her. Fun and games for those two tonight, she thought.

In the meantime, Stephens and the LA detectives, using contacts on the streets, learned of a 'new guy in town' who'd been looking for cover—for anyone to take him in, he promised to do anything for a place to lay low. Of course, that vague description might apply to any new arrivals every day in LA, a mecca for runaways, misfits, and miscreants. But when shown Kiley's photo, they had several hits—people who swore it was him. He appeared to be hanging about a rough neighborhood, a place where he could as easily get himself knifed as knife someone else.

The word was out on how hot Kiley was, and just how anxious the LAPD wanted this man for multiple murders in Chicago. As a result, anyone with half a brain, criminal or not, wanted nothing whatsoever to do with him.

"He's come to LA without any idea of how to locate the Elders, it would appear," Stephens suggested to his LA counterpart, Stiles, whose partner Kilborn looked to him for a reply to Stephens.

Max took his own time answering. "Got to put yourself in his shoes, from his point of view. We get into how he likely feels to be on the run—how in every face there is an element of treachery. His fear at any moment of being spotted and surrounded by cops who will open fire on him and fire away before giving him a chance to surrender. After all, he's killed vets, vets and nuns, for Christ's sake!"

Nightfall in the city was coming on, but Stiles and Kilborn told Stephens that the real rats show up in the late hours of darkness. As a result, the trio had sought out a place to eat and wait. The LA detectives had a couple of stops in mind.

While at dinner at a place called the Texas Grill, Stephens's phone alerted, telling him Rachel had forwarded several pictures. He opened on a photo of a rough-looking, long-bearded beady-eyed biker with caption, "This one broke my lip."

The other two photos depicted similar biker types with cryptic captions. Stephens was unsure what the photos meant. He then found a text from Sybil, and the text explained that he should be watching for photos sent from Rachel that were photos of persons of interest in the case who needed to be found and grilled on what they know about Kiley.

Stephens shared this news and the photos with Max and Joe, who began a discussion over the photos. They were not familiar with the faces, but they recognized the gang insignia on one fellow in the background. They increased the size of the photo to zero in on the insignia, which read "The Elders."

"By God, we've got them," Stephens said.

"No, hold on. This is too pat," said Max to the others. "Like...like a setup."

"What are you talking about. These are our guys. Otherwise, why smack Rachel?"

"Just don't think it's wise to jump to conclusions," countered Max.

Joe counseled Wayne, saying, "Max has a second sense about these things. I'd listen to him if I were you."

"Second sense or no, we need to find these guys and shake something loose from them."

Between chews on his steak, Max said, "We can do that. If someone's trying to start this race war you've been talking about, then they need two sides to go to war, right? The black population on one side, then who's on the other side they setup as their straw man? Who better than bikers in LA? Bikers whose gang affiliation is The Elders?"

Stephens sat back in his chair. "That...that may well be."

Joe added, "And who'd want to set them up? Should their plans go off the rails? Feed on our stereotypical beliefs about bikers?"

"You guys may well have something there, but again, all the more reason to question these guys. Maybe we could get information on who might have a grudge against them."

"A grudge of admiration for them," countered Max.

"Admiration, eh? Sure, I get that. Either way, maybe they know more about Kiley's connection with the term 'Elders' than they let on with Rachel and her Times buddies."

"Can you imagine Kiley going about these streets asking where he can find the Elders?" asked Kilborn, laughing now. "Could get him killed and he doesn't even know it."

"Do they have that kind of reputation?" asked Stephens.

"That and more, according to my buddy in the Gangs Division."

"Murder?"

"Worse than murder," Stiles said. "Try rape-murder."

"Triple murder."

"Torture."

"One guy was found skinned alive."

"So why are they running around free?"

"They're very good at taking out witnesses and terrifying the ones they don't get rid of."

"Sounds like they might also be racists?"

"The word puts it mildly, but yeah. Many are also card-carrying members of the KKK."

"Then maybe they are the ones behind the Unborn Child Killings and the snuff films that reach from here to Chicago and God knows where else."

"They do deal in random violence."

"We need to talk to them then, one way or the other," Stephens said.

"I think we'll need more help from our Gangs Division on that," said Max. "No telling how many operations they've got going to infiltrate."

Kilborn agreed. "Wouldn't want to step on any toes or get those guys and possibly the FBI pissed off at us, now would we, Chicago?"

Max added, "You agree?"

"I know you've got gangs in Chicago," Kilborn said. "You know about such protocols in Chicago, right, Chicago?"

"Yeah, yeah, sure...I know we have to step carefully; that it's a minefield."

"When we finish our steaks, we'll go by their hangout, announce our intention of finding Kiley to put him away, and see if anything shakes out. After that, we'll go talk to our experts in Vice on The Elders."

"Sounds like a reasonable plan." Stephens dug into his own steak.

The ladies from Chicago had already broken a few of Grant's demands and rules, which he'd made them swear to before allowing this venture to go forward. Jude felt badly about it, but they had not kept Grant in the loop. Things were just happening too fast to keep up. Sybil had felt no compunction over it, telling Jude that the least they shared with Dean the better for them.

"I know we've had to break a few rules," Sybil said over the phone. In the background, Jude could hear Rachel calling Sybil back to bed.

"A few rules? Come on, Sybil, call it what it is."

"And what is that?"

"We're going to...we're headed toward going behind Grant's back."

"Sometimes that's necessary with Dean. You know that."

"I didn't sign up for this."

"Let me put it in simpler terms, kiddo. In order to get at the tip of the spear and end this deadly game of making snuff films for online club-members' *pandering entertainment,* we have to do whatever the hell's necessary. Now, look, we are both headstrong women, and when this is over and we come out heroes—heroines—whatever, it will still reflect well on that bombastic overlord in Chicago."

"There will be fireworks. You know that, I know that."

"Since when are you afraid of a few fireworks?"

Rachel shouted in the background, "Naturally, *three* strong women, so of course there will be fireworks. Count on it!"

◆ ◆ ◆

Kiley had found the corner where he was supposed to await The Elders, but now night had fallen over LA and they hadn't shown themselves.

He understood the need for caution. Perhaps they thought instead of fleeing the police in a masterful plan that began with his faking his own death, that the Elders somehow believed he was leading the police to them. He felt confident that such a notion could be dispelled quickly and easily. He'd seen some of the work of the Unborn Child Killer, and he'd volunteer to help continue in that vein for the Elders, if only they'd take him in and promise him the safety of the group.

As it was, he felt absolutely vulnerable here on the street. There were only so many store windows a stranger in the area could fake staring into. Besides, he kept seeing his clean-shaven self in pictures on the front page of the LA Times below a headline reading:

Killer of Nuns and Vets Believed to be in LA—Fugitive Keith Kiley

He'd seen himself on the TV through storefront windows. He realized he'd made a serious mistake coming to LA, that the Chicago heat on him had followed him here like a stench he could not rid himself of. He could feel his every fiber tighten in fear each time a car passed with someone inside looking out at him. Whenever an LAPD cruiser came by, he had to duck into an alleyway, hide like a rat behind a Dumpster, and wait.

"Where the hell are they?"

Just when he most feared capture by police, a cadre of bikers came out of nowhere, and on seeing him, they came menacingly closer and closer until they stopped, all idling, all with their handlebars and front wheels pointed in one direction as if one animal with one thought in mind. Thus distracted, he did not at first see the black, unmarked van that pulled alongside him, nor exactly when a door at the rear and then at the side flew open, nor exactly how two burly men in ski masks grabbed him and dragged him kicking and screaming to the van.

Kiley put up a fight, but he was finally cold-cocked into submission by what felt like a sap. He lost consciousness and went limp and was unceremoniously thrown into the van while the bikes all around the van idled.

Sometime later, Kiley awoke to a huge, blue, cloudless sky over-head. He also awoke to restraints. He'd been tied to a tablet-like rock in the desert. There were people, but they were at some distance, a party atmosphere from the sound of it. He heard a crackling fire someplace nearby. He could not turn his head as it, too, was restrained against the table rock he lay on.

He could not see the discoloration of the rock he found himself on—the years of sacrifices that had created a rough crust of dried blood from the previous people dispatched here in the lawless desert. As he was not gagged, he screamed out, "What's going on here? What're you doing to me? I'm one of you!"

From the party goers, he heard one man shout, "He's conscious."

"Can we get on with it now, Cappy?" shouted another.

"You just hold your horses, Wilford. We'll do it *all* in good time."

"Maybe we ought to hear the man out," said a calmer, more ratio-nal-sounding voice.

"Yeah, hear me out, please! I just came to join The Elders. I should be named an Elder for all I've done. I killed for you! In your name!"

"Hear that, boys? Says he killed for us, in our name."

Laughter followed, intermingling with the crackling of the fire.

"Let's just find out what this sucker knows," said one voice author-itatively. And suddenly before Kiley's eyes, a torch appeared. "Gonna burn you bad, boy, if you don't tell us what I wanna know."

He was a huge, long-bearded man, a Viking look to him with his red beard and hair. The beard was tied in a small knot at the end.

"I made the films for you; it was me in the vet and nun killings."

"Anyone know what in hell this dumb fuck's talking about?" asked Red Beard of the others.

"Not a clue."

"A second man showed himself. "I read it in the papers," he began.

"You read the papers?"

This had many of the others laughing.

The man sheepishly ignored the laughter and said, "This is the guy they run out of Chicago for killing those nuns up there, and he thinks we put him up to it. That's how I read it."

"You're the Elders," said Kiley. "You're the Unborn Baby Killers, right?"

"Damn you for saying that!" Red Beard's face flashed anger and hatred, and he shoved the burning torch at the helpless man's eyes, scorching the side of his face and eye as Kiley was unable to pull away.

Kiley had instinctively closed his eyes and screamed on taking the brunt of the fire to his forehead and hair, which caught fire, making Red Beard laugh and call others over to watch Kiley's head of hair burn to wirelike shreds. Kiley continued in screams of pain.

Finally, he shouted, "I didn't come here to be killed like a mangy dog!"

"You're worse than a mangy dog, son!" Red Beard howled.

"Brought the pigs down on us, you did," shouted the rational one.

"Let me waterboard him," another said. "I'll get it out of him."

"Waterboarding's too good for him."

"Turn us loose on him, Red," called out a female voice in the biker gang.

"If you kill him," the rational one shouted, "you won't know the whole story."

"You stupid shit, bringing your ass to LA, asking all kinds of questions about us," said the person who appeared in charge of the group. "Well give yourself congrats, KKboy, b'cause here we are. Now what're we going to do with you, son?"

"Hey, hey," Kiley pleaded, "I'm one of you. I—I killed those nuns for you, those vets—in Chicago!"

"Then you stupidly brought all your problems to us—straight down on us," one tall blond, Aryan-looking leader replied. Kiley saw the prison tattoos on his hands and forearms.

"I killed for you guys!" Kiley wailed.

Keith then had a flashback thought of the innocent, sweet face and curvaceous body of Suzie Young, the girl he'd hoped so many years ago to make his, the secret love of his life. He'd read somewhere that what a person determines as beauty was extremely personal and that the notion of beauty was formed in a child's mind at a very early age—as early as first gazing on his mother's face. Keith gave a thought to his long ago, passed-away mother, too. He realized that Suzie Young had similar features to his mom's. He determined to have his last thoughts be of dear old mom and sweet Suzie here and now.

The others, some twelve figures behind their leader moved in closer, and Kiley saw that they were all holding huge carving knives with hilts like small swords. "You guys! I'm one of you. I came home to you for help! Help!"

"Shout it out, KKboy, scream for help."

The entire group took it up as a chant, "Scream for help! Scream for help!"

Keith could only move his eyes, and they went wildly from side to side, trying to see past the group of young, doped-up people with their knives coming at him. He only saw that they were surrounded by rocks, cacti, and desert. His screams, just as everyone here knew, went into the big sky where Kiley saw the last billowing clouds he'd ever see before the Elders began carving on him.

Kiley's last sight was the end of the camera lens and the knives penetrating him, and his last forceful plea came out as, "But I'm one of you!" Beyond weak now, life draining from him, he muttered in near whisper, "*One ovvv youuu?*"

Red leaned in over the dying Kiley and said, "Coyotes gotta eat, too, son."

The biker gang known as The Elders was a relatively new outfit put together by their leader. They'd had some success in getting cooperation with some of the older biker families in LA, and they had carved out a small area they could rely on for income. Their leader was Red Beard, otherwise known as Carl Buford. Buford ruled with an iron fist, and once he made a decision, there was no dissuading him, although the biker known as Tony Discenta tried his best to keep young Kiley alive—for questioning, torture if need be, to learn who sent him and how they'd been implicated in his crimes in Chicago, because it made no sense.

"Why'd he come looking for us, Carl? You gotta be wondering about that? And snuff films like they're talking in the press, and how did this creep end up here," he paused to point to the bloody heap of flesh on the stone slab, "and—and what they're after him for? Jesus, I hear they're linking him with the Unborn Child Killer, and hell, that's not us, but why'd Kiley here think it was us, and what kind of heat is that going to bring down on us, and how's Snake and Bullseye and your uncle going to take it when they find out?"

"They're not going to find out! That's why I had the bastard killed."

"But now we can't learn anything else about who's behind fingering us for multiple murders, Carl...Carl."

"You questioning my authority?" asked Red Beard, his eyes those of a madman.

"No, hell no! I'd never, but we need answers."

"That's why I got you around, Tony. You go find me some answers. Talk it up and don't come back until you have something for me. I want to get the rest of these dickheads on my slab."

Tony felt threatened. If he could not come through for Carl, he might find himself on that blood-stained slab of orange desert rock. He didn't relish the idea of his carcass chewed to the bone by desert varmints. He skulked off, found his bike among the horde of others, and to the tune of *Bad to the Bone* being played on fifty or so phones at once, he cranked up his Harley, turned her, and sped off, kicking up sand, gravel, and a cloud of dust in his wake.

Only when he got out of sight of the others did Anthony Benatar, aka Tony Dicenta begin to find himself, his true self. It took time and an adjustment to return to his identity as a father, a husband, and a cop, and the raw power and roar of the Harley Davidson didn't help in this regard. He'd just witnessed a brutal murder, and he'd been in no position to stop it. Instead, he'd even had to pretended to be a part of it, fearful his part in the stabbing death of Keith Kiley was on film now. He had to convince himself that he'd not truly been a part of the killing. After all, he'd come in late, stabbing the body long after Kiley was dead. "Had to make it look good," he told the desert around him. It had been the hardest thing he'd thus far witnessed as a member of the gang he'd infiltrated.

The Elders were a relatively new spinoff from Hell's Angels, actually in their infancy, and the only reason Red Beard Carl Buford was allowed to run his own little operation was his being a blood relative of the main guy at the top of the food chain. And everybody knew this. Those in Red Beard's camp and every member of Hell's Angels knew he was connected and couldn't be screwed with.

This fact was also quite well known by the Gang Division of the LAPD. There was the belief that if they could nail Carl on serious charges, that they could get him to rat out captains, lieutenants, even his cousin on the throne. As far as Tony knew, no one had fingered the Elders for the Unborn Child Killings, snuff films, or anything to do with what'd been going on in Chicago. This new ripple had only come to light when Kiley had logged into the gang's website—the brainchild of one Tony Dicenta as a way of sending coded information back to HQ without anyone's knowing. Anyone in the gang, that is. LAPD Gang Enforcement was on top of it.

He'd left a cryptic message regarding RB's plans for Kiley, but he'd thought it'd be an interrogation, not a murderous rage filmed in the desert. Tony's contacts at HQ hadn't reacted fast enough, and they had no idea where, in the vast desert areas that surrounded LA, the club would descend to torture information out of the fugitive from Chicago.

By the time Tony Dicenta arrived in LA, he was back to being Anthony Benatar, and he found his way to his real home, his wife, his child. After hugs all around, and after stripping off his biker clothes, showering but not shaving, after arranging for his daughter to go on a visit to the zoo with friends of the family, after making love to his wife, and after changing into casual clothes, he was prepared to go into headquarters to bring the team monitoring his field work up to date.

He had every belief that he'd be arrested if he told the entire truth. He knew he'd have to hold back somewhat if he wished to see his family again.

Then something troubling crossed his mind. What if someone on the team, monitoring the Elders, what if it had been a team member and HQ who had implicated them in the snuff film business? What if they'd set the Elders up for such charges in order to drag them in on trumped up charges to get at Syd Dupree, the top man at the LA Hell's Angels?

Would they be that crude? Were the Unborn Child Killings all staged for such a purpose? Had the online Elders site been used to create a contest of violence that extended all the way to Chicago? It was one of those thoughts that most men would quickly discard as absolutely fantastic and unbelievable, and easily denied, but Anthony had been living in a world of viciousness now for over a year, and he knew how frustrated and deeply angry his team at HQ had become. While it felt impossible, it did not feel altogether implausible either.

When he entered the police precinct out of which Gang Enforcement operated, Anthony was immediately met by members of the team, familiar faces—Joe, Jack, June, Matt, and the boss, Captain Nicholas Abel, but he also saw three unfamiliar faces—two with LAPD badges, one with a Chicago gold shield. As usual, he got a parade of pats on the back and kind words, "Great job you're doing, Tony. Keep up the good work. Something new to report?"

"You guys are as useless as the FBI," Tony joked as he always did. "What do you do here all day?"

Captain Abel quickly introduced Detectives Kilborn and Stiles, and Stephens from Chicago, explaining who they were trying to run down, and wondering if there were any gangs in LA who'd harbor a multiple murderer.

"Depends if they like the guy," said Tony, unsure how much now to share with the strangers present.

"Anything on the street about this guy, Tony?" pressed Abel, showing him a photo of Kiley and a BOLO order out for the man.

"Who's in charge of getting my messages through the Elder's website?" asked Tony. "I sent word we were picking this guy up hours ago."

"Shit, no!" said Abel, looking around at his people. "Who's dropped the ball?"

June Danner stepped forward. "It's my fault. We were hacked, and I was only able to get it back and running fifteen minutes ago. I saw the coded message, took it down, and we were hashing it over when Tony showed up."

"It's been down for hours then," said Tony.

"All we want to know," said Stephens, "is where Kiley is now, and who's running this Elder club?"

"The website, I'm running...or at least, I thought I had the controls."

June and Tony took Stephens and the other detectives not in Gang Enforcement into a secure room where the website was displayed on a screen for them. "This looks pretty tame for a biker website, selling shades, boots, hats, and shit," said Stephens.

"That's just the front," said June.

Tony added, "The real sales and money is in prostitution, drugs, racketeering, you name it."

"Behind a firewall that Tony set up for Red Beard."

"Red Beard?" asked Stephens.

"Carl Buford, the head honcho in this region."

"So where in all this is the snuff film contests that're going on? The Murder, Inc. part?"

"There's nothing like that on the site," said Tony. June agreeed.

"Are you sure?"

"I set it up, all of it, the legit stuff and the illegit stuff. I'd know if there was something like that going on, on my own site."

"Are you sure?" pressed Stephens who felt so close to a breakthrough and wanted no more frustration.

"I am sure, unless..."

"Unless what?"

"It's too crazy," said Tony.

"What the devil are you thinking, Tony?" asked Captain Abel. "Spit it out."

"Sir, the only way this site could have been modified to create an invisible chat room is if someone inside...inside here was involved."

"That's rubbish, absolutely preposterous," said June. "No one here has corrupted this system, sir."

"Then who?" asked Tony. "Tell me who?"

"Tell me all you know about Kiley's whereabouts now, Detective Benatar," said Stephens, "and while at it, tell me about this Red Beard guy."

"The whole team needs to hear your debriefing, Tony. Boardroom, now, everyone. You three, come along," Abel instructed Stephens and his two LAPD nurse maids.

Once everyone associated with what they were calling the Red Beard Operation were assembled, Captain Abel told Tony to bring them all up to date and to tell them the whereabouts of one Keith Kiley, aka KKboy.

"Kiley is dead, thanks to what, a hacker someplace whose infiltrated our system? I did all I could but Red Beard was determined to pull him off the street, and I thought it'd be a questioning session, an interrogation, maybe some torture involved until Carl got the information he *and* I wanted from Kiley, but Carl went nuts. He was on meth as usual, but he was also flexing his power for the girls in the gang, so far as I could tell. I pleaded with him to let me do the interrogation, throw a scare into Kiley, and get what we wanted, and then just leave him out there in the desert."

"They took him out to the desert?"

"To a g'damn rock, a stone slab, and it was caked, believe me, *caked* with blood. Carl wanted it to go down exactly as it did. I think he was testing me again to see what my reaction would be."

Tony dropped his gaze, shook his head, studied the tabletop.

"Go on, Tony. What happened next?"

"He wasn't interested in what Kiley knew; he just wanted to sacrifice him to his power over the others. Hell...it was like Charlie Manson all over again. He gave a little signal and all of a sudden a couple of the girls began filming while other gang members began stabbing Kiley, and I mean stabbing him everywhere."

"And where were you during the stabbing?" asked Abel in a stern voice.

"I only stabbed a corpse, captain. He was long gone by time I pulled my knife."

"But you participated and it's on film somewhere?"

"I was careful to keep my face out of it, and like I said, he was dead as the stone he was strapped to when I played my part."

"What'd they do with Kiley's remains?" asked Stephens.

"To be fed to the coyotes by order of Red Beard."

"We need to recover the body," said Abel, nodding at Stephens. "Can you take us to this table rock area you're talking about?"

"Sure, just came from there as Dicenta. And Captain, I was pretty sure Red Beard was going to strap me on that slab next."

"If we bring in the girls doing the filming," said June, "do you think they'd fold and give up Red Beard?"

"For murder? Not sure, but then who knows if we strike a spark of fear or decency in one of them. Get hold of that film."

"In the meantime, no one goes near the Elders website that Tony set up, no one."

"What's that all about, captain?" asked Jack Doyle.

"Just do like I say. Tony's the gatekeeper for that site. If someone's hacking into it and changing data and information, I want to know that it's not from inside *here*."

"Sowing a lot of distrust, aren't we, captain?" replied Doyle.

"Just do it. Put a lock on it from this end."

"Yes, sir."

"Okay, everyone load up, everyone with vests, and Tony, you're with me. Detective Stephens, you, too, in my car."

"You expect the bikers to still be there?" asked Stephens.

"Can't be sure. Want to be on the safe side."

13

"Where do we begin?" asked Sybil of Rachel.

"We begin at the beginning," the reporter replied. "With the Unborn Killer's first victim."

"Easy to say, hard to do since she's dead," Jude said, sipping at her drink through a straw. The ladies had eaten on the run, snatching a bite at a fast-food joint in the rough-looking neighborhood where a woman named Leeanne Bozeman had lived, had become pregnant, and who'd become the first known victim of the Unborn Child Killer. Somehow her movements had crossed with that of a serial killer, and Rachel believed if they could determine where those two lives crossed that the juncture would or could point like a compass to the killer.

"We don't have videos like we did in Chicago with Kiley and Goodwin. All we have are the results of these horrendous murders," Rachel ruminated. "So we have to go by the crime scene reports alone. It's how I got her last known address."

"Says she lived with her mother," added Sybil.

"Down on her luck, I'm sure."

They located the flat where, on the main floor, Mrs. Fiona Bozeman lived. They explained to the small, demure, sad-looking white-haired mother who they were and that they were working diligently to find her daughter's killer and the man who'd taken the life of her unborn grandchild.

"Sydney, she was calling the baby. She said it would work for a boy or a girl, didn't matter."

"She could easily learn the sex of the child at any clinic," said Jude.

"Oh, she wasn't in no position to get any prenatal care. She was out of work, had that bad spinal disc problem from the accident. I pleaded with her to stop riding that damn motorcycle, but she didn't. Not until the accident. Almost killed her. Still getting hospital bills. Bastards won't believe she's dead and buried along with the baby."

"Hold on. She rode a motorcycle?"

"Said it was tons cheaper than a car, but I knew it was not good."

"Was she, you know, involved in any biker clubs?"

"You mean gangs, don't you, officer?" she replied, taking Rachel for a police woman in plain clothes, despite Rachel's having been honest with her. "Oh, don't look so surprised, you three. I know cops when I see them."

The trio let this go. Jude asked, "Did she belong to a group called the Elders?"

The mother gave this a moment's thought. "No, no...said it was the Angels. Said angels can't be bad, mom."

"Hell's Angels," Rachel said in Sybil's ear.

"Did she have a boyfriend in this Angels' club?" asked Jude.

"You think her boyfriend killed her?"

"No, ma'am, we're just here to get background information, talk to anyone who knew her, go over the ground, so to speak."

"Oh yes, of course, like CSI on television—you have to know her every movement for the twenty-four hours leading up to her death."

Rachel nodded at this. "Exactly."

"Do you know her boyfriend's name?" Sybil pressed the point.

"She talked about Tony a lot, but then she talked about Danny, too, and Tommy, and a slew of girlfriends. Let me see, one in particular she took a shine to, that'd be Sydney, like the baby. She said she'd named the baby after the father, and we argued. I feel awful about that."

"You argued?"

"I told her if the man was not decent enough to marry her, and her with child on the way, that the man was not worthy enough to have his name on the birth certificate. I watch a lot of daytime TV, too, and I know how things get so bad between men and women when a child comes into the picture if the man don't want no child."

The ladies left Mrs. Bozeman's flat wondering if the Unborn Killer was a guy named Sydney who covered his murder of a pregnant girlfriend by creating a serial killer personae. "I say we ask around the neighborhood," suggested Rachel. "See if we can uncover anyone who knew her other than her mother to corroborate the stories the old girl had to tell."

"Good idea," agreed Sybil.

"If we can get enough on this creep Sydney—"

"Then we might have something to take to the LAPD to look into," Jude finished for Rachel. "Maybe get an arrest."

"An arrest leading to an interrogation leading to a confession?" asked Sybil.

"That's pretty wishful thinking, Sybil." Jude looked up and down the street. "Whose windows look out on the driveway here. Right, left, across the street."

"I'll take the neighbors to the left," said Sybil.

Rachel quickly said, "Jude, you take the right; I'll cross to the other side."

Jude saw that there was someone at the curtains across the street watching them. "Good luck, Rachel," Jude said, and the three ladies split for their separate destinations.

It was not a half hour later when the threesome reunited on the semi-rural street beneath a stand of trees. A light rain had begun, and the drizzle seemed to reflect the mood. None of them had anything substantial to add to Mother Bozeman's account. It really amounted to the neighbors repeating what the dead woman's mother had said about her daughter and her 'invisible' boyfriend.

They were getting drenched now and discouraged as well, when suddenly two bikers came barreling down the street, gunning their motors, and heading straight into the ladies. Jude shouted, "They're coming right at us! Jump the fence!"

A chain link fence offered them their only protection, and all three climbed over it, having to ignore cuts and scrapes to avoid the bikes that didn't slow down. From some neighbor's lawn, Rachel, Sybil, and

Jude squatted with their wet bottoms as soggy as could be, watching the threatening bikers career around the corner. Jude and Sybil had pulled their weapons but it was too late and useless now. All around them, people stared from windows, but no one dared step outside to help.

"Somebody called those creeps," said Jude, angry and annoyed as the raindrops increased in size and intensity.

"Let's get out of here," suggested Rachel. "You okay, Sybil?"

Sybil was nursing a cut to her forearm, while Jude realized her own gun hand was bloody and her knee was burning in pain.

"Over here," said Sybil, swinging open a nearby gate.

To get in out of the increasing rain, they located a coffee shop a few blocks away. Over lattes, they talked.

"You think Leeanne got herself killed because she was attracted to bad boys?" asked Rachel.

"You seem to be building a pretty good profile of the victim," said Jude. "I suspect she was attracted to that lifestyle, the gang lifestyle. A lot of women are."

"When you've got nothing else to hang onto, maybe," said Rachel, who had a faraway look in her eye now.

"What're you thinking, Rach?" asked Sybil.

"I fell for a bad boy once, same as Jude—and it turned sour fast."

"How bad did it get?"

"Bastard made a slave of me. As bad as it gets. I turned over every decision, every thought had to be cleared through him. I lost myself. Lost all power to even breathe."

"How did you get out of the relationship?" asked Jude.

"Damn whole thing began as sexual mischief, going against my family's values. I wanted to rebel and as a rebel I fell into this constant self-pleasuring lifestyle. Drunk all the time, getting high on whatever was at hand, and debasing myself for what?"

"Then it turned ugly?"

"Quick as a snake turns to bite you, yeah. Just as quick, I found myself helplessly caught up, psychologically hog tied, like—like as if I was his animal, his property, and there was nothing I could do to end it."

"Sounds awful," replied Jude.

"You bet it was. I never thought myself capable of thoughts direct-ed at another person, thoughts of hopefulness that he'd crash and burn to death, thoughts that someone would put a bullet in his head, and when nothing of the sort happened, I began thinking of how I could do it and get away with it."

"Jesus, Rach, you never told me about this." Sybil placed an arm over Rachel's shoulder and pulled her close.

"So did you ever act on those impulses?" asked Jude.

"If I gave those thoughts a moment or two, I'd dismiss them, but you know those death wishes for him were the only thoughts that fi-nally brought me around to my senses. Told me that this is not the kind of person I am or ever was. So the dark thoughts actually woke me the hell up."

"Being attracted to bad boys is one thing," said Jude, "but being attracted to pure evil as some sort of idea of pleasure and enjoyment... well, there is a pleasure too far."

"I'm just glad you found your way out, sweetheart," Sybil said to Rachel, kissing her on the cheek.

"What do any of us know," began Jude, "that is about...well, what constitutes pleasureful enjoyment and how easily we can, you know, find ourselves easing into that which...which makes us happy."

"And how often we confuse acceptance with happiness," replied Rachel. For Jude, she flashed a look that said 'thanks for understand-ing.' Jude got the distinct impression that Rachel felt that Jude under-stood more than did Sybil in this case. Then Jude wondered if Rachel might some day break Sybil's heart.

"Well...drink up, ladies," Rachel said. "We have a lot more shoe leather to burn up before nightfall."

Jude had gotten on her iPhone and had called Wayne, bringing him up to date on their movements and limited findings. Stephens half-jokingly replied, "You ladies are doing better than the menfolk. I'll see you later. Maybe for dinner."

Jude switched off with a half-smile. Rachel said, "You like him lots, don't you? Stephens."

"How could you possibly tell?"

Sybil added, "How could we possibly not? We're all for you two. Don't let him get away."

"I'm going to do my part so long as he does his."

"And if he fails you?" asked Rachel.

"I've got that covered."

Rachel smiled and shook her head. "No you don't."

"Whatever do you mean by that?" Jude lifted her glass and sipped.

"We always think we have an escape plan should something catastrophic happen, like a death in the family...a divorce...or a break-up, but there's really no way to prepare for such emotionally charged blows. Tell me that's not true."

"Are you sure you didn't kill that creep who turned you into his slave?" asked Sybil of Rachel, releasing an abrupt laugh. "And would you please not kill me?"

Jude suddenly realized that Sybil wasn't getting the message. Deeply wounded, perhaps since childhood, Rachel needed far more help than Sybil's unrelenting love could provide, and Sybil's own dependence on the unconditional love she expected from her lover was instead driving Rachel away. Inside such a delicate mine field of emotions, even the most Earth-shaking intimacy could not make up for all that was missing. Their relationship, Jude silently judged, was doomed, and while Rachel knew it, poor Sybil, for all her intellect and expertise in the medical world, was blind to this fact.

"Be right back," Jude lied, anxious to step away from the lovers. As she went for the ladies' room, she heard Sybil again laughing, blithely unaware that Rachel hadn't been talking about Jude and Stephens but Sybil and herself.

◆   ◆   ◆

Stephens stared out at the vast expanse of the southwestern desert stretching out before them for as far as the eye could see, an ocean bottom baking in the sun. Cactus plants waved at the police cruisers as they whizzed by at speeds of over a hundred miles per hour. It seemed like Abel's driver and those following behind were bent on breaking land speed records, or at least that was how it felt to a Chicago cop used to crowded streets.

"It all looks the same," said Stephens. "How could anyone find a specific rock in a place like this?"

"I'll get us there," Tony assured him.

"In this lunar landscape?"

"In this landscape, yes. Lived here all my life. When I was a teen, we'd come out to the desert to do the nasty."

Abel said, "Nasty is relative, now isn't it?"

Tony fell silent. "If I coulda done something, you know...you know I tried."

"I know; you'd have blown your cover if you had overdone being human with these people."

"That's about it, yes."

"Here, run off road to your left, Campbell, where the cluster of cacti are. The bikers call it the council tree. Beyond that, you'll go toward those rocks."

"Don't see anyone out here," said Stephens, sitting alongside Abel in the rear. Tony rode shotgun in order to direct the driver.

"Come up to a stop here."

The men exited the front car as the three other cruisers came to a halt behind and around them. "There're signs all over here of bike tracks," Abel said. "Appears they're long gone."

"Quite the observation, captain," said Jack Doyle who'd come alongside them. His remark got a frown from Abel.

"Point the way," Abel told Tony.

"Gotta go through this little pass ahead, too narrow even for a bike unless you jump your Harley. One fool took his muffler off doing it."

"How many times have you been here, Benatar?" asked Abel.

"This last time makes twice."

"Twice in a year?"

"It's only used to kill *unwanteds*, and to throw a scare into new members like me. First time, I was tied to the slab and given a water boarding, but I passed muster."

"Damn...little wonder you were concerned for yourself," said Abel as he now stared down at the rock Tony called the slab. It was covered in blood; small rivers of it discolored the rock like so many tentacles. "Kiley's blood's on top. I think we need to get some forensic types out here, take some scrapings and photos."

"I've already called a couple of ladies who can handle it for you, Captain Abel. They've come all the way from Chicago to find Kiley."

"Tony," began Abel, "where's the body you said would be here?"

Tony shrugged and looked around but saw nothing.

"Spread out," ordered Abel. "See what you can find and call out if you, *ahhh,* stumble on something."

Wayne, Max, and Joe went in one direction, while Tony, Abel, Doyle, and the others spread out in another direction. The desert floor was alive with scurrying creatures, and Stephens confessed to having a dread of snakes. Max said, "Snakes, most of 'em anyway, are smart enough to get out of your way, but now a Gila Monster, he'd come right at you, so take that into consideration."

Joe laughed at Max's remarks. "See anything?"

"Sun's going down. Hardest time of day to see shit."

They came on a rise, and the slope had been so gradual that Stephens hadn't a clue they were standing on high ground until he realized they were looking down over a desert meadow with grass and a small ravine, and in the near distance movement. A flash of movement, a sight of a human leg, and arm, dragging along. "Could Kiley be alive? Dragging himself off?"

"No, no! He's being dragged all right," said Max.

Joe Kilborn sadly said, "I see three, maybe four, Max."

Without warning, the two of them began firing their weapons at the body. Instantly covering his ears, Wayne saw the four coyotes loping off with various torn parts of flesh, disappearing beyond the next rolling hill of sand and brush. Stephens realized that Max had asked him if he'd like to get in on the 'turkey shoot' but it was already too late for that.

"Don't ever get much chance to fire our weapons except at the range," said Joe Kilborn.

Captain Abel had reacted by shouting for all the others to follow as he raced for the location of the gunfire. When he stood beside Stephens, he saw the body at the ravine. "Wonder how they got the body all that way without a sign of being dragged, no damn blood trail, nothing," said Wayne to the others, who just looked at one another and shrugged.

Abel explained, "Look behind you, Detective Stephens, and ask where's your footprints?"

Stephens turned and studied the ground behind him. He saw the faint outline of Captain Abel's prints where he'd rushed to them, but his own prints had disappeared. "Holy shit."

"It's not even that windy today," said Max.

Abel added, "The desert covers its own tracks, you might say; covers itself over and over every moment. No two moments alike out here."

"How do people, you know, like the Natives around here track animals?"

"Those who are good at it, and they are rare, never say it's easy, but I hear a desert rain helps."

"We'll guard the body until your forensics people get here," said Stephens, loosening his tie, the sweat now plastering his white shirt against his expansive chest.

"You mean you will guard the body," said Max. "I'm going back to the cruiser and the AC."

"I'll hang with you, Wayne," said Joe. "Wouldn't want the coyotes to get you." Kilborn smiled his most charming one.

Stephens smiled back. "Guess KKboy ended up like he lived."

The pair of detectives shared Joe's last two pieces of spearmint gum, plopped down on a pair of handy rocks, and watched over the mutilated body with countless stab wounds, all encased now with sand. "Nothing of Kiley would be left if Tony hadn't led us here."

"If he hadn't been here; if he hadn't been working undercover."

"Well...I mean there'd've been a scattering of bones, but look out there. Those coyotes would have eventually scattered his bones to the far winds, and the desert would've eaten 'em up like it did our footprints."

"Kinda has a man wondering about just how important his life is," Stephens said, "to the larger scheme of things."

"Hold on, not going there, Chicago. How about we instead check our phone messages?" With that Joe snatched out his iPhone and found that he could get no reception here. "Damn, we're in a dead zone."

"Luckily, I called Dr. Shanley and Dr. Avery before we got this far out. So...what do you want to talk about, Joe"

"Look at them desert critters there. Pernicious and tenacious, they are." He whipped out his gun again and fired. Two of the coyotes had crept back like a scouting party to test the waters, to see if they could get another bite of the corpse.

"Kiley sure came a long way to die."

"At least he got a chance to see the beauty surrounding us here, eh?" joked Kilborn, who began stripping down. First his coat and tie, and next he unbuttoned his shirt down to his navel. "Damn hot. How long before you think our replacements might show?"

"They're on their way, I'm sure, but they'd have had to get a police escort or some van from Dr. Hunsucker's department."

"A while then, you say?"

"Yeah, a little while.

Joe stripped away his shirt. "Pants are going next. May's well get a tan while we're here."

◆　◆　◆

Kiley's body, Sybil agreed with Jude, was the most riddled with stab wounds that either had seen in their careers. Every area of the body was pierced. He died from blood loss due to each painful jab. Death of a thousand cuts, Jude thought as they did what they could in the way of forensics at the ravine where the body lay. A small, shimmering rivulet of water shone in the moonlight where it rippled over shiny stones.

"I thought there was no water in a desert," Jude said to Captain Abel who'd remained behind after excusing his people. Stephens and Abel's driver, Campbell were the only others present now, and they worked under difficult circumstances in the starlit desert, the three men holding army issue flashlights over the evidence gathering duo.

"It's a definite ID," Jude said now. "There's a birth mark on the back of the ear we used, and it's his face below the beard."

They'd turned the body, and the eyes were agape, staring into the infinity of the desert sky and stars overhead. A van had been sent out from Hunsucker's to cart the body back to LA. Sybil looked up at the men, the flashlights blinding her. "Okay, you can tell Hunsucker's men it's time."

"And turn off those damn lights," added Jude. "Just about blinded me."

The desert night had brought on a strong wind coming out of the south, and while it felt playful and springlike, something about how the breeze jostled around Jude and Sybil as they worked, crouched over the corpse, had been irritating and annoying. "A poltergeist lives in that wind," Jude said to Sybil just as it sent a tumbleweed slapping into them, frightening a squeal from both of them.

That same night wind had created strange, scurrying noises all around them until Sybil said, "It's just the wind moving the sand is all."

Then Jude pointed her scalpel at how the wind was moving the sand into Kiley's bloodied wounds. A nearby cactus plant even began to groan, causing Jude to stare up at the plant only to see a live bat crawl from its interior to take flight.

When Sybil suggested they get out of here, Jude needed no second telling. She replied, "We can do a lot more good in a lab than out in a desert. Nothing more here's going to help us in the least."

On their way back toward the cruisers, Hunsucker's men, the *haulers*, passed them, going for the body with a black bag in hand. When a gunshot went off, followed by a second in rapid succession, the ladies jumped in unison, turned and saw that Stephens had fired off his weapon into the darkness on the other side of the body. Wayne shouted for all to hear, "Damn coyotes are back. They want their catch."

Sybil and Jude had seen the rents and tears from animal teeth—absolutely distinctive from the neat, piercing knife wounds, many of which had left dark hilt mark abrasions on the skin. Back at the cruiser that had brought them here, the ladies leaned against the hood.

"They ought to seal this place off," said Sybil.

"Stop these *jerkoffs* from using it as a killing ground," agreed Jude.

"From the look of that tabletop slab, the bikers use it for their sacrifices, damn straight."

"It's been in use for a damn long time," Jude stated the obvious.

Sybil had taken several layers of blood scrapings from the sacrificial stone. Jude had carefully labeled each scrapping by number to indicate layer one, layer two, and so on. "Likely used by Hell's Angels before the Elders."

"No doubt. Still we're in the dark as to who the Unborn Child Killer is."

"Yeah, and we're running out of time here."

Sybil nodded. "Dean hears that Kiley's dead, he's going to order us right back home."

"Imagine you're right about that, but we haven't uncovered the people behind the snuff films and the killings yet, now have we?"

"I was so sure Kiley was leading us to them, weren't you?"

"Exactly, yes...but now, looks like all is lost."

Shanley and Avery were not wrong about Dean calling them back to Chicago 'immediately' as he put it on learning that their Chicago killer was found murdered in a ritualistic mutilation killing in the desert. "Your backlog of work is waiting for the two of you," he added. "I want you on the next plane out of LAX."

Sybil tried to reason with him, listing all the rationale she had for at least one of them remaining behind, campaigning for the job. "At least let me stay behind while Jude returns. She can get started on that backlog of cases awaiting us."

On a separate call, Jude said the same of Sybil. "While I finish up here," she'd added for Grant. "Dr. Hunsucker sends his regards, by the way. Says really nice things about you, Dr. Grant."

"Hunsucker, eh? You two are getting along then?"

"Wonderfully, yes."

"Has he offered you a job?"

"Well...no, nothing like that."

"Well something like that is waiting for you here!" He hung up before she could find another word of argument to hurl at him.

He clearly wanted them both back now.

That's when Lionel and Ralph called on a conference with Sybil and Jude. "Lionel's found the true address belonging to the IP address where the Elders contest of snuff films is originating."

"You're kidding? What have you got?"

"It's a location in a residential section of Brentwood."

"Do you have a precise address?" asked Jude.

"We do, yes," said Lionel.

"Well?" replied Shanley. "Lay it on us."

"Only if you two promise not to go storming in there like Thelma and Louise," said Ralph.

"Ralph, we're not nuts. We've got the LAPD eating out of our hands, and we've got Stephens with us still."

"All right, but promise us."

"Promise, we promise."

"Both of you, one at a time."

They did as Ralph and Lionel wished.

"1124 Derringer Drive, Brentwood."

"Excellent. This is so helpful, guys!" said Jude.

"Thanks a million. Calling for backup now. Thanks guys!"

"Shall we call Uber?" asked Sybil, once off the phone with Chicago.

"No, we call Stephens. We don't take any more chances with our lives than is necessary."

"Stephens will call the LAPD guys, and we'll be marginalized."

"Marginalized in these circumstances sounds good to me."

"It's our case to crack."

"Nothing's cracked but you if you think we're going to go snooping around this address all on our own. These are vicious killers we're talking about."

"You're right, of course."

"Besides, Max and Joe have earned the right to be in on the raid."

"Raid. *Hmmm*...sounds like a lot more fun than going back to the lab in Chicago right now."

Jude called Wayne and informed him of what they had. An excited Stephens then called Max and Joe. "Can you get a search warrant, gentlemen?"

At the other end, the LAPD detectives said they were familiar with the address and that it was notorious, and that getting a warrant might be difficult as they'd raided it only a few months before.

"Looking for what?"

"Guns, ammo stashes. It belongs to the Hell's Angels."

"Are you shitting me, Max?"

"No, it belongs to the them."

"Damn...that doesn't compute if you know what I mean."

"We didn't go in looking for tapes or any connection at that time with the Unborn killer. We were just in for unregistered and illegal weapons caches."

"And you found what?"

"Nothing. They'd been tipped off, we believe. Hell some think it was Tony Benatar who tipped them off as part of his way of, you know, getting in deep with them. Anyhow about the same time, Red Beard as they call him, took Tony under his wing."

"Well, let's not share this with Gang Enforcement just now, shall we? Sounds like they have some holes and leaks over there."

"What about Captain Abel?"

"No one. Trust no one. We raid for films, videos, computers, we might just get lucky."

"All right, it's our play, but if we come up short, we're all going to catch hell."

Jude slapped up loose leaf lined paper onto the motel wall and began drawing lines between and among names of people, places, and things as well as events. In essence, she began creating an outline of their twisting, churning case. After drawing the lines, calling them connective tissue in her exercise at brainstorming, she stepped back to stare at her work.

Some of the papers stuck to the wall with Scotch tape had furled and were threatening to fall away but they held. Sybil now stared at the names and the connecting lines. They began with Goodwin and Kiley to a straight line like a laser beam to the LA Elders with a large red question mark. Then a line to the LA biker group—to Hell's Angel's—Red Beard.

"So why does Red Beard, the LA bikers known as the Elders kill Kiley?" Jude asked Sybil.

"I have no idea; I couldn't tell you, except that maybe, perhaps..."

"Spit it out. I want to hear it from a source other than my own head."

Rachel had been preparing drinks for the three of them from the booze she'd found in Jude's minibar. She came closer now, handing out drinks while staring at the 'map' on the wall. "What do we know about biker gangs?" she asked and answered with, "They abhor bad publicity, while operating like the Mafia, right? They have generals, majors, lieu-tenants, captains, like that."

"Like the military, yes." Sybil downed a third of her Vodka.

Rachel hummed as the wheels in her head began to turn. "Sup-pose...just suppose."

"Suppose what?" asked Jude.

"According to my sources, Kiley was killed by this new guy on the block called Red Beard. Suppose someone involved with the Angels wanted to get Red Beard on the General's shit list? How better to do that than to bring down heat on the club?"

"Someone inside the Angels wanting to see the downfall of this Red Beard?" asked Jude, mulling the idea over. "So they set up this dummy website for the Elders, create a private chat group dealing with the snuff videos...and, and..."

"And why not?" finished Sybil. "As good a theory as anything I've heard so far."

"So Kiley brings his Chicago heat down on the Elders, Red Beard knowing shit about what's really going on right under his nose, with regard to the Unborn Child Killers or Kiley and Goodwin, retaliates against Kiley without ever getting to the truth of the matter. How ironic."

"Sounds like Congress, doesn't it?" joked Jude.

"We have a workable theory here, ladies," said Rachel. "So do we take it to the men?"

"I think so, sure," said Jude. "They've worked hard on this case, too. And besides, we need them. We're not likely to be able to raid the Hell's Angels without a warrant, that's for sure."

◆　◆　◆

At police headquarters in LA, Jude reproduced her killer's 'map' or chain of events and persons of interests on a wall there. Everyone involved in the case, including now Tony Benatar, were nodding. It made sense to the men, and Tony added the name of the head man of the Angels, Syd Dupree, onto the 'map' of names, places, and events. "Red Beard is his nephew. He's the guy who put Carl in charge, gave him his own territory."

"So who is close to the headman and possibly jealous or enraged or both?" asked Stephens.

The final red line went straight to the top of the operation.

"Blood relative at the top," mused Max, nudging Joe. "How many times in our line of work is it a relative on one end of the gun?"

"Usually the shooter is known to the victim in one way or another," agreed Joe.

Benatar and others in the gang division immediately slapped up photos of Red Beard, Syd Dupree, and a mug shot of a young man said to be Syd's illegitimate son, a fellow named James 'Jimmy' Proust.

"Proust has been hanging around dear old dad since, hell, '89," said Benatar. "And he's got superb computer skills. That's what Dupree keeps him around for. No love lost there, according to Carl."

"So he could well be the brains behind the Elder's surprise contest that none of them seem to know a damn thing about," added Doyle.

"So long as it was masked—even from me," said Benatar, "it proved no threat to the Elders. But it sure brought down attention on them now."

"How did it get by you, Tony?" asked Doyle. "I thought you were an expert with this stuff?"

"Doyle, it's not all I was doing for the gang. I spent most of my time on a hog."

"So who is the Unborn Child Killer? Could it be Jimmy Proust?"

"The way it worked with Kiley and Goodwin," began Jude, "the site lured them in. The Unborn Child Killings are the most recent addition to the contest site.

"How can we be sure that Big Daddy, Uncle Syd, head of the real club, isn't directing all the killing and pinning it on his nephew?

"It wouldn't surprise me, and if not the uncle, someone else in the club who is angry that Red Beard got the territory handed over to him. Crazy Carl some call him," said Benatar, the cop in a position to know more about the inner workings of the gang than anyone else present.

"If we go back to basics," said Jude, twirling a red marker in her fingers, "people kill out of love and hate, for reasons of jealousy, money, greed, and revenge."

"Sounding more and more like the ignored son, Jimmy Proust," said Sybil.

"We tip our hand, raid the factory out of which Jimmy appears to be working and if we get lucky..." began Stephens. "It's a gamble."

Max quickly replied, "Gamble or not, we have to take action before another unborn child is killed."

"So our unknown suspect, be it the son, the nephew, the old man, or whomever, he starts this mad contest to see who can kill in the most outrageous ways, killing the most innocent people among us, the most vulnerable, and somehow Kiley and Goodwin stumbled on it when it was meant to be a local LA thing to bring heat down on the Elders, maybe put Red Beard away for life, maybe even get him killed in a gun battle—the real war this *unsub* wished to start."

"Not between the races but between lawmen and outlaws," added Stephens.

"So the Unborn Killer is a creation, same as the Chicago Nun and Vet Killer," said Rachel, who'd slipped past any gatekeepers. No one in the room had any idea how long the Chicago Tribune reporter had been in the room. "A filmmaker's creation come to life?" she rhetorically asked.

"Crazy, I know," replied Jude, as Sybil put an inviting arm around Rachel, "but it ultimately goes back to the person who put that murderous contest on the internet."

"Yeah but taking it all in," Max said, "I still vote for the family connection here."

Joe instantly agreed. "Max is right. Family is a sure bet."

"And with the sheer divide in this country, think about it," said Captain Abel.

"Yeah...with the upcoming elections," agreed Doyle.

Max said, "And how to spin it as an attempt to start the mythical race wars."

"Figures in just about right," Joe said. "Pit Hell's Angels against the LAPD and after the chaos, see how things shake out, who comes out on top, who's imprisoned, and who's dead."

Stephens nodded, rubbing his chin. "All has a kind of sick poetry about it, but then revenge always does, right?"

Joe smiled at this. "Like a damn picture puzzle coming into focus."

Max added, "More like an Agatha Christie ending."

Captain Abel put a damper on the discussion with a handful of words. "Right now, it's sheer speculation. Not a thing proven, gentlemen, ladies. We've got our work cut out for us, and I'd like to see it done without a war breaking out."

Captain Abel then gave them all jobs to do, speaking in rapid-fire succession. The Gangs Division would get the warrant to raid the target, the homicide detectives would secure all the findings and prepare for the raid. The forensics team would be on hand at the raid to secure anything of value in the way of scientific evidence. "Use that new DNA testing you people are talking about. Tell me who in that location is spending all his time on which computer."

"As for you, Ms. DuChampe," the captain said, glaring at the reporter. "You get the exclusive after the raid. Not a word goes out of this room, people—not a peep—until this raid is over. If the Angels learn of our plans, then we know we have a mole in this room, and if that occurs, I will leave no desk unturned to find you."

14

It took some time to get all the paperwork in place, and to get a SWAT team on board with the idea of raiding a Hell's Angels location, but by nightfall all was a go. Some bikers were leaving the location as the police arrived, setting up a perimeter a half block away. These bikers were taken into custody one by one, each shouting police brutality as he and the occasional she were put into patrol cars. A SWAT team negotiator had a chance to grill each for information about the interior, the layout, the purposes to which the warehouse was put. Next to no cooperation got the team little to no useful information. It soon became apparent that they'd be busting into a large, sprawling warehouse, with many areas to cover at once.

The LA SWAT team proved to be the best trained officers in law enforcement for this kind of work. Most had a military background, and it came as no surprise to Jude and the others from Chicago when simultaneously the front, back, and sides as well as the warehouse rooftop came under attack with perfectly coordinated timing. The helicopter used was a silent-running, state-of-the-art stealth Blackhawk. When it came over the warehouse, it did so with lights off, and men on board rappelled to the roof as men in other divisions moved in on all sides. Whoever and whatever was to be found inside, there was no escaping the SWAT members, who had the bikers surrounded and helplessly so. Every SWAT member had an AK-47 going in ahead of him or her.

This left Stephens and the LA detectives at ease, way behind the line of action, and Jude could see how much the detectives wanted to be a part of the initial attack, but orders were orders. Captain Abel was calling the shots here, and Abel had turned that chore completely over to the captain of the SWAT team. "This is a perfect operation for the experts," Abel had assured his men, Stephens, and the others. Still, Jude could see that Wayne, Max, and Joe in particular wanted to get inside now as quickly as possible.

The raid went down in smooth, militaristic fashion. The word *summarily* popped into Jude's mind as she watched the operation unfold like fate itself. Then shots were fired, a few bursts at first, followed by a fusillade of ear-piercing fire. The bursts of gunfire signaled that there'd been some resistance. No doubt there'd be casualties, perhaps on both sides.

Captain Abel gave the nod to his men when the gunfire had gone silent. "Let's get in there, see what we've got ourselves into, Max, Joe, Detective Stephens."

"We're coming in, too," Jude said for herself and Sybil who stood firmly at her side.

"You're going to want all the forensic help you can get in there," Sybil added.

"All right," Abel relented, "but you two stay well behind until we can be sure all the gun play is at an end."

They went through the front entrance. Inside, their first view was of some thirty or more bikes parked and awaiting their owners. To their left stood a sound stage for film-making, an encouraging sight. To their right, another sound stage.

"Looks like they're making movies, all right, just like we suspected," said Stephens in Jude's ear.

"They'll have a legit film business going to cover the snuff films," she replied.

Sybil added, "They'll also claim they did not make the snuff films we find here—that they were sent to them from outside sources."

"If we find them," said Rachel. "Besides, to these creeps, watching snuff films is a form of entertainment and their right, same as you and I enjoy a Dirty Harry film."

Stephens nodded. "They'll argue that all the way to the Supreme Court."

"They already have is what I'm telling you," Rachel said to Wayne. "They ruled on smut in their favor years ago."

"Killing and inciting others to kill is all we can charge these people with," said Max, his face a mask of anger.

Joe added, "So we need to locate the computer from which the master mind of the Elders' contest has been working."

"And determine whose fingerprint is on the entire enterprise," said Jude.

"Spread out," Captain Abel told his men. "Find every computer in the place, bag it and tag it as to precisely where in the warehouse it was found."

"There's an office at the opposite end of the facility, second floor," said Captain Dave Sands, SWAT. He led the way for Jude and Sybil with Rachel following. As they made their way, they saw bikers being led out, hands cuffed behind their backs. They saw actors as well, male and female. Someone was shouting, "We got every right to make porno flicks. It's in the Constitution!"

"Like to see where that's written," said Sybil.

"No doubt slipped in by Ben Franklin," replied Jude.

They then began seeing covered bodies, dead bikers, and a handful of wounded SWAT members. The sound of ambulances roaring into the open warehouse now was deafening. There would be a lot of sorting out, and already the LA press was outside pressing for answers.

In the office area, they found young Jimmy Proust, immediately identifying him from his photo at HQ. A burly SWAT member had him in custody and said, "Saw him coming up here. Think he was trying to destroy evidence, maybe drugs?"

"Screw you! I'm no druggie. I'm a film maker, a director, that's all."

"With bigger ambitions, eh, Jimmy?" asked Jude.

He glared at Jude and spat at her like a trapped creature. Proust was hunched over, and at first it appeared to be a defensive stance, but after he took another step back, it became obvious that he was something of a cripple with one leg mangled, likely from a biking accident, but the pronounced hunchback was something of nature's doing. "You got no right coming in here like this!"

"We have a warrant to search and a warrant for your arrest," replied Jude.

"And a warrant to kill bikers?"

"Your men put up a resistance and fired first," Jude assured Jimmy. She realized that she'd been staring at his deformity and thinking how handsome a face to be trapped in such an ugly body.

"Check the surveillance cameras. They don't lie. They came in shooting. You'll all pay for this!"

"Pay for what?" asked Sybil, who'd been looking about the office and was now at the man's computer.

"Raiding us! Wait till my dad hears about this."

"What if he hears about what you've been doing here, Jimmy? Implicating his nephew, Carl and his band of murdering rowdies?"

"A real family affair, the whole of it," added Jude while Proust squirmed in the darkest corner of his lair. "I'll sue the hell out of all of you all. Every damn one of you!"

"Is that before or after big daddy learns about your treachery, Jimmy?" asked Jude, smirking. "We know what you've been up to."

"You don't know shit, and you can't prove shit." Jimmy sneered.

"We know you're angry and vindictive," began Sybil, "and we know you have been doing your best to destroy Carl 'Red Beard' Buford."

"Make it look like his Elders were behind the Chicago murder videos," added Jude, "and the Unborn Child Killer videos here."

"We're going to find the evidence to put you away for the rest of your miserable life," Sybil assured him in an icy tone as she searched through the computer files.

"And your dad, Syd Dupree? He's going to applaud us for it," said Rachel, standing over Sybil at the computer. She flashed a grim smile for Proust.

"To help yourself now, Jimmy," finished Jude, "the best you can do is cooperate with us to locate the Unborn Child Killer."

"You can all go to hell!"

Captain Abel had entered the office and had stood silent, listening, as Jude now said, "He won the contest, didn't he, Jimmy? The Unborn Child Killer, and you and your studio here created him. Even your ugly-assed contest was a sham and a lie, as ugly as it was to begin with."

Captain Abel then said to Proust, "So you know who did the killings here. You know and you're going to share that with us, unless you want the death penalty applied to your case."

Jimmy hesitated a moment.

"He's a member of the Elders, isn't he?" Jude said in a flash of realization.

Proust remained silent and obstinate. "I want a lawyer."

"Sorry. Just went deaf," said Abel. "How about you ladies? You hear anything?"

"Not a thing."

"Nothing here."

"Nada," finished Rachel, urging Sybil out of the desk chair and climbing in the driver's seat at the computer.

"This thing's for the legit business only," Rachel concluded. "He's got the death contest computer stashed elsewhere."

"It's got to be somewhere in this building," said Jude. "It'd be too risky to take it anywhere else. Jimmy here controls this environment only. Have your men search for fake walls, hidden rooms from top to bottom."

Captain Abel had twisted the suspect around and had handcuffed him with flashing metal cuffs, and now Max, Joe, and Wayne Stephens arrived at the office. Abel gave them orders to take units of men and search the entire premises for hidden rooms and false walls. "We've got to find that computer."

The hunt was on. Harshly, they sat Proust down and asked, "What do you know about people disappearing in the desert, Jimmy? Maybe you can curry some favor with me, shave off some years in prison. No lawyer's going to help you with that."

Proust only spit and seethed more.

"Reminds me of an angry opossum, captain," said Sybil.

"Richard the Third, eh, Jimmy?" said Jude. "You got good cause to implicate Carl. With him gone, you doing a bang up job here at the factory, you figure King Syd will give you the attention and rewards you deserve, right?"

The armor in his act softened only slightly. She realized his hatred had been growing in cancerous fashion for a lifetime—his lifetime.

"After getting rid of Red Beard, you'd have gone on to destroy your father next. Visions of grandeur, visions of taking over control of the entire gang—as if..."

"As if, yes! Yes, as if a cripple like me could lead Hell's Angels. Crazy idea." His expression had turned to that of a hurt child, but he quickly wiped that away, replacing it with a sneer. "How simple you people are, and how stupid. Me with any ambition at all. Please! Bunch of disgusting liars trying to pin all this on me because of your bloody failure to catch a serial killer."

"Tell you what, Jimmy," replied Jude. "You're going to make some prison shrink in a federal facility for the criminally insane a wonderful guinea pig and a full-blown case study. Might even make the doctor's reputation. Hell, might even inspire a Clive Barker horror novel before it's over. You and Richard the Third having so much in common. A tragedy of the ill-born. A family destroyed by ugliness at the core. Think of it."

"You go to hell, lady! All of you, straight to hell."

"Rather an extensive vocabulary," replied Rachel. "I'm a storyteller, and I'll be the first to describe your part in all this horror. Are you sure you don't want to tell it to me from the beginning? I can make you famous." She flashed her Chicago Tribune press ID.

Jimmy sat stone-like, uncooperative, belligerent.

"We'll let him sit and think about it in lockup," said Captain Abel.

It took another hour and forty minutes to locate a secret room with a shoddy little desk and a Mac computer atop it. This was quickly brought to Captain Abel's attention, and he in turn escorted Rachel, Sybil, and Jude to the location. Rachel, who knew more about this story than anyone, began working on a code to get into the files. She attempted so many and failed that Captain Abel called for an end to it. "We have experts at HQ that we can take it to."

Rachel pleaded for one more try from a suggestion given her by Jude. "Try Syd and if that fails, King Syd."

On using King Sydney, the program files opened to Rachel. She quickly found one marked The Elders. This opened on the website in question, and she moved the cursor to a file marked Unborn Killer.

The file opened on a video that first depicted the murder of a young woman by a frightfully large presence that hung over her like a beast. Its anger had been unleashed on her as the killing could only be described as a slaughter. After multiple stabs, the woman succumbed.

The camera then moved in close on the bloodied stomach where a specific C-section-style cut was made and a child was removed by the overly large hands of the monster. The child could not have survived outside the womb for long; it was as yet unformed. It was so small as to fit into the palm of the monster's single right hand.

Then there was a distinct cutaway but quickly the film continued. This time with the knife coming down repeatedly into the unborn child. The brutality was too much for Rachel and even for the forensic team of Shanley and Avery. The police present were also unnerved by this shocking sight.

"Shut it down, Ms. DuChampe," ordered Abel. "Do it now! I've seen enough to last me a lifetime."

"Who's the guy with the big hands wielding the knife over the mother's stomach?" Stephens asked Abel. "Any ideas? Do we have him in custody with the sweep?"

"Not sure, but we're going to have a closer look at every man jailed tonight and those among the Elders."

"There's a lot of large men riding bikes," said Sybil. "Good luck with that."

"The camera never shows his face" Jude said. "Wonder why that is."

"You think that was purposeful?" asked Wayne.

She shrugged. "Who can tell with these heartless predators."

"All right, bag and tag this computer, Dr. Avery, Shanley. We'll get it logged in as exhibit A to put that prick Proust away for life."

"Death penalty off the table is it?"

"DA's working a deal to get information on his accomplice. It's out of our hands now, but this item will leverage things nicely for our side." Captain Abel took the bagged, tagged computer in hand and carried it out personally to his car. He meant to see it took not a single detour to lockup.

Processing the aftermath of the raid at the warehouse was a job for Hunsucker and his team, but as they concentrated on the results of the raid and those 'judiciously' killed in the firefight, Jude and Sybil concentrated their forensic skills on the film sets in the warehouse. Each set was meticulously searched for blood evidence in particular, and when one set was found to be a crime scene, they concentrated on it.

This took hours and in the end most of the next day. They were supposed to have been back in Chicago long ago, but there simply was too much here now with their combined teeth sunk deep into it. Processing the on-set murder scene took great care as it hadn't been recent. In fact, Jude surmised that it well could be the scene of the first Unborn Child Killing murders, mother and child. The victim of the first known case had been a woman and an unborn child known to Syd Dupree. In fact, when questioned about the first victim, Dupree reportedly broke down in tears during questioning, saying he had loved Leeanne and their unborn child.

"This gets more Richard the Third than ever," Sybil said on learning of victims one and two from the record. "Forensics shows that at least one of the Unborn Killings took place on a set in the warehouse," she told Stephens, who'd come looking for her.

"They've sweat it out of Jimmy in lockup," he told Jude and Sybil.

"Made a deal with the devil, did they?"

"It's imperative we get the actual killer behind bars, Jude."

"So the state will spare Jimmy's miserable life for info on the Unborn Killer."

"That's about it, yes, and as for us, the damn clock's running out. My captain wants me back, and Dr. Grant wants you two back ASAP."

"We've got unfinished business here in LA," Jude said through gritted teeth.

"To run down a madman, I know but..."

"A dupe of Jimmy's making, no doubt. Someone in his employ at the warehouse. Someone easily led."

"His biker name is Hoss, and his real name is Billy Hodges. Hoss Hodges."

"Then where is he?"

"No one's seen him since they killed Kiley out at that rock in the desert."

"I suppose he took part in Kiley's murder as well?"

"Actually, according to Tony, he held back and didn't take part in it at all."

"Really?" asked Sybil. "And Red Beard was okay with that?"

"Billy's got the IQ of a six-year-old, it appears."

"I don't get it. If he had trouble killing Kiley, why not mothers and unborn children?"

"The stories put in his head by Proust. How these mothers were evil, how they'd beat and torture the child if brought into this world."

"And this big idiot believed every word of it?"

"Apparently, if Jimmy said it, it was the gold standard."

"God...think of it. The man killing unborn children and their mothers, rips open stomachs and rips out the unborn child is hardly more than a child himself. But even a child, you'd think, would blanch at so much blood and guts."

"Well...for all we know, Jimmy's not telling the whole truth. He claims all he did was film. Sound familiar?"

"Yeah, very."

"Suppose Jimmy's the one who actually mutilated the infants after the big dummy killed the mothers to get at the child?" asked Jude. "I mean he could have concocted a story even for his accomplice."

"What sort of story?" asked Stephens, with Sybil hanging on for an answer to this as well.

"I don't know, a kind of Rumpelstiltskin tale...how he had a connection with a man who adopted out the babies to good mothers."

"If that sonofabitch Proust lied about all of this...if his testimony is false, all bets are off, and his deal goes South, and he knows this."

"Put it to him, just like Jude said, and see how much he flinches," Sybil suggested. "Tell him we found blood matching Leeanne Bozeman's in the warehouse studio—his first Unborn Child Murder victim, mother and child." Jude paced as she threw out these suggestions. "Also add that we have reviewed the murders, and that we've had expert analysis that proves the hand wielding the knife in the final cuts of the unborn child video murder belong to him.

Stephens had begun jotting down notes, trying to keep up. "We have expert analysis of that?" he asked

"No, but we will as soon as Sybil and I revisit the videos."

Sybil tried to imagine where a dupe of Jimmy's making might go to hide. A monster-sized six-year-old, a fellow so easily directed in a 'film' as to be turned into a real life monster. A phone call to Tony revealed the same name that Jimmy Proust had fingered. "Easily directed, easily turned into a Frankenstein monster and a cousin of Jimmy's," Tony finished, "and we think we know where he's hiding."

"Where would that be?"

"Uncle Syd's, of course."

"Whoa, that's going to mean another huge firefight," said Stephens on the conference call. "Unless Syd Dupree gives the man up."

"We're counting on that. Going to Syd's residence with SWAT backup, but we're going to try to reason with Dupree. Explain the whole sordid business with Jimmy at the center of it, and how Red Beard went off half-cocked and killed the wrong man over it. Killed Kiley thinking he was behind the set up of the Elders."

"Sounds then like you guys have it well in hand. You've got Red Beard and most of his gang in custody—except for that smart handful who took off for Texas. You have Proust and his crew, some of whom are bound to turn state's evidence against Jimmy. All you need is the Frankenstein monster now. Guess we Chicago folks're headed home."

"All but Rachel DuChampe. She has been promised the whole story, not just part of it." Tony hung up.

"What do you say, ladies? We write up our final notes and suggestions, turn it all over to Captain Abel, and take the next flight home. Get us there in time for tonight's Cubs' game."

"Sure...why not?" said Sybil. "Appears we're done here."

"I want to prove my theory about Proust's hands in the video. We'll need to take photographs of his hands and compare them to what we see in the video. Hopefully, we can find a number of distinguishing features."

"Well...once we get that chore accomplished," said Sybil, shrugging. "Guess the rest we can leave to the LAPD."

"Okay then," said Stephens. "I'll go ahead and arrange for a flight back via our pals at UPS."

"Do that, Wayne. And Sybil, I think you're right. I think we're done here."

15

It appeared the Chicago authorities were packing up, getting all their ducks in a row, pulling together all the threads but one. Where was the second Unborn Child Killer? He was the subject of an all-points bulletin, considered armed and dangerous, and on the run like a frightened animal. He knew of the warehouse bust. He wasn't there at the time, but the news spread like wildfire across LA and beyond as the news hounds were all over it.

Rachel was in her glory. She had all the inside information, the real scoop. She'd already flown back to Chicago to work on her Pulitzer-winning story, or so she hoped. She'd given short shrift to saying goodbye to any of them, including Sybil.

Everyone assumed it was only a matter of time that someone in custody or on the street, some member of the biker gang would give up Billy 'Hoss' Hodges and his whereabouts. It seemed a foregone conclusion, but when hours went by and still there was no clue as to Hodges' whereabouts, all manner of speculation began bubbling to the surface.

Max suggested to Wayne and Jude, now readying to board the waiting plane along with Sybil who had already boarded, that the big cheese in the gang likely had 'Hoss' Hodges boiled in acid. "We may never find that big boy," Joe finished for Max. The foursome shook hands, well-wishes all around, and the LAPD detectives marched off while Jude stood firm. Detective Stephens took her arm and gently guided her toward the idling plane, but Jude pulled away.

"What is it?" he asked.

"I have a hunch where Billy Hodges might be."

"What're you talking about?"

"The sacrifice rock out in the desert."

"Why would he go there?"

"Orders, conscience, who knows, but it's worth a shot."

"We've got to board now, Jude."

"You go. You and Sybil. I'm staying at least long enough to scratch this itch."

"I'm not leaving you here to go off on some wild-goose chase alone."

"I wasn't planning on going out there alone."

"Max and Joe?"

"Maybe we can catch them before they get too far."

Wayne waved off the pilot, who'd been frantically waving for them to board, alternately pointing to his watch and a clipboard from where he sat in the cockpit.

The plane began to move off like a giant-sized pachyderm, lumbering toward the runway. Jude gave a final wave to Sybil who's face became a mask of confusion, arms and hands raised at her window seat.

Wayne had phoned Max and Joe, and just outside the terminal at LAX, they awaited Jude and Wayne.

"What's this all about?" Joe asked while Max frowned, adding, "I thought we got shed of you two."

"It hit me where Billy could be hiding."

"We've determined he's in Texas," said Joe with a shake of his head. "Harbored by the bikers in the club there."

"That's what our expert, Tony, tells us," added Max, "and appears the Gangs Division is in agreement."

"There's only one way to be certain," said Jude, her green eyes making the appeal.

"You tell us your theory, Dr. Avery," said Joe.

"Everything we know about Billy Hodges points to some degree of remorse. If he really feels guilty about what he's done, and there appears a probability of that, he could well think he deserves to die, and what better biker way than the table rock out where we found Kiley's body?"

"Makes a certain amount of sense," Wayne said to the other two men.

"Twisted sense," said Max.

"Hell's bells and Hell's Angels," muttered Joe. "You think even a half-wit follower led by the nose, that he has to make some sense sometime?"

Max asked, "You mean feel some sense of guilt?"

"Maybe Dr. Avery's right, Max."

"Let's do it," said Max. "What's the worst that can happen? We have a nice ride out to the desert in this heat."

Sunrise temperatures in and around LA had begun at 92 degrees Fahrenheit, and they'd climbed to a sweltering 99 and rising now. The desert would be scorched by the time they might arrive at the table rock.

"It's been a long stretch of time between our taking Jimmy Proust into custody and this 'Hoss' guy's disappearance," said Max as he drove.

"What're you saying?" asked Jude from the rear seat.

Joe translated for Max. "He's saying that if big Hoss is out there anywhere, unless he's made friends with the Devil and the coyotes, his carcass will be in a semi-melted state by now. You know, given the temps we've been 'enjoying' as they say."

"Whatever condition we find him in, at least we will have wrapped up the final loose end," said Jude.

"Dr. Avery," replied Max, "with gangs like this, there is never a final loose end; there's always another and another and another."

"I was referring to this case, not the gang ascension."

"Fine, okay. We all want the same thing here."

Contentious to the end, Jude thought of Max Stiles. She imagined nothing would ever please this man. She wondered how Joe put up with him.

Wayne remained stubbornly at her side but silent, unsure of the wisdom of their having not gotten on the plane with Sybil. "My captain's going to have my ass," he said in Jude's ear.

"Dr. Grant's going to have mine, too."

"No way; that belongs to—"

"Don't finish that sentence," she warned him.

"You two need us to pull over at the next motel?" suggested Joe. "Max and me can check out the rock ourselves."

This remark had Jude pulling her hand out of Wayne's grasp. "No, thank you. We want in on this."

"You really think this goofball's out there alone doing what? Trying to cut his wrists?"

"Who knows? He may not be alone. Not if the gang has held court and made a ruling."

"We'll know soon enough, but in case the place is crawling with bikers, I'm calling for backup."

"Not a bad idea either," said Wayne.

"We're in sight of the turnoff, and I see no evidence of bikers coming or going," said Max, turning off road now for the stand of mounds and rocks that created a kind of Stonehenge meeting place for the bikers.

"Nobody here," said Wayne, somewhat relieved.

"But somebody's definitely been around here, detective," countered Max. "Multiple people—tracks in and out tell the tale. Recent, too."

"You think they were tipped off to our coming?" asked Jude.

"Can't be sure, but from the tracks, well the wind's as strong today as usual out here, and those tracks aren't covered, so...yeah, they beat a hasty retreat out ahead of us, heading South...likely Texas."

"You think someone tipped them off?" Wayne repeated Jude's question.

"Benatar, Tony," suggested Joe. "He's still working undercover. He was never compromised during the bust. Kept back to preserve his status with the club. If he tipped them off that we were on the way, King Syd Dupree would be impressed, and Tony could infiltrate even deeper than before."

"To fight another day, eh?" said Max.

The unmarked police car pulled into the circle used by the bikers, and indeed there were fresh prints everywhere along with beer cans, cigarette butts, candy wrappers, and Styrofoam cups. Along with the plastic and paper debris, there was also human debris left behind.

Billy Hodges was still tied to the slab, his enormous body bleeding from what appeared to be a thousand cuts. What the Elders had done to Kiley, Syd Dupree and his followers had done tenfold to the giant Billy, whose eyes slowly opened to reveal the depth of his pain. He blinked away blood streaming from his head, trying to see who the newcomers were.

Jude realized immediately that she could not save the man. The blood loss had already covered the stone slab he was tied to. His forehead and facial characteristics made him a throwback to the cavemen. The gang had subdued him with drugs and had stripped him bare of clothes. He could barely speak, but he was muttering something to Jude. She leaned in close, getting his blood on her blouse, to hear him speak, hoping he'd name his killers and who gave the kill order. Instead, the giant, who seemed as if he were twelve feet tall and built like the comic book Hulk, whispered, "Plea...cuvva me up."

Jude realized he was embarrassed to be seen nude like this by a woman. "Get a blanket from the unit," she called over her shoulder. Then she said to the bleeding young man who appeared no older than a high school kid, "Billy, we're going to get you help. You hold on. You're going to be all right now."

"Give us his name, Billy," pressed Wayne. "So we can punish him and his puppets."

"I—I did it. I—I asked 'em t' pun—punish me."

Joe threw a blanket over Billy at the moment of his death.

"Damn, damn, damn," Jude said, pushing up from the bloody rock, her hands red with it now. She accepted a handkerchief from Wayne and used it to alternately wipe away the blood and wipe away tears welling up and spilling over.

"Why're you shedding tears for this monster, Dr. Avery?" asked Max in an angry tone. "Even he said he got what was coming to him."

"Yeah, he did, didn't he, and the rest of us?" she asked, shaking her head. "Could we have done more?"

"What more could we've done, doc?" asked Joe.

"Well now, given what's happened, all we can do is forgive ourselves."

"Forgive ourselves? Bullshit. I got nothing to forgive," said an angry Max as he stomped the earth below his feet.

"Forgive our kind, mankind, Max," Jude finished and went back to the car to get away from the fetid smell of so much blood in the hot desert air. Wayne escorted her back. "If we'd only gotten here earlier," she began to beat up on herself. "Why did I get the notion if it was too late to do any good?"

"The gods love to screw with us, Jude. You know that," Wayne said. "But thanks to you, we've made a positive ID that the murder of the children from their mother's wombs, that those murders were done by Jimmy Proust, and his plea deal's been thrown out as a result of his lies and half-truths. He'll go to the gas chamber. No doubt about that, so we didn't need Billy's testimony."

"I didn't rush out here for testimony, Wayne. I came for *him*. I suspected what King Syd would do to Billy."

Wayne shook his head in confusion. "For him; you came for Billy?"

"To show him that at least one person on this planet gave a damn about him, and to understand, at least somewhat, how he could...how Billy could be talked into murdering the innocent by a devil like Proust."

"Well, you sure have a lot more forgiveness in you than I do, darling."

"Think of it, Wayne. This man, no matter what he looks like to you, he's a child in here!" she pointed to her head. "He was used like a tool to murder those women. Same as Kiley's baseball bat, his level. Same as Jimmy's knives."

"A tool, yeah. I guess if you look at it that way, yeah—yeah, I get it. I get where you're coming from."

"This work, it hardens us all to stone. We get so...so jaded. We all become like Max over there."

"Max isn't so bad."

"No, none of us are so bad, but what are we left with after seeing these unspeakable, unthinkable acts performed by creatures we call human beings?"

"We look into the abyss. It's part and parcel of the job, Jude."

"We look into it, and it looks back—reflects back. The abyss's eye is our collective soul, and it has such dark despair at its heart."

"What can I say."

"Nothing. Say nothing. Just hold me."

"That I can do." He took her in his arms.

Behind them, Max shouted, "Whataya wanna do now, Dr. Avery?"

Joe added, "We got Hunsucker's ETs on the way. You want a part of this?" Joe pointed to the bloated form below the blanket.

Jude pulled her head from Wayne's shoulder, realizing that the other two men were actually being solicitous, stepping across a tightrope with her. She was the professional here, the only medical person, the Chicago ME. They could simply cut her out of the deal now and adamantly do so. This was after all, the end of the road for their relationship unless she did take control of the murder scene and process this one. In his way, crusty old Max was telling Jude that it was her call; that no matter what she decided, it was fine with him.

"I'll process the scene," she firmly said as beads of sweat formed across her forehead and just about everywhere on her body.

"I thought your Gangs Division was going to keep an eye on this place," Wayne asked Joe.

"They sent out a chopper twice a day, but someone higher up decided the cost was too great."

"Sure was too great for Billy Hoss Hodges here."

"Can't do much until Hunsucker's people get here," she said to Wayne. "Haven't got my medical bag. It's on the plane with Sybil."

"I'd call my captain and Grant for you, but I'm not in the mood to be yelled at."

"Nor I."

Joe joined them. "Hey, Jude...Dr. Avery, a closer look at the ropes holding Billy down, and Max and me, we agree, he could've broken loose had he wanted to, but he didn't. So maybe what you were saying back there...maybe you were right."

She nodded. "Thanks, Joe. Not that that's much comfort under the circumstances, but thanks. Tell Max thanks too, and hey if you can hurry up those ETs, it's getting damn hot out here."

"Only dogs and fools go out in the noonday sun. A line from some damn poem I learned in fourth grade. Always stuck in my head."

"It's mad dogs and fools, Joe," she replied. "I kinda recall that one myself."

"And so here we are, all of us, mad dogs and fools," shouted Max, overhearing the chatter.

They all fell silent, conserving their energy, awaiting the Medical Examiner's van. They found what little shade the desert afforded, hunkering in close to the rocks. Max and Joe chose the car, running the AC, but the gas tank was low, so this didn't serve them for long, when in the distance, they heard the rumbling of motorcycles.

A huge, long parade of motorcycles out on the highway, all heading back toward LA. They were going nowhere, certainly not Texas. Syd Dupree and his followers were flagrantly going home. Syd and the others even waved as they passed the sacrificial rocks, seeing the police car there. Then another noise sounded overhead, and looking up, Jude saw the police helicopter, and it was descending nearby. The chopper pilot located a safe place for a soft landing, and when they began to leap out, Jude recognized Dr. Hunsucker himself, and beside him, Sybil. She'd obviously gotten off the UPS plane, contacted Hunsucker's office, and here she was.

"Thought you guys might need help," Sybil said as she approached.

Jude rushed to her and threw her arms about Sybil. "Dr. Shanley, Dr. Hunsucker. So glad you're here. We have a sad situation on our hands."

Sybil only frowned and said, "Again?"

Jude then thought of how this entire case had begun with the crushed skull under the dead man's hat in her lab. How Corporal Dewalt's death investigation had meandered as it had so far from home. And how there was something to be said for the safe confines of a laboratory.

◆　◆　◆

Once returned to Chicago and the familiar confines of the ME's office, Sybil and Jude were surprised to find a jubilant Dr. Grant awaiting them. It was difficult to tell, however, if his happy exterior was real or not. He shared the fact that he'd just gotten off a conference call with Captain Abel and Captain Mendes, detailing the results in LA. While Syd was still in charge of his gang of thugs, life in LA had returned to normal with Jimmy looking at the death penalty and Kiley's body in dispute as to which jurisdiction was responsible for his remains. Whether he would be entered in a Potter's Field in LA or Chicago, since so far *no one* had come forward to claim the corpse. As for Billy Hodges, Dupree's family had offered to provide a biker's funeral. Captain Abel had starkly said, "Nothing like being buried by the people who murdered you."

"I suspect you're building a case against Dupree?" Captain Mendes had asked.

"Yeah, sure, have been for two decades."

Captain Abel had next praised the work of Drs. Shanley and Avery, along with Detective Stephens. "You've got top-notch people working for you."

"Yes, we do," replied Mendes and Grant in unison.

"How's your case against this creep Goodwin going?" asked Abel.

"Forensically," Grant said, "he's nailed down tight."

"We're confident he'll spend the rest of his life in jail," added Mendes.

Their goodbyes were professional and terse.

Grant had given Jude and Sybil a play-by-play of how authorities in LA had been impressed by their tenacious work and expertise. This gave the two MEs smiles, but then Grant turned serious. "All that being said, doctors, we have a backlog awaiting you both. I suggest you get to it."

"What, no press conference?" asked Jude, a comment that left Sybil's jaw agape.

"Actually, I want both of you at a 3 PM news conference to put this case to bed."

"You want us at the podium with you?" asked Sybil, her tone telegraphing confusion.

"You two are celebs now or haven't you heard?"

Jude shrugged at this, and Sybil did a slow, slight shake of the head, speechless.

"Come now. It won't be hard for you two. Not much to tell the *newsies* now is there? I mean it's pretty much out there as is *since* the Chicago Tribune has a play-by-play on it already!" Dean slapped down the copy of the Trib on a stainless steel instrument tray on wheels so hard the tray ran across the room. He'd been tightly clutching the paper the whole time. Before the tray came to a stop, Dean had turned and left.

Sybil and Jude exchanged a look and a shrug as they went for the paper. Sybil got to it first and grabbed up the newspaper. Pulling it open, raising it to her eyes, she read the front page headline:

Chicago MEs Chase Down Killers in Snuff Film Competitions

Sub-titles included the words Chicago's Nun Killer and LA's Unborn Child Killer. Photos littered the page as well. Jude's picture, Sybil's alongside those of the killers. On the continued page, more photos—a pair of crime scene shots.

"Jesus," complained Sybil, "you'd think this was a Criminal Minds episode on TV."

Avery had been peeking over Sybil's shoulder to see Rachel Du-Champe's byline along with the full story. "Rachel got what she was after," she said, her eyes trained on the paper.

"She used me, used us both, Jude."

"Well it works both ways, and we *knew* she was in it for the story."

Sybil said nothing in reply, her lower lip quivering, on the verge of tears. "Yeah, sure, mutual consent."

"Right, it was a mutually agreed upon arrangement. I mean our following her leads and her following ours."

"I'm not talking about our case or her damn story! The bitch *used* me." Sybil burst into tears and stormed off for the changing room, upset but obviously bent on going back to work. Jude imagined that when they'd gotten back to Chicago, Rachel had chosen the time to kill her and Sybil's relationship. Jude imagined Sybil had had a horrible night.

She wanted to catch up to her, console her, but she believed Sybil would need some alone time, which meant 'left alone' time.

For now, Jude had to see to a literal stack of bodies awaiting her attention, most being uninteresting 'drawer' cases, but all deserving of respect and a proper going over. The heat wave had not abated in the City of Big Shoulders, nor had the death rate. Nor had the murder rate.

In fact, while absent from her new home, a gang war incident had broken out, leaving twenty-six dead in one night. Such carnage had to stop. Authorities needed to get a handle on gang violence on the city's South and West Sides yesterday. She wondered why there were not mass arrests of entire gangs like those that plagued LA and Chicago, and then she realized all the laws put in place to protect the average citizen from unlawful arrest applied to gang members as well. To this thought she said to herself, shit.

Many an innocent death due to crossfire and bad aim had come though the door this summer as well. Then there were those clever killers who used such carnage moments to plan and plot murder, thinking it the perfect kill time, a time to get away with murder by masking it as part of a larger event like this weekend's rampage. It had even been known to happen in a bombing event when a man set off a bomb in order to mask the murder of his wife.

Jude knew that she could not get complacent with gang victims any more than she could get complacent with heat stroke victims, not since discovering what was under the dead man's hat in the Dewalt case; not after the journey his murder had put her on. On this job, she thought as she now suited up for her next autopsy, anything's possible.

Jude hoped that she and Sybil could remain friends, and that they would have many more debates like they'd had and enjoyed in LA. Like the debate over what strange and odd behaviors constituted the plethora of what the human animal thought of as pleasurable enjoyment, such as snuff films, such as murder, power over another's life, torture, or playing with a victim over a long period of time.

Most importantly now, for Dr. Judith Avery, she hoped to work on and close more cases with the CPD, with Wayne, with Sybil, and with Dean, but the ins and outs of the job, the nuances, the politics—all conspired to make it a shaky tightrope walk. She'd have to be careful to stay balanced, that was certain. According to the Chicago Tribune, however wrong and unfair DuChampe's reporting felt, however biased she was toward the LAPD and the CPD, Rachel had made the team of Shanley and Avery local celebrities. That couldn't sit well with the local celeb in Chicago forensics, Dr. Dean Grant.

No matter how he might mask it.

DuChampe had played up the forensics over the shoe leather and street work of the cops. How Wayne, Dennis, Captain Abel, and the other detectives as far away as LA were treated in the two-page article was another story. Officers in uniform who'd contributed mightily to the team effort to catch Kiley and to uncover Proust's scheme, even the efforts of Ralph and Lionel, had been ignored completely. How they felt about this news account, Jude did not know. She worried about its impact on her and Wayne's relationship in particular, and about other relationships as well. So much depended on the reactions of others, and she knew no one capable of controlling the reactions of others, not to what Rachel had printed or how she was depicted as some sort of Superwoman.

Evidently, Rachel had her own agenda the entire time. She wanted to see high-ranking officials in the CPD and possibly the LAPD as well brought down. Jude recalled how she'd gone on about how shabbily the LAPD had treated her counterparts at the LA Times. Her article insisted that the case could have been 'solved far sooner had competent men been at the helm' in both cities. It went further, calling for resignations since 'unborn children did not need to die.' The article totally ignored the attempt on Proust's part to usher in a race war, beginning with his father's gang going after people of color.

The ending of Rachel's story bathed Sybil and Jude in a bright light, lauding them as passionate crime fighters, overdoing it to the point of purple prose, Jude felt. She feared a backlash would come her and Sybil's way as a result. Who'd want to work with them in future?

It'd been obvious that Dr. Grant was none too pleased with their sudden celebrity, despite how it had shone a positive light on his department. All Jude had wanted was to earn the respect of all her colleagues and Dr. Grant in particular, not that of the bloody mayor or the governor, but on her cellphone were messages from both the mayor's office and the governor's office. Calls she had not as yet returned. Calls she had no intention of returning, not without speaking to Dean first. Certainly not before the end of the day. She had work staring her in the face. Today's cases to tend to and fences to mend. Many fences to mend. She wondered why she hadn't heard from Wayne since they'd gotten back from LA. She wondered if she, like Sybil, had sacrificed love for her career.

She shook off such thoughts and, just as she got back to working on the victim of an ugly stabbing, Luther and Lisa wheeled in a dead man that Noble said was the son of a senator named Cauldwell, a hugely powerful man in Illinois. Noble rather respectfully said, "Dr. Avery, I coulda given this one to Dr. Shanley, but I owed ya a red ball case."

"Why? For not reporting Lisa?" Jude asked.

"Or me!"

Jude shrugged. "Dr. Grant got wind of it anyway."

"I went to him right after you jumped on me," explained Lisa. "I took full responsibility."

"Well now, good for you."

"Besides, we know you got the killers out in LA. Heard all about it."

"Trust me, that was a team effort."

"Whatever," said Lisa.

"Yeah, all the same, doc, young Blake Cauldwell here's all yours."

Lisa yanked Noble to the door. "We got another call to run."

With that, the ETs were gone, and Jude exchanged a laugh with Ralph. "You up for more overtime, Ralph?"

"Sure, doc."

"I gotta call Boomer's sitter."

Robert W. Walker

Robert W. Walker has written & published over 74 novels, 3 short story collections, and the how-to *Dead On Writing*. A graduate of Northwestern University, Rob holds an MA in English Education & teaches at West Virginia State University. While born in Corinth, MS, Rob grew up in Chicago, the setting for many of his novels. Rob's Instinct Series, begun with *Killer Instinct* and his Edge Series are Rob's longest running series, alongside Bloodscreams, a horror series. His first novel, completed in high school, *Daniel Webster Jackson & The Wrongway Railroad*, won Rob a full scholarship to NU. Rob's favorite authors are Twain and Shakespeare. He lives in Hurricane, WV with his wife and step-children.

Learn more about Rob and his books at www.RobertWalkerbooks.com